FIRSTS

FIRSTS

A NOVEL

Laurie Elizabeth Flynn

Thomas Dunne Books
St. Martin's Griffin New York

THOMAS DUNNE BOOKS
An imprint of St. Martin's Press

FIRSTS. Copyright © 2015 by Laurie Elizabeth Flynn. All rights reserved. Printed in the United States of America. For information, address St. Martin's Press, 175 Fifth Avenue, New York, NY 10010.

www.thomasdunnebooks.com
www.stmartins.com

Designed by Molly Rose Murphy

The Library of Congress Cataloging-in-Publication Data is available upon request.

ISBN 978-1-250-07596-3 (hardcover)
ISBN 978-1-4668-8732-9 (e-book)

Our books may be purchased in bulk for promotional, educational, or business use. Please contact your local bookseller or the Macmillan Corporate and Premium Sales Department at (800) 221-7945, extension 5442, or by e-mail at MacmillanSpecialMarkets@macmillan.com.

First Edition: January 2016

10 9 8 7 6 5 4 3 2 1

For Steve—my last, my only, my everything

ACKNOWLEDGMENTS

Writing is something you mostly do by yourself (or in my case, with an entitled Chihuahua on your lap), but publication is a journey that involves a whole team—and I'm lucky enough to have the best team of all. *Firsts* would still be a Word document on my computer if not for several supremely wonderful people to whom I'm eternally grateful.

First (pun intended!), a million thanks to my rock star agent, Kathleen Rushall. This has all been possible because of you, and your fearlessness and unfailing positivity made this process not only less stressful, but a whole lot of awesome. Thank you for sharing your great instincts and your listening ear, for your words of encouragement, for believing in this book (and in me), and for making my dreams reality. I'm so very thankful to have you in my corner.

To my brilliant editor, Kat Brzozowski: thank you for taking a chance on Mercedes and turning *Firsts* into the best book it could ever be. You are full of amazing ideas and understand me and my book in a way I never could have imagined anyone would. Not only that, but working with you has been incredibly fun—I'm glad we were able to bond over haikus and nostalgia for the Backstreet Boys. (I'm still Team Brian.)

Before I had an agent or an editor, I summoned up the nerve to enter a contest called Pitch Wars. Massive thanks to Brenda Drake for organizing this contest, because it played a huge role in *Firsts* getting out in the world. Thank you to Evelyn Skye for teaching me the fine art of pitching and supporting me at every bend in this crazy road to publication. Enormous tackle hugs to Lori Goldstein, who saw the potential in an edgy manuscript and continues to provide guidance and advice whenever I need it. Lori, *Firsts* wouldn't be *Firsts* without you. I never thought when I entered Pitch Wars that your mentorship—and friendship—would last long after the contest ended, and I'm so happy it did.

To Emily Martin, my fabulous critique partner, thanks for being everything—an honest critic, a passionate cheerleader, a trusted confidante, and a good friend. Your sharp eye helped *Firsts* become a stronger manuscript, and your willingness to read over anything I write is appreciated more than words can say.

To the members of The Sweet Sixteens and Sixteen to Read debut groups—thank you for being so welcoming, supportive, and enthusiastic. You're all so talented and kind and I'm honored to be sharing this journey with every single one of you. Group hug!

Thank you, or should I say *grazie*, to Taryn Fagerness, foreign rights agent extraordinaire, for bringing *Firsts* to new audiences around the world.

To the amazing people at Thomas Dunne Books/St. Martin's Press who helped *Firsts* become an actual book—you have made me feel like the luckiest writer out there. Special thanks to Karen Masnica and Michelle Cashman for your stellar marketing and publicity efforts, and to Danielle Christopher for designing a gorgeous cover I still can't stop staring at. To Kristin Roth, thanks for being so incredibly perceptive and polishing *Firsts* to a shine.

To Fernanda Viveiros at Raincoast, thank you for handling the Canadian sales and events for *Firsts*.

To Amanda Maciel, Caisey Quinn, Jennifer Mathieu, and Lori Goldstein (again): thank you for your generosity in providing blurbs for *Firsts*. I admire your writing so much and your support means the world to me.

To my fourth-grade teacher, Ms. Parrack—thank you for always looking excited when I asked for more paper to write on because my stories were taking on a life of their own.

My friends and family all deserve a huge round of applause. Thank you to Tory Overend and Lauren Badalato for keeping my secrets and loving me even when I'm a hermit. To my in-laws, Jim and Doreen Flynn, thank you for taking such an interest in my writing (Dad Flynn, you and your blacksmith may be on to something). To my brother-in-law, Jermaine Shakes, for your optimism and faith that good things will happen. To Erin Burns, my sister and best friend, for sharing a thousand inside jokes, being proud of me no matter what, and always wanting to celebrate my successes with wine and shopping.

My parents, Denis and Lucy Burns, were my very first supporters. They always knew I wanted to be a writer and gave me everything I needed to make it happen. Thanks, Mom and Dad, for being there through the highs and lows, for putting up with all of my crazy whims, and for supporting me in every way possible. You taught me that the most important thing in life is to try, even if you fail. I've fallen down many times, but because of you, I'm never afraid to get back up. You're my heroes.

Last, but definitely not least, thank you to my husband, Steve Flynn, for marrying and loving a writer who spends an awful lot of time with made-up people. Thank you for not getting mad when I spend hours holed up in my office, for buying me the best desk chair imaginable, for our walks and talks in the woods, for endless pots of coffee, for endless hugs, and for just being you.

And to all of you, my readers—thank you for being the reason I do what I do, and for giving me the chance to do it. I couldn't be happier to be sharing this first with each and every one of you.

FIRSTS

1

Tonight, I'm doing Evan Brown's girlfriend a favor. An awkward, sweaty, fumbling favor. Melanie, or whatever her name is, owes me big time.

Except she'll never know it.

"Wait there," I tell Evan before slipping into my walk-in closet.

I sneak a glance back at him, at his crouched-over stance on the edge of my bed, his skinny shoulders hunched forward and his hands on his knees. He looks like he's getting ready to play a video game. I stifle a laugh. This is one level he won't beat on the first try.

When I'm carefully ensconced in my walk-in, I wiggle into a pair of pink satin boy shorts and a matching camisole. I know by the fear on his face and the smell of nervous sweat emanating from his armpits that Evan can't handle the black lacy negligee, and especially not the red slip, the one with the slit that goes all the way up.

I open the drawer containing my garter belts and collection of fishnet stockings, then close it again. Evan wouldn't know what to do with a garter belt or fishnet stockings, and it's not my intention to embarrass him any more than he already is.

I apply pink lipstick and leave my hair loose around my shoulders. It's wavy, still damp from the shower. Normally I'd flat iron it into stick-straight submission, but this time, maybe I'll drop the getup. I rub the lipstick off, but the judgment in my eyes remains.

Evan will get what I'm most definitely not—the good girl.

"God, Mercy," he says when I emerge. His voice cracks and he blushes redder than his hair, which makes the pimples dotted across his cheeks stand out. Puberty wasn't kind to Evan Brown.

"Don't say that," I command, climbing onto his lap. His legs are trembling.

"Don't say what?" His voice is trembling, too.

"Mercy. That's not my name."

"But that's what Angela calls you."

"Angela's my friend. You're not. You're somebody I'm doing a favor for. You don't have to call me anything. But if you want to, my real name will do."

"Mercedes," he says, squeaking out the extra syllables. "My mom always wanted one of those." He slaps his forehead. "Shit, I didn't mean to bring up my mom. I'm not thinking about her or anything." He removes his glasses and rubs his eyes. "I just didn't think I'd be so nervous."

I used to like my name. Mercedes. That is, until I figured out I was named after a car. The shiny red car that my dad loved more than anything—the one he waved from as he drove away. I remember liking that car, too. My dad used to let me sit in the front seat and pretend to steer. "You're going to have a lead foot," he would say over my childish *vroom, vroom*s. "Somebody'll need to teach you how to slow down." But he didn't stick around long enough for that person to be him.

Out of Evan's mouth, my name doesn't sound fancy or fast. It just sounds complicated, like he's trying to speak a foreign language. I guess for Evan, I *am* a foreign language.

I smile and run my fingers through his hair. Or at least I try to, but he put so much damned gel in it that my hand gets stuck.

"Don't worry about it," I say, wiping my sticky fingers on the back of his shirt. "Everyone gets nervous." I kiss his neck, where I can feel his pulse beating against his skin. I move my hands to the base of his T-shirt and pull it over his head.

"I brought these," he says, jamming his hand in his jeans pocket and pulling out a roll of condoms. There must be about ten of them. He attempts a smile, but it looks more like a grimace.

"It's always good to be prepared," I say. "But save those for Melanie. I'm prepared, too."

I lean over and open my nightstand drawer, where the boxes are piled neatly like little soldiers. Ultra Thin, Ribbed for Her Pleasure, Second Skin, Magnums. I pull out an Ultra Thin. No matter what they think, most guys are Ultra Thins. Just enough for protection, no extra frills. This fact was drilled into me early. My mom started teaching me about birth control when other moms were still on tampons.

Besides, Evan doesn't look like a Magnum kind of guy.

"How far have you got with Melanie?" I say.

"Melody," he says. "Melody—that's her name. Not Melanie. Melody, like a song." He looks down to where my cleavage is propped in front of his face. "She let me feel her up. And one time when her parents were out of town, we almost did it. We did other stuff."

I put my hands on my hips. "You've got to be more specific. Other stuff, like you've seen each other naked? Like you went down on her?"

He nods and blushes an even darker shade of red. "But she didn't want to go all the way. She wants it to be the best night of her life. So I have this whole thing planned, a dinner and stuff."

"Very romantic," I say, smiling broadly. *This* is the reason I do what I do. "Sounds like you like her. And she likes you."

I love when guys take the time to make a plan. And even though Evan mumbled "a dinner and stuff" without making eye contact, I know he means much more. He took the time to know Melody, what she likes, and what will make her happy.

"That's the problem," he says. "She says she loves me. She says because she loves me, she just knows I'm going to rock her world."

I nod. I understand this part. Melody sounds like every other girl, the kind who expects fireworks the first time. I know better. Fireworks don't just happen. They need to be carefully arranged and then ignited slowly.

Which is exactly what I'm doing for Evan.

"But you don't think you're going to rock her world," I say slowly. "That's why you're here."

"Well, yeah," he says. "She's way hotter than me. And my friend, Gus—he's still with his girlfriend because of you."

I know exactly who Evan is talking about, except I remember him more by his nickname, the one I secretly gave him. The Crier. Gus was number six, the one who acted all tough and practically tried to instruct me—until he broke down and sobbed into my pillow afterward.

I brace my hands against Evan's shoulders. "Well, you're a lot farther along than some people. You've already seen each other naked. You got that out of the way. For some people, that's the most awkward part." I slip the straps of my camisole down my shoulders. "Like now. What would you do if I was Melody?"

"I'd tell you you were beautiful," he says. "I'd ask if I could touch them."

"Right and wrong," I say. "You're always right to tell a girl she's beautiful. But never ask if you can do something. Be bold, because confidence is one thing you can absolutely fake until you actually feel it."

Evan continues to stare at my breasts. He's breathing heavy, and I can feel his erection through his jeans. Maybe Evan will need a Magnum after all.

"So go ahead," I say. "This is the place to make mistakes."

And he does—he makes plenty of mistakes. He palms my breasts like they're baseballs, slobbers on my neck, sticks his tongue halfway down my throat. They're rookie errors, the kind most people don't get right the first time. But that's what I'm here for. I tell him to close his lips, follow the curves of my body with his hands, use his fingers to trace an outline for his tongue to follow. I teach him how to open the condom packet, how to pinch the tip before rolling it on to make sure all the air gets out. I dim the lights for the final act, help him guide himself into me, don't chastise him for the first fifteen seconds of fumbling in the dark but give him credit for his improved technique in the last fifteen.

But when he asks for a round two, I shake my head firmly. I have never allowed a round two. "Save it for Melody," I say.

He stretches out under the covers and turns his head on the pillow. His breath is still coming in ragged gasps. "Should I stay over?" he says. "We could do it again in the morning. I bet I'll last longer."

I cover my breasts with my hands and stand up, searching for something to better cover myself with but only finding a sheer robe. I curse my lack of actual pajamas. This is the part I don't like. In the dark, when I'm the one in control, even with everything on full display, I feel less naked than now. Then the lights come up and they want to talk. To ask questions. Questions I can't answer for myself, let alone for them.

"You're not staying over," I say, fastening the robe around my waist. "You'll get there. Girls care less about that than you think. Especially in the beginning. You can work up to it together."

He grins. He looks different, more handsome somehow. In the softer light, his pimples aren't as evident and his jawline seems more pronounced. One day, I think Evan Brown could even be a heartbreaker.

But that day isn't today.

I glance at the clock on my nightstand. Eleven p.m. on a Tuesday. "It's a school night, Evan. Time for you to go. Your mother will wonder where you are." Or I assume she would. Most mothers do. Not mine, of course.

His grin turns into a frown. "Do I, you know, owe you something? I don't know how this works . . ." His voice trails off.

"You don't owe me anything. Just be good to her, okay? Remember everything we talked about."

I know he will. He even took notes. *Open her car door for her. Bring her flowers, not something generic like roses but her actual favorite flowers. Have dinner reservations in advance, not necessarily somewhere fancy but somewhere meaningful, like where you had your first kiss or where you realized you loved her. Kiss her, not just on her lips but in unexpected places. On the nape of her neck. On her forehead. On her wrist. Push her hair behind her ears gently. Take a picture. She'll want to remember the night.*

I swallow against a lump that has risen up suddenly in my throat. It's not that Evan is different—he's a nice guy, a kid who loves his girlfriend and wants to please her. Maybe I'm the one who's different. Maybe this speech is starting to feel too familiar. I told myself five favors for five deserving virgins. Five was the line I drew in the sand, and I trampled over it like it wasn't even there. Evan is the tenth, and ten is a line I can't just trample past.

But I'm certainly not going to get into this with Evan, so I put on a fake smile. I gesture around the room at the chaise lounge and walk-in closet and floor-to-ceiling shoe rack. "Besides, I really don't need your money. Spend it on Melody."

He pulls his boxers and pants back on. His movements are more measured, not the bumbling, terrified movements of the Evan Brown who entered my bedroom an hour ago. Even his voice seems deeper, like he came here a boy and is leaving as a man. I suppose that's not far from the truth. I allow myself a little smile, a real one this time. It's easy to reaffirm what I do. What happened to Evan in my bedroom will change him, make him into a more considerate lover, even a better boyfriend. Moments like these are what made that line in the sand so easy to obliterate.

Moments like these, I could see an eleventh, even though I promised myself that's not going to happen. I'm starting the second half of senior year with all of my good karma already under my belt.

"I don't know where you came from, but you saved my life, Mercy. I mean, Mercedes. I don't know what I would've done without you."

"You would've ripped five condoms by accident, and you might've drowned the girl in saliva. But now, you're going to nail it. Literally."

He tugs his shirt over his head. "When Gus told me how you helped him, I didn't believe it. But he was right—you're an angel." He pauses. "But can I ask you—"

I cut him off midsentence. "No, you can't. Don't spoil it."

"But you didn't even let me finish," he protests.

8 LAURIE ELIZABETH FLYNN

"Oh, I let you finish," I say. "The one thing you can do for me is not ask me any questions."

He nods. "Fair enough."

"Goodnight, Evan," I say.

"Goodnight, Mercy. Uh, Mercedes." He gets to my bedroom door and pauses with his hand on the doorknob.

"This won't be awkward at school tomorrow, will it?" he says, looking back at me.

"Of course not," I say, folding my arms over my chest. "It's not going to be awkward at all, because what happened in this room becomes just a figment of your imagination the second you walk out that door."

He gives me a tight-lipped smile and pulls the door shut after him. I can see his shoes underneath, can tell he's lingering there, wondering if he said too much or not enough, not entirely convinced that his secret is safe with me.

But he has nothing to worry about. His secret, like those of nine of his fellow seniors, is safe with me. At Milton High, I'm my own statistic. People fail to see the great equalizer, the one thing the band geeks, the drama nerds, the jocks, and the preppies all have in common.

Me—Mercedes Ayres.

The girl who took their virginity.

2

My mom's car is still in the driveway when I head out the door in the morning, which means I have to maneuver my Jeep around it to avoid hacking a side mirror off. Despite the time it takes, I'm relieved. The obnoxiously yellow Corvette convertible in the driveway means my mom made a smart decision last night and didn't drive her car to happy hour at the martini bar. Kim's DUI last summer cost her a three-month license suspension and would have entailed a couple days in jail if not for her excellent lawyer. Kim would never admit it, but I know she's secretly proud of her DUI. Now she shares an extracurricular activity with D-list celebrities everywhere.

Needless to say, Kim fits in perfectly with the housewives of

Rancho Palos Verdes, gossiping relentlessly and spending the money from her divorce settlement on expensive champagne and the kind of plastic surgery that everybody gets but nobody admits to. She blends in, but I can't wait to get out, and this particular morning marks the start of my last six months here. I know exactly where I'm going and how I'm getting there. Massachusetts Institute of Technology. MIT. The mecca, the holy grail of chemical engineering. It will be a fresh start, as far from Southern California as I can get, in a state where people wear black instead of pastels and the seasons actually change. My grades will get me in, and once I'm there, I'll work hard to stay there. No guys. No distractions. Nobody there will know who I am or what I have done or how many people I've slept with.

When I have safely cleared the driveway, I gun my Jeep down our suburban road, hoping to make up some time with my lead foot. Angela hates when anyone is late for prayer group, and I don't like making my best friend upset.

The great thing about getting to school this early is a guaranteed prime parking spot, which I slide the Jeep into. After a breathless run down the hall, I dump my extraneous textbooks in my locker. That's when I see it in my locker mirror—a small hickey at the base of my collarbone, no doubt Evan Brown's handiwork, most definitely unintentional. I swear under my breath and duck into the bathroom to cover it with a blob of concealer, knowing that despite my best intentions, I'm going to be late anyway. But covering this up is worth a scolding from Angela.

I rush into the library right when Angela is about to start reading. She smiles at me over her Bible and gives me a little shake of her head, almost like she expected me to be tardy. I take a seat beside Angela's boyfriend, Charlie, the only other person who attends prayer group on a regular basis. Charlie's eyes flicker over my face, and I swear they come to rest on the hickey, although I must be paranoid.

I met Angela at prayer group in grade nine, which I only started going to because Kim was pushing me to find a boyfriend and naturally, I told her I wanted to join a convent instead. Angela is why I kept the charade up. And this year, the bonus has been that it makes an excellent cover for my pay-it-forward scheme. Even if there were a rumor or two, who would suspect the girl who's almost a nun?

But I would never tell this to Angela. Angela thinks sex is a sacred gift that you only give to your husband on your wedding night. She has been dating Charlie for nearly two years, and the farthest they have gone is "petting on top of the clothes," and that was only the night he gave her a promise ring.

In today's prayer group, Angela has a revelation. Literally. As in, Revelation 1 of the Bible. "'I am the Alpha and the Omega,' says the Lord God, 'Who is, and who was, and who is to come, the Almighty.'" She asks what this means to us. Angela is big on making prayer group interactive.

Charlie spouts out something about the suffering of Christ, which I tune out. *Who is, and who was, and who is to come.* Angela would freak at my answer, because for me, that's a loaded sentence. Who is: today, Zach is. Who was: I would have to refer to the notebook I keep in my nightstand under the boxes of condoms. The notebook has a white pearly cover—it was a gift from Angela for my last birthday. Angela would be horrified that the pages are filled with details of my sex life, although I think of it not as a record of my conquests but as a remembrance of my good deeds.

Angela and I walk to chemistry together after prayer group. It's our first class of the day, and the only one I consistently enjoy.

"You should tutor me," Angela says.

I shake my head adamantly. This has been happening every semester for the past two years: Angela asks me to be her lab partner, and I turn her down.

"You'll distract me," I say. "We'll spend too much time talking about the Gospels of Matthew, Mark, Luke, and John and not enough time talking about the quadratic acid compound."

I stop in the middle of the hallway, suddenly wanting to throw up. It was meant as a joke, but the third name might as well have reached up and punched me in the face, like it always does when it comes up during prayer group. *Luke.*

"The what?" Angela scrunches up her face and keeps walking, not noticing my momentary panic.

"Exactly," I say, readjusting my armful of books and pasting on a wide grin.

I don't like mixing friendship with anything else. If I'm thinking in chemical terms, friendship is an undiluted solution, something weakened by adding more to it. Unlike Kim, I'm a firm believer that the different compartments of your life should be kept separate—I can't just up and switch schools the way she changes gyms when the backstabbing gets too intense to bear. This is why instead of Angela I sit with Zach Sutton during chemistry, and why every Wednesday at lunch, Zach and I slip back to my bedroom to make chemistry happen there. And if sex with other guys is a science that I teach them, sex with Zach is more like art.

Zach is not my friend, nor my boyfriend, although he has asked at different times to be both. It's not like I haven't toyed with the notion of us becoming a couple, but we have absolutely no base upon which a relationship could be built. We've had sex more times than we have had conversations. I don't know Zach's middle name or even where he lives, but I do know that he wears boxers with goofy cartoon characters and loves when I wear thongs.

"What am I, then?" he always asks.

"My chemistry partner," I always say.

After our morning classes, Angela and I walk down the hall and stop in front of her locker. "You're doing lunch with your mom today, then?" she says, turning her combination lock and swinging the door open.

I nod. Ever since Zach and I started sleeping together, I have let Angela believe that I have a long-standing lunch date with my mom on Wednesdays. She thinks it's cute. I think it's just far-fetched enough to actually work.

"See you later," Angela says, pulling out a brown bag lunch from her locker. "Have something fancy for lunch that I can't pronounce." Her lips curl into a smile. I wave and head out toward the parking lot, trying to shake off my nagging guilt.

Before Zach, and before the virgins, Angela and I spent more time together. Nights spent sprawled on her bed, drinking tea, and reading the celebrity gossip magazines her mom loves to buy. Afternoons in my kitchen, trying to make chocolate-chip cookies but mostly just eating the dough instead. Sleepovers where we argued about which movie to watch—always romantic comedies for Angela and action for me—and talked about everything.

Almost everything.

Not lately, though. Now I can barely open my mouth without a new lie slipping out. And Angela never doubts me, because I haven't given her a reason to.

But the Kim excuse is convenient. It gives me ample time to meet Zach in the parking lot, smuggle him into the back of my Jeep, and drive to my house. Chemistry class is all the foreplay we need. Zach considers himself the master of sexual innuendos.

"You're getting my beaker all wet," is his favorite line, even though it makes no sense whatsoever to somebody who actually pays attention in class and knows that a beaker is in fact a receptacle.

But as bad as his sense of humor—and attention span—is at times, Zach knows exactly where and how to touch me without being told. His first time was definitely not with me. According to Zach, he lost his virginity back in the eighth grade to his older sister's best friend. I have no way of knowing if this is true, but I don't ask questions, and neither does he, which is one of his best qualities. Zach knows when to shut up. Considering all the vocal instructions I give the other guys I sleep with, it's nice to be completely nonverbal with Zach.

"You looked so hot today," he says as he drops his backpack at the front door and kicks off his shoes. Shoes at the door aren't a problem in my house, since Kim never comes home at lunch. Lunch is always reserved for manicures and gossip with her equally divorced and equally Botoxed friends. And probably for boning her Pilates trainer, too, although I'm not one to judge.

"Don't you mean I still look hot?" I say, throwing my coat on the floor. "Looked implies past tense."

"Your level of hot is omnipresent," he says, coming up behind me and biting my neck.

"I see you learned a new word." I turn around and meet his mouth with mine.

"I don't think I can make it upstairs," he says as he pulls my shirt over my head and expertly unhooks my bra. His fingertips alone send jolts of electricity through my skin, and he trails them down my back, starting feather-light and getting harder as he nears my tailbone. I grab Zach's hand and pull him down the hall into the kitchen. Behind me, I can hear him undoing his belt and unzipping his fly.

"The kitchen?" he says when I press him against the stainless steel refrigerator. "I never did it in a kitchen before." He grabs me around the waist and lifts me onto the granite counter, where he puts his hand up my skirt and pulls my panties off. The counter happens to be the perfect height for sex, a fact I never noticed until yesterday morning, when I bent over it to paint my nails and purposely mess up Kim's daily ritual of polishing the granite. This has been on my mind ever since, taunting me in prayer group and distracting me all through chemistry. This is a regular occurrence for me, using Zach to play out my little fantasies. Somehow I don't think he minds being a guinea pig.

"These are my favorite," he says, clutching my pink lace panties in his hand. All of my panties are either lace or satin or sheer—no dingy whites or high-waisted monstrosities. I don't even want to know what those would do to my reputation. Lucky for me, Kim tossed out all my childish floral panties back in elementary school, the day I got my period and she decided I needed something more grown-up.

Zach lets his own pants fall to the floor and abruptly closes the gap between us. He stands right between my legs, ready to go—until I reach out and slap him in the face.

"Condom, Zach," I say, snapping my fingers. "You didn't want to make it upstairs, so you should be ready."

"Come on," he says, leaning in to bite my lip. "I'm clean, you're clean. I got tested six months ago. And we're not sleeping with other people. It would feel so good without it."

I reach out like I'm about to slap him in the face again. "No condom, no love, Zach," I say. "Those are the rules."

He exaggerates a frown, but there's a smile behind it. "Hit me again," he says. I roll my eyes. I forgot that Zach likes when I get rough with him.

"Lucky for you, I come prepared." He bends over and rummages in the back pocket of his discarded jeans. When he stands up, he's holding a condom in a purple packet. I recognize it as a Trojan Ecstasy. I have a box upstairs with one missing from last week's devirginization of Bobby Lewis.

"You're the one who's lucky," I say, opening the packet. "Come prepared or don't come at all."

He doesn't waste a minute. I lean my head back and put my arms on the counter to steady myself. A low moan escapes my lips. Evan Brown could definitely learn a thing or two from Zach about how to handle a girl's breasts.

Today, neither of us lasts long. Zach has the distinction of being the only guy who has ever gotten me off, although I'd never tell him this. I don't even want to know what that would do to his ego.

"God, Mercy," he says, collapsing his upper body on me. "You're amazing. *We're* amazing."

"Mercedes," I say, heaving him off me and straightening out my skirt. "My name's Mercedes."

He frowns. "Even after four months of this?"

I kiss him on the cheek and mock gasp. "Has it been four months? Is today, like, our anniversary?"

He clenches his jaw, an indicator that Zach is about to get serious. I turn away and survey the handprints—and butt prints that could be passed off as handprints—on the countertop with pride, half hoping Kim notices and cares enough to ask me what happened to her pristine kitchen.

"Seriously. It could be our four-month anniversary. I'd treat you right." He grabs my arm and twirls me around. "I think I'm in love with you."

I zip up his fly and buckle his belt. Everything in reverse. I hate this part, the part where the physical act is over and the mental act begins. This is the part where one of my secrets is most likely to slip out and I'm more likely to stop being Zach's dream girl and start being something else.

"That's your orgasm talking," I say. "You're not really in love with me."

"You can't tell me how I feel," he says. His voice gets quiet, trails off at the end. "I could be your boyfriend."

Zach hasn't told me he loves me before, but I sensed it building up. I dreaded hearing the words, knowing they'd be the end of our Wednesday lunch dates. I can't have a Wednesday date with somebody who loves me. Not when I don't love him back.

I look Zach squarely in the eye. He's making his sad puppy-dog face, which makes me feel even worse. The stakes of our relationship—remaining chemistry partners and nothing else—depend on the delivery of my next line.

"You can love me like a friend," I finally say. I almost wish I could relent and give him what he really wants—relationship status. When I started with the virgins, they were my excuse to keep Zach at bay. There was no way I could have a boyfriend. But now my pay-it-forwards are done, completely finished. There's no real reason, besides the nagging feeling that I know I'm going to let him down, and letting him be my boyfriend would just end badly for both of us.

"I thought we weren't friends?" he says, his mouth turning up at the corners.

I sigh. "We're chemistry partners. But I guess there's no reason chemistry partners can't be friends."

"I'm going to call you Mercy, then," he says. He squeezes me in a tight hug. I can tell he's smelling my hair, but I don't stop him. "You so love me, too."

I find his balled-up shirt on the floor and drive it into his stomach. "I so don't. Now let's get out of here before we're late for school."

"No way," he says, dangling my panties in the air. "You can't go back without these."

I head for the door and grab my backpack. "Sure I can," I say. "But I bet you can't get through the day knowing I have nothing on under my skirt."

He pulls his shirt over his head and shakes his head. "You're evil," he says. "What do you say about a sequel to this, after school?"

I shut the door behind us and give him a soldierly pat on the back. "The sequel's never as good as the original." He staggers and pretends to fall over. "Besides, I'm busy after school."

"Busy doing what?" he says.

"Big assignment. Group project. Not in chemistry," I add quickly.

"Can I come?" he asks.

"No, Zach," I say. "But I think you already did."

He laughs and slings his arm around my shoulder. "Next Wednesday, then," he says.

"Until next week," I say, trying to keep the relief out of my voice. Next Wednesday is part of our routine, another chance to spend lunch hour doing it somewhere else in Kim's immaculate house. Maybe on the white leather couch next time, the one she loves too much to even let me sit on. Zach wanting to see me next Wednesday is almost like Zach asking me on a date, if I were a regular girl wanting a regular relationship.

But I'm not a regular girl. I don't want to hold hands in the hall at school and slow dance at prom and see a movie with Zach. I don't want to be the girl he dates senior year and loses interest in when he goes off to college. I want to be just fast enough for Zach to have to run to catch up, because if I stay ahead, I won't ever have to see his retreating back.

3

I wasn't lying to Zach. I really do have an assignment after school. I'm meeting with two other people from my French class, people I have to work with not by choice but by where my name falls in the alphabet. Adams, Ames, Ayres.

"Adams" and "Ames" are friends outside of class, which makes me feel like even more of an outsider. Adams—whose first name is Laura—went to my elementary school and we actually used to be friends, before life got complicated by boys and boobs and the hierarchy of high school popularity. I toyed with the idea of inviting Laura and the other girl over to do the assignment at my house but chickened out. Anything could go wrong at my house. They could stumble upon my negligee collection or my condom stash. So I suggested the library instead, which screams (actually, whispers, since screaming is disallowed) professionalism.

Or, is supposed to, until Laura shows up in tears, interrupting the silence at our table.

"Babe, what's wrong?" Ames—Britney, "spelled like the singer"—jumps to her feet and wraps an arm around her sobbing friend.

"I think Trevor is going to dump me." Laura wipes her face on her sleeve. "We had this whole plan. For this weekend. You know." She drops her voice, as if she's just now noticing I'm here and realizing she hasn't spoken to me in years. I lower my eyes and pretend to be intensely interested in the list of French verbs we're supposed to be conjugating.

"You can talk in front of Mercedes," Britney says as Laura slumps into the chair across from me. She opens her mouth to say something else but shuts it promptly. I know what she was about to say. *You can trust Mercedes—she's a prayer group geek.* I arch my eyebrow at her serious face but try to soften my expression.

Laura looks up at me through her tears, as if deciding whether I'm an ally or an enemy. I smile weakly, not sure myself.

"So, what happened to the big plan? Did your parents decide not to go away? Or did Trevor get cold feet?" Britney chews the top of her pen.

Laura drops her head onto the table. Her hair spills onto my pencil case. "All I told him was that I was nervous. I was scared it was going to hurt. And he wasn't sensitive at all." She looks around, even though the tables beside ours are empty and there's nobody in sight besides Mrs. Woods, the ancient librarian. "He kept saying all these positions he wanted to try. I guess he was watching porn and got these ideas, and I just freaked out." She frowns and looks directly at me. For a terrifying second, I think she knows everything.

"Sorry. I'm sure you don't want to hear all this." She half laughs, half sobs.

I shake my head and shrug at the same time in an attempt to look both nonchalant and considerate. Laura would flip out and most certainly violate the library's vow of silence if she knew that I specialize in hearing stories like hers.

Britney pats her friend's arm sympathetically. "I remember my first time. It does hurt. But Orlando was, like, so sweet. He kept saying how beautiful I was." She flutters her eyelashes.

I rest my head against my palm and pretend to take study notes, but my jaw is tightening. I taught him that, told him to say beautiful when he really meant hot. There's only one Orlando at Milton High. I remember him as the Watcher, because of the way he stared at me before, during, and after I took his virginity. Except he wasn't with Britney then. He was with a girl named Clara, a girl he told me he loved. I helped him make a special night for her, even told him a romantic out-of-the-way hotel to take her to. He told me he planned to be with Clara forever. I guess forever didn't even last halfway through senior year. I don't know if I'm angry or disappointed to hear that Orlando and Clara are over, or if I even have a right to be either one.

Orlando was number five for me. He was supposed to be the last one.

Until six happened.

"Anyway, I don't know if I can be with a guy who doesn't care about my needs." Laura wipes her face, leaving streaks of smeared mascara behind.

Both Laura and Britney seem to have forgotten I'm here, which is part of where prayer group comes in handy. Everybody assumes I'm still a virgin, so they're never going to ask to hear my first-time story. Which is probably for the best, because I would never tell them, and they wouldn't believe me anyway.

"Just give him another chance," Britney says, rubbing Laura's back. "He's probably nervous, too."

Somehow Laura calms down enough to get through our list of French verbs. By the end of the hour, Laura and Britney are even laughing, comparing stories about their boyfriends' penises.

"I'm glad I at least saw Trevor's first," Laura says. "I don't know if it's big or small since I have nothing to compare it to."

"I'm pretty sure Orlando's is huge," Britney says with a giggle. "He told me it was nine inches."

I cough into my hand. *Nine inches?* Orlando is definitely not the guy he was when I slept with him, when he was kind and considerate and eager to learn. And he was definitely not nine inches of anything. I wish there were a way I could take the Watcher off my list, but that's the thing about sex. Once it happens, it can't unhappen.

I'm relieved when the project is done. Laura and Britney are more than happy to let me do the grunt work of typing it up and putting our names on it, and I'm so glad to get rid of them that I don't even care. My heart is pounding and I'm nowhere close to figuring out what just happened. I sit in the library until I'm the only one there, and Mrs. Woods comes over to tell me she's about to close up. The look she gives me from behind her bottle-cap glasses—a mixture of pity and annoyance—makes me want to cry, although I don't know why.

The lights are dimmed in the hallways as I head to my locker, so I don't notice the tall, lanky kid until he's almost right in front of me.

"Sorry," I say under my breath, holding my books protectively over my chest. But he doesn't move out of my way and doesn't let me past.

"You're Mercedes, right?" he says. I look up, wishing my face wasn't in such close proximity to his armpit. He's wearing gym clothes, and the basketball under his arm means he's probably on the team, although I don't recognize his face. It's a good-looking face, though, with a strong jawline and a sprinkling of freckles across his nose and really dark eyes, the kind where you can't tell what color they are until you're inches away.

"Yes," I say, letting him trail behind me to my locker. I open the door and busy myself putting my books in. I can tell from my locker mirror that he's staring at my chest.

"I hear you can do things. You know. Help guys like me." He crouches down to my height, like he's afraid someone will see him, even though we're the only two people in the hall.

"Guys like you?" I say innocently, not meeting his eyes. I know exactly what he's talking about, but I'm not letting anything on. Yet.

"I'm a virgin." He says it almost inaudibly. "And I could use some help."

I close my locker door with more force than I have to. I don't exactly know how to tell him that my legs are closed for business. Ten guys was my absolute ceiling. It's in the double digits.

"I'm sorry," I say, slinging my backpack over my shoulder. "I can't help you."

He looks down at his scuffed sneakers. "I wouldn't ask if I wasn't desperate," he says in a small voice. "It's just, Laura expects that I'm this stud now. I talked myself up to cover up how scared shitless I am that I'll disappoint her. I think I made a huge ass of myself."

I turn to leave, not wanting to look at his face. I can't get attached to his story, but I'm anchored in place at the mention of her name. Laura. My former friend, the one who still wanted to play with her Barbie Dreamhouse long after I outgrew toys.

"What's your name?" The words tumble out of my mouth before I can stop them.

"Trevor," he says. "Trevor Johnston."

I know I should keep walking down the hall and let Trevor Johnston figure things out for himself. He made a rookie error by pretending to know what he's doing and might have ruined things for good. It's not my problem. But when I think about Laura's teary voice and the smudged mascara wiped across her cheek, I talk myself out of it. Laura might be a bit flaky and she's terrible at conjugating verbs, but she deserves a perfect first time. Maybe if I help Trevor, he and Laura will have the future Orlando and Clara apparently won't. It'll be a double-pronged good deed: I can erase my loathing for the Watcher and do Laura a favor at the same time.

Besides, Trevor's cute. This won't be a complete hardship.

I clear my throat. "Trevor Johnston," I say. He looks up hopefully.

"Five twenty-four Silverberry Run. Be there at nine tomorrow night."

He breaks into a huge smile and extends his arms like he wants to hug me, but I keep walking, and when I'm far enough away I smile, too. It's not like going from ten to eleven is going to make *that* much of a difference. The line will still be basically intact.

I'll just blur it a little.

4

I'm surprised to see Kim's car still in the driveway when I get home, parked haphazardly, the wheels on the right side halfway into the flower garden, which would mean nothing except the dining room lights are on, too. Coming home to a darkened house is part of my routine, but that doesn't change the flurry of hope in the pit of my stomach when the lights are on. Maybe Kim has finally realized that I'll be out of the house after this semester, so if she doesn't get to know me now, she might never get a chance to.

Or maybe she just wants to pick my brain about the hot date she has tonight.

"Honestly, I never thought he'd be interested," she says, throwing her coat over a high-backed leather chair as I enter the foyer.

"I mean, I lied about my age, but I don't really look thirty-eight, do I?"

I drop my backpack on the floor in defeat. I can't believe I was stupid enough to equate the lights being on with Kim actually having dinner here or wanting to spend time with me.

"You're not thirty-eight," I say, watching her lips curl into something resembling a smile, or at least as much of a smile as her most recent Restylane injection will allow, and deflate when she hears the end of my sentence. "You're forty-five, Kim. Actually, forty-six in a month."

"Well. Age is all about how you feel, right? And I don't feel a day older than twenty." She arches an eyebrow and taps a long crimson fingernail on the granite counter, chipping away at an invisible stain. I stifle a laugh, wondering how far up her forehead her eyebrows would go if she knew what happened this afternoon.

"And let me guess. Your date is really twenty? Is it the Pilates instructor?"

She cocks her hip and narrows her eyes at me. She's going for a sarcastic expression, but the amount of Botox in her forehead prevents it from being fully formed. But the most disheartening aspect of her stance is how much I can see myself in her. We have the same green eyes, the same cheekbones, although Kim's eyes are rimmed in too much dark makeup and the hollows in her cheeks are more pronounced. People always tell me how much I resemble my mother, but really I think it's the other way around. She resembles me, thanks to her eternal quest to look younger and younger.

"God no, sweetie. He's out of the picture. My date tonight I met at the bar."

"That sounds promising," I say, opening the fridge to a total lack of food. I stand there anyway feeling the cold air on my hot cheeks.

"Don't be so cynical," Kim says. "He's a great dancer. And you know what I say about great dancers."

I shut the fridge door and stand in front of it with my arms crossed. "I don't know, Kim. What do you say about great dancers?"

Her face sags just a little bit. She hates when I call her Kim, but that's the name she was born with. Mom is something she has yet to earn.

"Great dancers are better lovers," she says, smacking her lips together. "So I probably won't be home tonight."

"That's fine," I say. "Maybe I won't be, either." This is a lie. I have absolutely no intention of leaving the house tonight, but she doesn't need to know this. It wouldn't hurt Kim to actually worry about me from time to time.

But instead, she fluffs her hair and slides her feet into a pair of black Manolos. *My* black Manolos, probably plucked from my shoe rack while I was at school. I make a mental note to padlock my bedroom door during the day.

"Honestly, honey, now's the time to live a little. You're never going to be as young and beautiful as you are right now. I don't know why you don't have boys over more often." She straightens the hem of her dress, which doesn't do any good. It still hugs her thighs too tightly, and when she sits down, I'm sure her date will see everything under it. The thought is enough to make me gag.

"I do have boys over," I say, leaning over the granite countertop, the scene of today's crime. "You're just never home."

It's meant as a jab, but she doesn't take it that way. She just laughs, the raspy laugh of somebody who smokes but pretends she doesn't, and kisses the air beside my cheek, because actually kissing it would mess up her lipstick. And when a car horn sounds impatiently outside—apparently her date is too afraid to come to the door—she's gone, in a flurry of cloying perfume and hair spray.

I walk upstairs to my room slowly, my eyes pricking with tears. I hate how I even still care, how even my shock tactics are completely lost on Kim. I could probably tell her exactly what Zach and I did on her countertop and she would give me a high five.

I should be working on homework, writing the essay on moral ambiguity in *Hamlet* that's due next week or typing up this week's chemistry assignment, which I'll finish by myself and slap Zach's name on. But instead, I pull the white book out of my nightstand and flip absentmindedly through the pages. I read it backwards, starting with Evan Brown—who I decided to call the Gamer—and end on page one. The only one without a nickname.

His name is Tommy Hudson. He didn't come to me—I found him. It was only a few months ago, though it feels so much longer. I have passed him in the hall almost every day since, but he never makes eye contact. Probably because he's always holding her hand. Jillian Landry, willowy, long-limbed Jillian, who most likely doesn't even know my name. But I know her.

Jillian will never know this, but she is the reason I started doing what I do. Or did. After Trevor it will be *did*. Honest. Jillian planted the seed on the very first day of senior year, when she burst into the girls' bathroom with her sobbing friend in tow. Annalise was Jillian's sidekick, the chubby best friend who never got out of Jillian's shadow until she made one huge mistake.

"I'm so screwed," Annalise had whined. I could see her thick ankles from my vantage point on the toilet, clad in those stupid juvenile jelly sandals she always insisted on wearing. At that point, I still only knew her as Jillian's friend. I lifted my Converse-clad feet soundlessly off the ground and tucked them onto the toilet seat.

"Seriously, Annie, it's going to be okay. I'm sure it's a false alarm. Everything's going to be okay." She hesitated a moment. "Are you sure you want to do this here?"

"It's not like I can do it at home. My mom's always watching."

They didn't even check to see if anyone else was in the bathroom, or maybe they didn't care. I knew exactly what they were doing. If the rustling of the paper bag or the sound of pee coming in awkward spurts didn't give them away, Annalise's terrified little whimpers would have. I should have gotten up, flushed, and left, but by that point I didn't want to give away that I was there, and I was way too intrigued to go.

"You look," Annalise had said to Jillian when they exited the stall. "I can't."

A long silence. I think I even held my breath.

Jillian didn't say anything. Through the crack in the stall door, I could see her shake her head in the mirror. Annalise burst into tears, giant sobs that wracked the whole bathroom.

"Now what?" she said. "My mom won't let me finish high school here. She'll make me go to some special school for pregnant fuckups. She's going to kill me!"

"Can't you get an abortion?" Jillian had said quietly.

"No way." Annalise's red face was quivering, but she shook her head defiantly. "I might be a fuckup, but I'd never do that."

In the stall, I started to feel heat creeping up my neck. I put a hand on the toilet paper dispenser to steady myself and remind myself to breathe.

"I can't believe it," Annalise said, blowing her nose into a giant wad of paper towels. "Matt never wanted to wear a condom, but he said it would be okay. And it's not!"

"You didn't make him wear a condom?" Jillian said, her voice raised at the end. I had a pretty good idea then, not from the question itself but the question in her voice, that Jillian and Tommy hadn't ever done the deed.

"He said it desensitized his cock. God, I'm such an idiot!"

Jillian rubbed her friend's back, but I could see her staring into the mirror at her own reflection. "I'm making Tommy wear one next weekend," she said.

"Wait. You're doing it next weekend? Don't do it, Jill. Wait till you're married or something."

"I don't know if I'll ever get married. But Tommy and I have been together for ages. I trust him. I'll be safe, Annie."

I heard the hesitation in her voice, but I'm not sure Annalise did, because she just broke into a fresh fit of tears.

I stayed in the stall long after they left the bathroom, so long that both of my feet fell asleep and I forgot about meeting Angela for lunch. I couldn't stop thinking about Jillian for the rest of the day. I had a nagging feeling that I would play some sort of role in her story. I didn't know Jillian, but I knew I didn't want her to end up like Annalise.

The next week, Annalise was pulled from school. I guess she was right about her mother putting her in a special school for pregnant fuckups. She went from anonymous to the most whispered-about student at school overnight. And while everyone was busy talking about Annalise, I figured out what I wanted to do. Or, who I wanted to do.

Tommy Hudson.

It was easy. I waited until after class and trailed him into the photography darkroom, alone. I pretended I was interested in the pictures he was developing, which were all of Jillian. I asked him about her, read his tense facial expressions and noticed the way his hand shook just a little when the topic of sex entered the equation.

"I don't know why I'm telling you this," he said. "I guess it's not like I can talk to the guys about it. They'd call me a pussy and tell me to just bang her and get it over with. And I can't talk to my folks. They'd freak out and try to homeschool me." He hung his head and chewed his lower lip.

"What if I had an idea to help you get rid of your anxiety?" I said.

"I'd owe you, big time," he said.

And I gave him my address and told him to meet me there the next night. I didn't tell him what I planned to do or give him any more information. I don't know if he had a clue, and I didn't even know if he would show up. I spent a long time on my hair and makeup that day, trying to make myself into Tommy's dream girl, even though I lack Jillian's long legs and tiny waist. For the first time, I was glad Kim had bought me a matching bra and under-wear set for my birthday every year since I turned thirteen. And when Tommy rang the doorbell, I took him up to my bedroom with-out saying a word. I was nervous, but I didn't want him to know that. I wore my hair down for a reason. The loose waves covered my trembling shoulders and gave the impression of a level head.

"Guide yourself," I said as I lay underneath him. "This is your turn to take the lead. Don't make her do it." I pulled him closer to me, watched his eyes widen and his lips tremble slightly.

Tommy took direction perfectly. When I told him to use his hands to cup my face, he did it and added a kiss on my forehead. When I let him know that he bit my neck too hard, he left tiny kisses over the bite. He listened to everything I said and put his own spin on it. As his confidence grew, so did mine. I told him to make eye contact and smile, not manically but sweetly. He re-sponded by holding my gaze and remembering to blink.

It might have been the longest and most vocal two minutes of my life.

Afterward, I could practically see the tension removed from him, the way he seemed to stand taller when he put his shirt back on. I helped him plan a dream date for Jillian, a night she would never forget, starting with her favorite flowers—carnations—and ending with a candlelight dinner and the perfect first time.

"I don't know what I would've done without you," Tommy said before he left, hugging me at the front door just a little bit too tight.

"Just make it special for her," I said with a smile.

He turned around again when he was halfway down the driveway. "Why me?" he said, shrugging his shoulders. "Why Jillian?"

I didn't know how to answer that, because I honestly didn't know. Tommy and Jillian were no more familiar to me than just about every other student I passed in the halls every day. I didn't have an answer, and I still don't, so I told Tommy the next best thing.

"I just saw a chance to make myself useful."

What I couldn't tell him was that I wanted, for some desperate reason, for Jillian's first time to be what mine never was. Jillian was everything I wasn't—pure, innocent, and unaware of how much pain the opposite sex could inflict, physically and emotionally. I wanted her to stay unaware. I watched them in the days following, watched their interactions with each other. Tommy was so respectful, carrying her books and holding doors open for her. Jillian would put her hand in the back pocket of his jeans and muss up his hair playfully. I was watching, waiting for some kind of sign that they had done it. And one day I could tell by the little smile they shared, a new smile that told a secret and held a deeper kind of love.

I thought I would be happier than I was. After all, the whole end goal was to make sure Jillian got a perfect first time. But I was sad that I never had a guy like Tommy to give my virginity to, and sad that I would never be a girl like Jillian for somebody to deflower. Mostly I was just empty, like the high had evaporated and left a cheap aftertaste in its place.

And that was when another guy in the photography club approached me wanting the perfect time for himself. I could have played dumb and said no, but I didn't.

I told myself that five would be my absolute maximum. Five good deeds, five pay-it-forwards. The guys were specifically instructed to tell no one, unless they knew another virgin who needed the service. But they were even more concerned about the secrecy of the whole operation than I was. They had more at stake— girlfriends and reputations. No guy wants to admit he's a virgin and lose face, especially when his friends know he has been seeing a girl for ages and assume he gave it up the first chance he got. I really feel for guys. They have the hard part, physically and emotionally. Virginity is supposed to be something a girl gives up only when she is ready and feels comfortable, something a girl discusses at length with her friends and flip-flops over a million times in her mind before actually doing it. A guy is expected to be born ready.

But what I realized after Tommy is that they're not. They're just as scared as their girlfriends, maybe even more so because the onus is on them to be gentle, make it last, make it memorable. And most of them haven't a clue. But thanks to me, five of them would.

When five turned into ten, I thought of it solely as a science. There's logic behind everything, and the secret to my formula for success was two parts instruction, one part passion, and one part planning. I operated under the unshakeable knowledge that they needed me more than I needed them.

Except when I turn the pages and dwell on each name and nickname, it's more than a science. It's a whole system. My system, the one I invented, complete with a rating that I assigned. Each guy gets a page, even though each page only has one line. Numbers have always made more sense to me than people, so narrowing each guy down to a decimal, a rating, made it something logical.

Tommy Hudson—*Maybe I should feel guilty, but I think I really helped.*
The Biter—*6. Point redacted for leaving a mark.*
The Nervous Giggler—*5. Couldn't get past creepy laugh.*
The Screamer—*4.5. The half point is for size only.*
The Watcher—*8. Very observant.*
The Crier—*7. Point redacted for waterworks.*
The Preacher—*6. Point redacted for talking about God, which killed the mood.*
The Dirty Talker—*8. Point added for impressive vocabulary.*
The Acrobat—*7.5. Half point added for serious flexibility.*

And lastly, the Gamer. I poise my pen beside his nickname and tap it against the page. I should give him a mediocre rating, maybe redact a point for his sloppy technique. But instead I don't rate him at all.

I start making neat point-form notes like the ones I take during chemistry. *This guy's actually sweet. He'll be handsome someday. Loves his girlfriend. I wonder if they'll still be together ten years from now. Or fifty.* My own urgency to get it on paper takes me by surprise. I don't know why the Gamer escaped the rating system and got cheesy feedback, like something out of the diary of a teenage girl much different than me. I glare at the lines I just wrote and cross them out. Then I take my pen and cross out the Watcher's rating with heavy black strokes. He doesn't deserve it. I write something else over it. *Asshole.* Then I release my death grip on the pen and toss it against the wall, where it leaves a dot on the paint. Seems like it should leave a stronger mark.

I roll over on my back and clutch the book against my chest; then I chuck it onto the carpet. It's too heavy to rest on me, too full of history. Not all of it is bad. Some of the memories make me smile.

Some of them make me mad. But more dangerously, some of them make me wonder what my life would be like as a girlfriend, what it would be like to have a regular relationship, with all its ups and downs and awkward moments.

I switch out my lamp and stare at the ceiling in the dark, taking a series of shaky breaths. I know that it's better this way, being the one in control. The one in control calls the shots, and the one in control sets the pace.

Most important of all, the one in control doesn't get hurt.

5

I always like to do some research into the person I'm about to sleep with. It's more for my benefit than theirs, so I can see what kind of a person each guy is. Who he is to his friends, who he is to his girlfriend. So I take the time before Trevor Johnston comes over to read up about him, starting with the yearbook and culminating with his Facebook page. He appears in the team photos for both basketball and field hockey, which makes me a bit wary—Angela's boyfriend, Charlie, is on the soccer team, and I know that jocks talk. But I also know that Charlie isn't like most guys. He doesn't have many friends and mostly just hangs out with Angela. Even so, I make a mental note to impress upon Trevor just how important the secrecy of this operation really is.

If the yearbook tells the story of Trevor's life in sports, his Facebook page tells me he likes to party. In most of his photos, he has a beer in hand and a sloppy smile on his face. Some boys are hard to read, but Trevor isn't one of them.

I have the same ritual before I see any guy. Living up to years worth of pent-up sexual frustration is a lot of pressure, and I want to play my part well. I always shower, shave, and moisturize—vanilla for the guys I think are looking for a good girl and the more exotic frangipani for the ones who might want to get freaky. After a semester of doing this, I'm pretty good at figuring out what a boy is looking for. Jocks like that sexed-up girl next door, sometimes a flexible cheerleader type with a crop top and pigtails. Preppies are even easier to please. Give them kneesocks and not much else and they're good to go. The brainiacs are the wild cards. Sometimes I break out the leather for them, and sometimes I go the simplest route—nothing at all.

Normally, before a guy is coming over, I put the finishing touches on my bedroom. I make sure the sheets are clean and lightly scented with lavender, the lighting is dim, and there are at least two candles burning. This is important, as I tell the guys, because it sets the mood. "No girl is going to want to sleep with you on top of your smelly gym shorts, underneath the Playboy posters taped to your ceiling," I remember saying to the Acrobat when he commented on the décor.

And this is the position I'm in—stretched across my bed, tucking in the corners of my duvet—when Kim strolls into my room, with the unmistakable smell of perfume and cigarettes clinging to her. Eau de Kim. The situation would be less awkward if I were wearing something other than a men's button-down shirt with lace panties and kneesocks, but Kim doesn't even blink.

"I didn't know you were home," I say, smoothing my duvet and sitting on it. Kim unfortunately plops down as well.

"I thought we could have girls' night," she says, putting "girls' night" in air quotes. Kim's air quotes look more like claws, courtesy of her crimson nail polish and ridiculously long acrylic nails.

I clench my jaw and ball my duvet in both hands. Kim never initiates mother-daughter time. Mostly I think she forgets we even share a house.

"I can't," I say. "I'm having company."

"Oh. Of course," Kim says. "I love what you've done with the place. Very romantic." I can't tell if she's being sincere or sarcastic. "Is this a new boyfriend of yours?"

"He's somebody's boyfriend, but not mine," I say brightly. I regret saying it almost immediately, but Kim's terrible timing and half-assed attempts to ingratiate herself into my life piss me off. Maybe if she discovers that I'm promiscuous, she will start to worry about me.

Kim narrows her eyes and smooths my hair back. The gesture almost brings me to tears. It's the one maternal gesture I remember from when I was a little kid, when Kim would brush my hair and put it in French braids for me. That was before she told me French braids were babyish and I should start looking more like a woman. I think I was ten years old.

"I think you should change your lipstick," she says slowly. "That red isn't doing you any favors. Here, try this." She rummages in her purse and presses a tube of lipstick in my hand, then pats my bare thigh before leaving the room.

"Thanks," I say numbly, but she isn't around to hear it. I roll the lipstick around in my hand and look at the ceiling, counting back from ten. This tactic, focusing on numbers, always makes me feel less like crying.

I change my lipstick when I hear Trevor ring the doorbell. I hate that I even care about Kim's opinion, but she gives one so rarely that I take it anyway. And she's right. Kim's lipstick is soft pink and Trevor sure seems to like it.

"God, you're hot," he says when I shut my bedroom door behind us and unbutton my shirt. Due to his jock status, I took Trevor for the type with a naughty schoolgirl fantasy and little in the way of imagination.

"Don't tell her she's hot," I tell him for what feels like the millionth time as I yank his jeans down. "Girls don't like to hear that. It makes them feel like objects. Tell her she's beautiful."

"You're beautiful," he says. "You have pretty hair. And soft skin." As if to prove his point, he starts groping at my stomach and chest like he's lost in the dark and trying to feel his way out by grabbing a wall.

"Even better, don't say anything," I say. I turn my iPod on, where I have the usual sex sound track ready. Except today, I turn the volume up much higher than I have to, just to piss Kim off.

"That's loud," Trevor says. "Can't we talk, too?"

"Not during sex," I say before biting his earlobe. "Never have the room completely silent. You don't want to force Laura to hear your weird grunting noises, do you?"

Trevor almost looks like he's about to cry. Usually I would be sympathetic and try to beef up his confidence, the one thing every virgin lacks. But tonight I'm full of aggression and short on patience. So after I show Trevor how to put a condom on properly, I get on top of him and do my best to moan even louder than the music. Trevor joins in with a chorus of "oh, baby" and "this is awesome!" I will him to last long enough to get me off, long enough to offer me some kind of release. But I don't get one.

"I'm sorry," he says when we're finished. I'm not listening to him. I'm listening for a telltale knock at the door, anything to let me know that Kim is at least a bit concerned that a boy she has never seen before is over having sex with her daughter.

Trevor goes to put his hand on my breast but settles for my shoulder instead. "I feel like I pissed you off," he says. "Whatever I said wrong, I didn't mean to. I told you I had no idea what I was doing."

I know I should put my shirt back on and help him with the mechanics of the nonsex part, setting the perfect scene. In the past I have helped with everything from location to brand of cologne to style of underwear (never briefs, especially not white ones). I critique restaurant selections and even veto food choices, like the time I had to explain to the Crier why Mexican food was a terrible choice of cuisine for anyone wanting to get laid. But tonight I'm not in the mood for any of that. Laura is just about the furthest thing from my mind.

"Practice makes perfect," I say, kissing Trevor's neck gently enough to not leave a mark but hard enough to get him aroused.

I do something I have never done before—let Trevor have a second round. I tell myself it's purely educational, but when I cling to his neck and wrap my legs tightly around his back, I know deep down that it's not. It's as much for me as it is for him.

When we're finished, he circles my jawline with his thumb and index finger, coming to a point at my chin. It happens too fast for me to realize what he's doing, and before my mind can formulate a reaction, my body does it for me. That touch, exactly how Luke used to do it, right down to pressing the pad of his thumb into the groove of my chin. I tilt my face into his hands and close my eyes. He pushes my bangs off my forehead.

"You're pretty," he whispers. His face is close to mine, so close that his hair falls onto my cheek. I open my eyes quickly. It's all too familiar, the way he's touching me and the way his hair is on my face. I can feel his heart pounding against my chest, his heavy beats out of sync with my light, erratic fluttering. And he's too heavy on top of me, like any minute he could smother my whole body.

"Off," I say, wiggling out from under him. "Off. I can't do this."

He pulls his hands away from my face. I can tell he's still looking at me, staring at the back of my head.

"I think we already did," he says quietly.

By the time we put our clothes back on and I show Trevor to the door, I realize Kim isn't even home. I must not have noticed the garage door opening over the deafening music. She took her purse and her car but left a note on her beloved granite countertop.

> *Leftovers in the fridge. Just don't eat too much—boys are hard enough to please. Love, MOM.*

MOM in capital letters, with a squiggly line underneath.

I shred the note into a million pieces and spend the rest of the night typing chemistry notes. I only pause to wipe the tears that insist on leaking out the corners of my eyes. It must be the hormones, or whatever endorphins you're supposed to feel after sex. It has nothing to do whatsoever with my mother not caring how many guys I sleep with.

Before I curl up in the sheets Trevor and I had sex in, I make another entry in my pearly white notebook. Trevor Johnston, number eleven. I give him a nine in loopy lettering, then add commentary. *Good looking. Strong. I bet he's a good boyfriend, the kind that's fun and can be serious when the time calls for it.*

The more I write about Trevor, the worse I feel, but I can't seem to stop. I'm afraid of what will happen when I stop. *The way he touched me. He touched me like only one person has ever touched me before. How can he touch me like that when he barely knows me?*

I give him a nickname, even though I almost don't want to. It's part of the system, a rite of passage. Every guy needs a nickname, so Trevor is forever immortalized as Round Two.

6

The next morning, I pretend I'm surprised to see Kim home, even though I heard her thump into the house sometime after midnight. As she clatters around in the kitchen, I change into something I know will raise her eyebrows as far up her forehead as they can go. One of my lingerie tops, a black one with lacy trim, tucked into a tiny denim skirt. Instead of my usual Cons, I pull on high heels. I grip the railing as I toddle down the stairs.

"Good morning," I say, forcing a perky voice. I reach into the cupboard for a coffee mug. Usually I have to stand on my tiptoes to reach, but the heels give me extra leverage.

Kim throws up her hands. "We're out of coffee. We're out of coffee and I can't find anything in this damn kitchen."

"Maybe you should try grocery shopping," I tell her, palming my mug and elbowing her out of the way. "Coffee's back here. With the breakfast food. Where it belongs." I should know. I'm the one who organized the cupboards in the first place. One trait I share with Kim is that neither of us can live in chaos. Everything has to not only have a place but has to occupy the right place. A place that makes sense.

"You look nice today," Kim says, pressing herself against the counter. "Very pretty."

I turn away to pour coffee grinds into the filter and try to ignore the rush of pride that ripples through me. I know I don't look nice today. I don't look pretty. I don't even look like myself. I have never let the persona I put on in my bedroom cross over into real life before, and I didn't do it today for any guy. My reflection is distorted in the stainless steel—pink lipstick and dark-rimmed eyes. I look more like Kim than I ever thought possible.

"Well, you look like you need some sleep," I say, spinning around to face her. I don't add that she also smells like she needs a shower and some mouthwash.

"Maybe we can go shopping today," Kim says, cocking her head. "You can help me pick out some new clothes."

I grit my teeth. This is what I wanted last night. I wanted Kim to act like a mom. But it's all wrong, the way she does it. She can never get it right. A good mom would take her daughter shopping on a weekend, not at seven in the morning on a school day. A good mom would remember that her daughter has school. A good mom wouldn't let her daughter leave the house dressed the way I am right now, not in a million years.

"I can't," I say, slamming the mug down on the counter with more force than I intended. "I have that thing. School. You know— that place where I go to classes and get straight As."

"Oh. Duh," Kim says, slapping her forehead with the heel of her hand. "Well, you can skip it for one day, can't you? One day won't hurt."

I grip the countertop behind me with my fingers. I want to scream, but when my voice comes out, it's flat and emotionless. Kim can't get the mom thing right, and I can never show emotion when I feel it. What a fucked-up family unit we are. I wonder who she blames, since I blame her.

"I can't skip it. In case you forgot, I'm going to MIT next year. I need to actually go to class to get the grades, and I'm not throwing that away so you can buy more clothes you don't need and shouldn't be wearing anyway." I grab my bag off the table and storm out the door with shaking hands.

"Well, have a good day, honey!" Kim calls behind me. I slam the door to the Jeep as hard as I can, but it still barely makes a sound. I don't look back and I don't return the wave that I know she's giving me, her red-talon nails extending to the ceiling. Why can't she ever get mad? Why can't she take something personally? Why does everything I say bounce off her, like her plastic skin is some freakish form of Teflon?

I'm already in the parking lot at school by the time I realize I'm here way too early. Class doesn't start for another hour, and prayer group isn't meeting today. The minutes stretch in front of me on the clock radio. I can't sit here, not for another second. I'm full of energy that I don't know what to do with, so I decide to channel it into something productive and go to the science lab. I can sit at my desk and read ahead on our next assignment. Zach will be thrilled that he'll have even less work to pretend to do.

I'm met with a warm breeze when I step out of the Jeep, and I reach down to tug at the hem of my skirt, willing it to cover more skin. At least I had the good sense to grab a cardigan. I wasn't actually planning on leaving the house like this. I was going to wait until Kim left and change back into my normal attire. I could go back now, but that would mean running into her again, and she would ask why I'm changing and then she would know I put this outfit on for her. And that's not a satisfaction I'm about to give her.

The hallways are dark and quiet. The only sound is my heels clacking on the floor. I remember being in grade nine with Angela, when we hated sitting in the cafeteria but she was worried about being caught eating in the hallway. At the first hint of clacking heels, she would shove her food back into her backpack, and I would always laugh because she looked so guilty. Usually it wasn't even a teacher, just a senior who would give us a weird look.

The door to the science lab is ajar, but the room is mostly dark. I set my bag down and flip on the lights. For some reason I wander behind the desk Mr. Sellers occupies at the front of the room instead of heading to my own desk. I pick up the whiteboard marker he uses and stand beside the board. I clear my throat and begin to speak to nobody.

"Today, we're going to be talking about electronegativity. It's more interesting than it sounds. It's all about attraction. The higher the electronegativity of an atom, the greater its attraction for bonding electrons."

I pause and prepare to draw a diagram on the whiteboard, until a soft knock at the door makes me drop the whiteboard marker. My heart starts pounding through my flimsy excuse for a top when I realize who is standing in the doorway.

Jillian Landry, with her perfect hair and perfectly appropriate khaki pants. She's hugging a textbook to her chest and smiling.

I instinctively pull my cardigan tightly around myself and bend down to pick up the marker with my butt facing the whiteboard. Why is she here? I didn't even know Jillian took chemistry. I have never been in a class with her. But I guess I don't know anything about her, really, besides what I gleaned from Tommy. I don't know anything about her except how much he loves her.

"You're good at that," she says when I come back to a stand-ing position. "I never understand it when Mr. Sellers tries to explain it. I always space out after five seconds of hearing him talk."

I roll the marker between my fingers. I guess I should be em-barrassed that Jillian caught me talking to myself, but there are a thousand other things running through my head instead. I won-der if Tommy loves her more now than before they slept together. I wonder if he tells her she's beautiful, if he remembers special dates and opens doors for her. I wonder if I helped him and in turn helped her. Then I banish that thought from my head. Would I be doing this if I weren't helping people?

"It's his voice," I say finally. "He's like a drone. Obviously he re-cites the same spiel, year after year. And year after year, nobody tells him how dry it is."

Jillian laughs and takes a seat at a desk. My desk. "Yeah. Well, I can't fully blame him. I have a terrible attention span. Which ex-plains the C I'm getting in this class."

I sit down at Mr. Sellers's desk, grateful that its big wooden bulk is covering my bare thighs. Jillian is staring at her notebook now. Maybe I should leave her alone and get out before this gets too awkward.

"I'm Jillian," she says. "And I suck at chemistry."

"I'm Mercedes," I say.

"I know," she says, raising an eyebrow. For a second all the blood rushes to my head. *I know.* Two words I never wanted to hear coming from Jillian Landry.

"I know," she continues. "He mentions you. You're his little superstar."

Suddenly I feel like I'm going to be sick. My stomach twists in a violent knot. "Who does?" I squeak out, my voice tinny and un-natural.

She smiles. "Mr. Sellers, of course. I think you're the yardstick he measures the rest of us by. And you set the bar pretty high."

I take a deep breath as my heart returns to its normal rate. She doesn't know. It isn't Tommy who mentions me. Why would he?

"I'm doing this thing," she continues, thankfully oblivious to my inner panic. "This Students Helping Students program. I came up with it last year to help my friend who was doing shitty in French class. Basically we pair a student who is doing well with someone who isn't. It benefits both people. The person struggling hopefully gets better grades. The person doing well gets to add tutoring experience to a college resume."

I lean back into Mr. Sellers's chair. I remember seeing Jillian during activities week, sitting behind a booth in the hallway. I remember Angela talking about the program but being too nervous to sign up. I remember writing it off because I'm not a joiner.

"Where's your helper?" I ask.

Jillian rolls her eyes. "Good question. It's supposed to be Bobby Lewis, but he's noticeably not here. Again."

I almost choke on the saliva collecting under my tongue, but I try not to react. I can't even imagine Bobby Lewis, aka the Acrobat, as a legitimate chemistry tutor. I figured he had no authority teaching anything besides gymnastics, at least according to what went on in my bedroom.

"I really thought this program would help people," Jillian says, shaking her head. "I guess I never considered that I'd be the one getting screwed over by it."

I stare at her, with the ends of her hair pooling on the cover of the textbook. Jillian is a good person, the kind who tries to help other people. The violent knot in my stomach returns. My insides feel like they're being wrung out like a wet towel.

"I'll do it," I say before I can take the words back. "I'll do it. I mean, if you want me to, I'll help you."

Jillian smiles broadly. She has a great smile, wide and open and honest. The smile of somebody who has never been hurt before, or at least not badly enough for it to leave evidence.

"It'll look good on your college application," she says, even though we both know college applications have already been sent and MIT will never know if I do or don't tutor Jillian Landry. "I hope I'm not too dense for you."

So before school even officially starts for the day, I'm the newest member of Students Helping Students. I'll be working with Jillian once a week as well as a junior named Toby, who Jillian says is desperate. I had no idea so many people needed help, at least not help in the classroom.

"I can't thank you enough," Jillian says when she closes her textbook after a crash course in electronegativity. "I would have been so screwed otherwise."

I paste on a smile, even though the inside of my mouth is cotton-dry. All this time I have been trying not to think about Tommy, to keep my mind on atoms and elements and ionization energies. But he keeps creeping in, invading everything that makes sense and dragging along something that feels a whole lot like guilt. I can't deal with it right now, so I push it out of my head and tell Jillian that I'm happy to help. And it's the truth, in more ways than one.

7

I'm vaguely aware when I walk into home economics later that day that I'm not anonymous in this class, and not because of my barely there outfit. I switched into this class at the last minute because I fulfilled my math credits in first semester, and because Angela told me it would be fun. I can already tell that fun isn't the word I'll use to describe it.

"Mercedes," Trevor Johnston says, turning around to where I sat down beside Angela. He winks at me and stares too long at my crossed legs, a gesture he probably thinks is subtle but definitely isn't. I look down at my notebook, willing him to not make eye contact. Then I notice who he is sitting beside: Chase Redgrave, aka the Dirty Talker. Chase at least has the decency to pretend he has no idea who I am.

"How do you know that guy?" Angela whispers in my ear. I shrug, aware that a flush is creeping into my face, but I'm spared coming up with an excuse when our teacher loudly admonishes somebody for coming in late—somebody I have gratefully not slept with. I do a quick sweep of the classroom to make sure I haven't slept with anybody else in attendance, but luckily Trevor and Chase are the only two. I inwardly panic when I see Trevor whisper something to Chase. How do they know each other? And how much do they know about each other?

I turn my gaze to the back of the room, where there are two vacant desks side by side. Maybe Angela and I can sit back there instead, far away from Trevor and Chase. Maybe it's not too late to move.

"Can we relocate? That guy's cologne is giving me a headache," I whisper.

"I can't see the board from back there," Angela says.

"Maybe if you wore your glasses you could," I hiss.

Angela frowns and turns around. "Wait, isn't that your lab partner?"

I grip my desk with my fingers and peer over my shoulder. Shit. Sure enough, Zach is slinking into the classroom, taking exaggerated tiptoe steps, no doubt to cover up the fact that he's walking in after the bell.

"Mr. Sutton," our teacher, Mrs. Hill, says. "Nice of you to grace us with your presence."

I watch Zach's face turn red as he plops into one of the empty desks. When he meets my eyes, he winks and gives me a little wave. I roll my eyes and turn around to face the board. Great. Now I'm trapped between three people I have slept with. It's like the worst kind of claustrophobia. Why would Zach want to take home economics, anyway? I figured he would hate this stuff. Although, I guess I kind of do, too.

Mrs. Hill is rambling on about our first assignment, the details of which I can glean later from Angela. I already hate her high, screechy voice and the way she insists on rapping the blackboard with a meter stick periodically, probably to make sure we're paying attention. I have more important things to pay attention to, like whether or not my secret is going to be exposed by the end of the day. I don't know what would be worse—the whole school finding out, or Zach finding out the real reason I don't want to be his girlfriend.

Trevor and Chase. Chase and Trevor. Trevor is a jock; Chase is a preppy with a seriously sick mind beneath all that argyle. I never thought their paths would cross. I know that guys were bound to talk within their own groups, but I didn't think there would be any cross contamination between other groups. So far I have been able to avoid awkward exchanges and judgmental stares and that chatter that stops the second you walk into a room.

I think back to what I tell every guy before he gains entry to my bedroom: *Don't wink at me, don't wave to me, don't talk to me. Don't even look at me. If you do, I don't have to tell you how much I have on you.* Most of them look at me with wide eyes and nod their heads in assent. The ones who don't at first do when I threaten to show them the door.

I try not to visibly cringe when Trevor and Chase give each other one of those lame fist bumps. I seriously hope that isn't universal guy code for "I slept with Mercedes, too."

"Mercy. Duh." Angela is poking me in the ribs with her pen. I look up to see the whole class, plus Mrs. Hill, staring at me. Mrs. Hill is even rapping that goddamned meter stick.

"Sorry. I missed the question."

"That's not surprising," Mrs. Hill says, bringing the meter stick to rest beside her desk. "That's what happens when you don't pay attention."

"Sorry, Mrs. Hill." I give her my sweetest smile, which feels like more of a grimace.

"As punishment, I'm going to make you my first victim. Today's topic," she says, hitting the blackboard with her meter stick with an ungodly amount of force, "is sexual education. Nobody wants to talk about it, but we have to make it a priority."

I want to curl up under my desk and disappear. This can't possibly be happening. As if Trevor and Chase and Zach in the same room wasn't bad enough, now Mrs. Hill seems to be in on the joke. I suddenly have to fight an unpleasant mental image of Mrs. Hill wielding that meter stick like a whip. Mrs. Hill, the dominatrix in an ill-fitting pantsuit.

"Although, I don't call it sexual education. I call it safer sex. We're not telling you not to do it. Just how to do it safer." She laughs, an unnaturally high-pitched sound. Her hands are shaking slightly as she opens her desk drawer. She comes up with a goddamned bunch of bananas.

"This is not going to end well," I mutter under my breath. By the look Angela gives me, I can tell she has no idea what Mrs. Hill is going to do with those bananas. Lucky Angela.

"Has everyone seen one of these?" she says, wagging a condom packet in the air. I recognize it as a Ribbed Ultra Thin. I wonder if it came from Mrs. Hill's own collection, yet another mental image I don't want to have.

The guys in the class snicker. Chase laughs the loudest of all. I pretend not to notice. Trevor, at least, has the good grace to shut up and stare at the blackboard, although I can see the backs of his ears turning red. I don't even dare to peek at Zach, but I can feel his eyes on me, boring holes into me. It's unsettling. Why does he have to look at me like that?

We all watch Mrs. Hill hastily rip open the condom and try to sheathe the banana. Some people laugh. Others, like Angela, cover their eyes with their hands. Somebody films it on a cell phone, unbeknownst to Mrs. Hill and her no technology rule. Although Mrs. Hill has a wedding ring on, I get the feeling she has never put a condom on a guy in her life. Her brow furrows under her frizzy hair. *You just ripped it with your fingernail, you idiot*, I want to tell her. *That condom's going to break. Mrs. Hill, you just got pregnant.*

"I'm leaving this stuff up to Charlie," Angela says through her hands. "When we're married, of course."

Yeah, right, I want to tell her. *Because men always know what they're doing.*

"Voilà," Mrs. Hill says. The condom sags loosely around the banana she waves in the air. *I hope he pulled out*, I want to say.

"Mercedes, do you want to give it a turn?" Mrs. Hill says, thrusting a naked banana in my direction with a nervous laugh. "I did say you'd be my first victim."

I stare at Angela, whose eyes are wide with terror. Chase laughs into his hand and tries to disguise it as a cough. The back of Trevor's neck turns an unfortunate shade of crimson. I'm just glad my face isn't turning the same color, and I'm about to stand up on shaking legs—either to give the class a better demonstration or to configure an escape route from this school—when somebody saves me the trouble.

"That's really a terrible example," says the female voice accompanying the knock at the door. "It's supposed to block the sperm, not give it a swimming pool."

Everyone turns at once. The girl in the doorway gives the guys in the front row whiplash. I see their reactions before I actually see her. I'm expecting rough, tough, maybe army-green cargo pants and a bad haircut. I'm not expecting beautiful.

"You call this sex ed," she says. "I call it a really lame Friday night."

One laugh breaks the silence. Mine.

"Who is that?" Angela hisses in my ear.

The girl pushes her honey-colored hair behind her shoulders, an amused expression on her face. She could probably commit murder and hide behind that face.

I make the mistake of looking at Zach now, of all times. He's not looking at me anymore. He's staring at the new girl, and I don't like the expression on his face. It's how he used to look at me, before we ever slept together. It's the face he makes when he's concentrating, when the wheels in his head are turning, when he's thinking about something he wants.

I didn't know he could look at another girl like that.

I watch the new girl sit down in the vacant desk beside Zach. His eyes travel from her face, make a detour down to her legs, and come to rest on her boobs, which are propped up inside a tiny tank top. *Gross, Zach. Way to be so completely obvious.*

"I have absolutely no idea," I say to Angela, and it must be what the thirty other students in the class are thinking, too.

Her name is Faye. I don't know her last name, or where she came from, or why she transferred to our school right when second semester is starting, when freedom from high school is a mere six months away. I only know that her name is Faye and that she's terrible at chemistry. I know the second part because as of Wednesday morning, she has displaced Zach as my new chemistry partner. Mr. Sellers's choice, not mine or Zach's.

"I guess we'll have to figure out a new label," Zach says as he gathers his stuff with a heaving sigh. "Like maybe 'Wednesday friend.'"

Faye watches him shuffle off with a raised eyebrow. "He's cute," she says. "I sat beside him in home economics yesterday. He even offered to share his notes."

I barely resist rolling my eyes. I'm sure that's all he offered to share.

"I wouldn't trust Zach's notes," I hear myself say. "They're probably more like doodles in the margins."

Faye stifles a laugh and I realize how mean that sounded, how sharp my voice was. I don't know why I even said that. Just because Zach sucks at chemistry doesn't mean he sucks at all his other classes, too. Plus, we're supposed to be friends. But before I can open my mouth to fix it, Faye cuts in.

"Well, he's probably pissed that I'm stealing his lab partner. I hope I didn't ruin chemistry for him."

I shake my head but silently vow to make it up to him today at lunch. "Zach's resilient. He'll be fine."

"So, what's your deal? You're like, a chemistry superstar? I got lucky, then." She looks at me from under eyelashes that must be fake. No tube of Maybelline Great Lash would give that much volume. I should know—I have tried out enough mascaras to bankrupt any drugstore on my eternal quest for the perfect bedroom eyes.

I shrug. "I just get it. I like how everything can be boiled down to a formula. Makes it almost impossible to fail."

She laughs, a harsh, grating sound, like some kind of animal should be making it instead of a teenage girl. "I guess I never understood the formula, then."

Today, we're making a volcano out of hydrochloric acid and sodium bicarbonate. The end result is supposed to be an explosion. It's a juvenile experiment, one that was done ad nauseam last year, but Mr. Sellers is intent on reincarnating it again this year. Either that, or he's going senile, which may be likely, considering he must be pushing eighty.

"I like watching things explode," Faye says as she pours solution into a beaker—the wrong kind of solution, too much of the indicator solution and not enough sodium bicarbonate.

"Just watch your mixing," I tell her. "You need to wait to add the diluted hydrochloric acid to the purple solution. Otherwise it won't explode. It'll just kind of be—"

"Flaccid?" Her laughter rises over the general din of the room. Zach, two rows in front of us, turns his head back and makes a pouty face. Zach's own volcano, I notice, is mixed with the correct proportions. I feel a swell of pride. When he catches my eye, he winks. I wink back.

Then I realize I don't know who he's winking at—because Faye is looking at him, too.

"I was going to say stagnant," I say loudly. "But flaccid is better." I dump the contents of Faye's beaker down the sink.

"So doing all this boring prep work is like foreplay," Faye says, flipping her hair over her shoulder. "Sorry. I'm afraid I have a bit of a one-track mind."

I open my mouth to say something, but Faye interrupts. I don't know what I would have said anyway. I didn't think my new chemistry partner would be so much like my old one, full of sexual innuendos and with total disregard for the lesson plan.

"So, what do you guys do for fun around here?" Faye asks.

"Depends on what you're into."

"Well, what're you doing this weekend? I could do it with you." She bites her bottom lip.

I shrug, feeling a flush creep up my neck and wishing she would stop looking at me like that. *Is she flirting with me, or Zach?* I recognize in her all of Kim's go-to moves. The lip biting, the hair flipping, the eyelash batting. Except Faye does them much better, with curiosity instead of desperation. If she is flirting, she's doing a better job of it than I ever could. She's all soft lines and finesse, where I'm sharp edges and instructions. She's subtle, where I'm just blunt.

And I don't like it.

"I'm studying with my friend," I say quickly. "She needs tutoring." I gesture toward Angela, who is shying away from her lab partner's hand-wringing proclamations.

"I need some tutoring, too," she says. "What time should I come over?"

I adjust my safety goggles and pretend to be studying the formula in my notebook. This is why I like chemistry: everything is straightforward; everything comes from directions. The end result only becomes an end result because of steps one to five and won't happen if any of the steps are missed or done out of order. Most people follow some sort of formula, too, or make some degree of sense. You can't be a football captain without putting in the work—going to practice, eating right, getting enough sleep, lifting weights. You can't be a math whiz without studying the material and putting in the time. I stereotype the guys I sleep with for a reason, because people's personalities develop from a routine, too.

Faye seems not to follow a formula. And it's extremely unnerving.

"Come over at noon," I say. "Bring your books. And be ready to work. I don't mess around." My voice sounds harsh, but Faye doesn't seem to notice. I almost want to shake her to drill my point across. I don't need another friend. Angela was my only one, until Zach insisted on becoming one, too. The more friends you have, the higher your chance of taking a knife in your back.

Out of the corner of my eye, I see Faye smile. Her teeth are perfect, either from genetics or years of braces. I self-consciously run my tongue over my teeth. I have always hated the two beside my front ones, which I think look like little fangs. Even Zach commented on them during sex. His exact words were, "You should role-play as a vampire. That would be hot."

I wonder what Zach thinks of Faye's smile. Yet another thing about her that one-ups me.

Our science project erupts in front of us before bubbling over.

"I think ours just came," Faye says.

9

I'm almost grateful to Angela for dragging me to Charlie's soccer game after school the next day, more for the distraction than anything else. But considering Angela is generally against all organized school activities (with the exception of prayer group, which she conceived of in the first place anyway), I'm a bit surprised that she has decided to become Charlie's cheerleader from the stands after two years of not going to a single game.

"It'll be fun," she says, but her tone of voice implies she's getting a root canal, not watching her boyfriend kick a ball around.

We take a seat in the first row of bleachers. I want to sit at the very back, just like I do during classes, but Angela won't let me. "Charlie wants to make sure he can see me," she says, tugging at her frayed shirtsleeves and squinting into the sun. "Except I can barely see what one he is. Why are they all wearing the same outfit?"

I smile and put my arm around her shoulder. "Because they're on the same team, Ange. They're uniforms, not outfits. And if you can't see what one Charlie is, you probably need your glasses."

Since I haven't ever seen a school soccer game, either, I don't know what soccer players are supposed to look like. But if I had to go by the preconceived notion I have in my head, they would all look exactly like Charlie. Tall and sinewy with lean muscles, with a faint hint of a tan from playing outside. The cheerleaders are stretching on the sidelines but keep whispering in a clump and pointing at him. Angela claims she doesn't notice the way girls look at her boyfriend, but I don't see how she's that blind. She really should start wearing her glasses.

Even if Angela can't see a thing, Charlie sees us. He keeps casting glances in our direction, along with winks meant just for Angela. When he scores a goal, he looks up to make sure she sees it, his face a mask of concentration and pride. I feel a pang of envy in spite of myself. Charlie and Angela have the kind of connection that you can almost physically feel. The kind of connection I have only felt with one person, who never felt it with me.

"This seat taken?"

I use my hand as a visor and look to where the voice came from, but Faye has already plopped down beside me and dropped her messenger bag almost directly on my foot.

"You're Angela, right? I'm Faye," she says with a wave to Angela. "Mercedes's new lab partner."

Angela smiles shyly. "I know," she says. "You're lucky. Mercy is the best lab partner ever."

Faye drops her gaze on my face. In the bright light, her eyes are a watery blue.

"Mercy," she says. I look down at my feet. I have never heard my name said like *that* before, almost like a little sigh instead of a name.

She points to the field. "I always thought soccer was an underrated high school sport. The players always have nice legs. And they have all their teeth!" She taps her fingers against her denim-clad thighs.

None of us says anything as we watch the action on the field. Faye starts moving her hands and arms subtly when the cheerleaders do their lame sideline dance. She's mimicking their motions exactly.

"Looks like you missed tryouts," I say.

But Faye just smiles brightly. "I was a cheerleader at my old high school," she says. "We all think we have an original routine, but really it's all a perpetuation of the same cliché."

I want to ask her why she left her old high school. But the question seems so blunt and would probably seem like an accusation leaving my mouth. There are only two reasons why somebody would do that. One involves a parent getting a job in a new city, and the other involves trouble. The kind of trouble you can't hide from.

"Number fifteen is hot," Faye says. "And he keeps looking at you."

I cast a glance at Angela, who is picking her fingernails. Most girls would be jumping at the chance to lay claim to the team superstar, but Angela says nothing.

"That's Charlie," I say. "Angela's boyfriend. He's looking at her."

Faye nods appreciatively. "Nice work, Angela," she says. "Your boyfriend has great footwork."

When the game is over, Charlie gestures for us to come down to the field. He wraps Angela in a sweaty hug, which she looks more disgusted by than anything.

"Ouch," I say, pointing out a bloody patch of skin on Charlie's calf muscle. "That looks like it hurts."

Charlie shrugs. "That Ridgewood guy was an asshole. I'll make sure he gets what he has coming to him." The sun glints in his eyes. He's smiling, but I can't tell if he's joking or not.

I pull my cardigan tightly around my shoulders, aware of a chill building at the base of my spine. Faye drapes her arm around my neck like we have been friends for years, not one day.

"So, which one's your boyfriend?" she says. "Please, tell me it's that young Antonio Banderas over there who keeps checking you out."

I follow her gaze to the edge of the field, where a guy with black curly hair is indeed staring in our direction. When I meet his eyes, he doesn't look away, so I do. I don't like when guys stare like that. It doesn't happen often, but when it does, I wonder exactly how much they know.

"I don't have a boyfriend," I tell her.

"Not even Chemistry Boy?"

"Nope."

"Come on. No lab partner is that upset to move desks. Something must be going on."

I grit my teeth. "I said no. He's just some guy who happened to sit beside me."

She doesn't take the hint. "Come on. So he's not an ex? A fling? Not even a drunken mistake?"

I shake my head. "None of the above. Just a chemistry partner, and I did the work anyway."

In other words, end of story.

She bites her lip. "Well, want to grab a bite to eat? I'm starving." She stretches her arms over her head, revealing an expanse of flat tanned stomach. Her belly button is pierced. I try not to notice, just like I try not to notice the beginning—or end—of a tattoo snaking out of her waistband when she turns around. But I guess I don't do a very good job of not noticing.

"I made some bad decisions the summer before ninth grade," she says with a smirk. "My mom wanted to kill me."

I force a smile, but the effort leaves my face strained. I clutch my own stomach instinctively. Faye isn't the only one who made bad decisions the summer before ninth grade. Except the bad decisions she made are ones Kim would have gotten on board with. I remember my first day of tenth grade, which Kim wanted to commemorate with mother-daughter eyebrow rings. That was the month she dated the drummer in some band and wanted to seem edgier. Thankfully, we never went through with it.

Somehow I don't think Kim would agree with my bad decisions, and I'll never give her a chance to know about them.

I tell Faye I'm not feeling so well and head to the parking lot. I don't know why she has decided to be friends with me, out of all the people at Milton. She'd fit right in with the bubbly-perky-C-cup-plus cheerleaders, or the preppies, or even the drama geeks. Anybody but me. *Pick someone else*, I want to scream. *I'm damaged goods*.

All I want to do is go home and be alone. Except when I get to my Jeep, somebody is waiting there for me. The curly-haired guy from the soccer game, the one who was staring at me.

"You should be driving a faster car," he says, pushing his foot against the tire of my Jeep. "How about a ride?"

"You should be taking the bus home," I say, crossing my arms. "I'm not a carpool service. Especially for people I don't know."

He leans in. I reach into my purse for my keys, unsure whether I'll use them to open my car door or stab him in the eyeball.

"I did not mean that kind of ride," he says, his thick accent punctuated with a nervous giggle. "I am sorry. Forgive my bad joke."

"What is it you want?" I say, thinking I might already know. "Because you're going to have to be more specific."

"I want to give you my virginity," he says. "If you'll take it."

I almost break out laughing. He says it so casually, like he's offering me some kind of gift. Except I don't laugh, because for some people sex is a gift. For some people, it's special. Even sacred. I stopped thinking of it that way long ago. For me, it's just science, formulaic elements combined together for an end result.

"What makes you think I'd be interested?" I say. I want to sound calm and collected, but my voice is rising. This guy is on the soccer team. Charlie is on the soccer team. If Charlie ever found out what I did, he would tell Angela. And if Angela found out, the one friendship that has gotten me through high school would be over.

"I hear about you from my friend. Trevor."

I narrow my eyes, resolving to give Round Two a talking-to if we're ever alone together again. Apparently he has a different concept of discretion than I do.

He bites his bottom lip, causing it to turn a cherry red shade. Despite my objections, this guy is attractive, and I wonder what it would be like to kiss those lips.

"Tell me in one word why I should help you," I say.

"One word. Isabella." He sounds out each syllable, making the name sound impossibly exotic. *Is-a-bell-a.* "I love her. But I did not tell her she is my first kiss. And my first girlfriend. When Trevor tells me what you do for him, I have to seek you out." He lowers his voice. "I love her."

I look into his eyes. He does love this Isabella. He would be number twelve. *Twelve.* I can no longer pretend I haven't crossed the ten line. But I can't bring myself to walk away from this guy. Trevor shouldn't really count. Round Two was a mistake, a mistake made when I was feeling especially vulnerable. I let my own agenda get in the way. I can make up for it with the guy standing in front of me, chewing his lip.

"Go home and shower, then come and see me." I give him my address before getting into the Jeep, before I can chicken out. As I drive home, my hands are shaking and my heart is pounding. I'm exhibiting all of the telltale signs of being excited about something. When I first started doing this, I felt wary before each encounter, almost scared. My hands would tremble when I unbuttoned a guy's fly and my legs would shiver when I climbed onto a lap. But somewhere between five and ten, this started happening. The sense that it's not just for them anymore. The knowledge that I like it, too. The fear that I want more out of it than all of them combined can give me.

And if all of them combined can't give me what I want, I'm scared to find out what will.

10

"I showered," he says when I open the door to him waiting in full-on formal wear: a dress shirt, dress pants, and a tie, almost like this is a date. "And I brought you these." He pulls a bouquet of red roses from behind his back.

He smells like too much cologne, but that's better than pulling down a guy's underwear right after he was at practice. I know from experience, unfortunately. The Nervous Giggler neglected to tell me that he "didn't have time" to shower, which led me to gently inform him that I "didn't have time" to tell him all the reasons why he would stay a virgin forever if he said that again.

"You're charming," I say, taking the flowers. "Charming works on your girlfriend, but not me." My voice is sarcastic, but I'm a little bit touched. I have never received flowers from a boy before. Actually, I have never received flowers from *anybody* before. I want to put them in water and inhale their scent, but this would weaken me, so I toss them at the foot of the stairs instead as I lead him to my room.

His name is Juan Marco Antonio, which makes me a bit wary. His three first names and lack of a real last name make me nervous. Unfortunately, after my experience with William Malcolm, aka the Biter—who had two first names and zero idea that biting is not considered appropriate unless discussed beforehand—I don't exactly have high hopes. I try not to put any bias on one guy due to a negative encounter with another, but it's difficult to shake off the baggage sometimes.

It just so happens that Juan Marco Antonio is my very first exchange student. I learn this by looking him up on Facebook before he comes over, where I also learn that his home city is Madrid and he loves taking photos of himself. He isn't in any of my classes, but I sense he is the target of much female attention, probably due to his newness and his sexy Spanish accent. So far, his relationship status shows that he is committed to this Isabella, even though I recognize her from my American History class last year and I'm pretty sure her real name is just plain Isabelle.

"Isabella is like the sun that shines over me. I want to please her. Show me how." He stares up at me from where he is already lying on my bed.

This is the other thing that's unsettling about Juan Marco Antonio. I find it extremely difficult to believe he's a virgin and that he hasn't tried to get Isabella into bed already. I wonder why a guy who looks like Juan Marco Antonio would need my help at all. He is beautiful, with molten chocolate eyes fringed by thick black lashes. And even if he doesn't know what he's talking about, his accent alone should be enough to get him a girl. But he doesn't want to get a girl. He wants to keep her.

"I want Isabella to come back and meet my family," he tells me.

"One step at a time," I say, slipping into my walk-in closet.

I think the most unsettling thing about Juan Marco Antonio is that I don't know how to read him. If I don't know how to dress up for a guy at first, I almost always know by the time he has strung together a few sentences and made himself at home on my bed. But not Juan Marco Antonio. My trusty black negligee won't do for him, and I don't want to go the slutty cheerleader route for fear of offending his precious *Isabella*. Juan Marco Antonio seems too sophisticated for an oversized men's shirt, and too foreign to appreciate boy shorts and a matching camisole.

For Juan Marco Antonio, I might have to break out the leather. It's my hardest outfit to get into but the one that has the best chance of making Juan Marco Antonio the hardest. Although that's never really a problem for any virgin.

But when I come out from the closet, he isn't looking at me. He's rummaging around in my nightstand.

"What exactly are you looking for?" I half shout from across the room. Nobody looks through my stuff. *Nobody*.

"I'm just searching for, you know, a rubber," he says, turning to look at me. "Wow. You are so very beautiful."

I put one leg up on the side of the bed and bend over it, giving him a view of where my breasts are bulging out of the leather straps binding them in. I might not be able to read Juan Marco Antonio, but I'm banking on the fact that he will respond to the universal language of cleavage.

And I'm right. His hands are out of the clutter on my nightstand and on my breasts in a second. Just when I think this might not be so bad after all, he has a very strange request.

"I want to blindfold you," he says. "I always wanted to blind-fold someone."

I raise my eyebrows. It's nice to know that I can still be surprised.

"I don't think so. I'd like you to keep your hands where I can see them."

"But it's my first time," he says, curling his lips into an exaggerated pout. "I want it to be very memorable for me."

I scrutinize his face, the way he combs his curly hair off his forehead. I don't like the way he smells, like he bathed in Armani Code, and I don't like his odd request. But he has a point. It's his first time, not mine.

"Fine," I say. "But one weird move and I'll be tying you up instead, and you won't like it. *Comprende*?"

Some girls might like being blindfolded or tied up, but I'm not one of them. Being restricted or cut off from any one of my senses freaks me out. He uses his tie to cover my eyes, which I hate even more because it reeks of his cologne. I try to hold back my panic. Did he wear that tie with this idea in mind? How much thought has this guy given to me, considering I only just met him?

"Such a pretty girl," he says, trailing his fingers down my arms. "Beautiful."

I can feel his fingers on my skin, but nothing else. He doesn't move in for a kiss, or make any moves to disentangle me from my leather bindings.

"There's nothing wrong with going slow," I say, hating the shrill tone that my voice has taken on. "But go too slowly and a girl might think you fell asleep on her." I suddenly wish I would have gone with Faye after the game and not found myself in this predicament. My breath starts to get shallow. With any luck, he'll think I'm turned on, not terrified.

"I certainly have not fallen asleep on you," he says, and

suddenly I feel the weight of him on my upper body, pushing me onto the bed. I immediately flip him off me and accidentally punch him in the chin.

"Whoa, Don Juan. Word of advice: never do that to a girl." I rip off my blindfold and brush my hands through my hair, aware that they're shaking.

"Please forgive me," he says. "I did not mean to disrespect you."

At this point, I don't want to sleep with him at all, so I do something I have never done before. I turn him down.

"You should go," I say. "I don't feel right about this. I'm sorry." I hand his tie back to him, expecting him to get off my bed and scamper away. But he just stares at me, unblinking.

"Please," he says, pouting his lips like a girl. What a turnoff.

"I'm sorry," I say again through gritted teeth, wondering why I'm apologizing and why my voice doesn't sound authoritative like I want it to. I'm so good at ordering guys around in my bedroom. Why am I so bad at ordering one out of it?

"Look. Mercedes," he says, his voice more like a purr. "I do not want to come across as, what you Americans say, an asshole." He rolls the tie around in his hand and peeks at me from under his eyelashes. "But Trevor told me a lot about you. He said you would do anything to help guys like us."

I finger the duvet cover, wishing I could tear it to shreds and strangle Juan Marco Antonio with them. Beneath his silky accent, his voice has a hardness to it that I recognize.

"Are you threatening me?" I fight the urge to wrap my arms around my body protectively.

"Of course not," he says. "I just would not want the wrong person to find out." He reaches for my hand. I know that if I let him take it, I'll be giving my consent. He will get what he came here for, and I'll get his silence.

"I don't think I have to tell you how crucial your discretion is," I say as he threads his fingers through mine and covers my arm with kisses. I force his face up with my hand, enjoying the power that has shifted back to me. "Do you understand me? Nobody finds out about us. Not your friends, not your buddies from the soccer team. *Comprende?*"

He nods and smiles. I'm not sure I like that smile, but maybe it's just because the atmosphere in my bedroom has gotten so weird.

And it gets even weirder. He doesn't want to do it on my bed, so we start doing it on the carpet beside my bed and then end up against the wall. As his hot breath wilts into my ear, I start wondering who exactly is in control and who is being dominated. I keep wishing he would just get it over with like every other guy, but he keeps going and going, like some kind of Energizer bunny. I fight off the fear that mounts as I consider the possibility that I have made a huge mistake. This guy isn't like any virgin I have ever been with. He has either watched a lot of porn or been blessed with a hell of a lot of stamina.

Either that, or this isn't his first time. But if that's the case, why would he choose me over his supposedly precious Isabella?

Afterward, he wants to lie on the floor with me, but I make him put on his pants and leave before he can mention a round two. I guess Trevor kept his mouth shut about that, a fact for which I'm very grateful. And as he's heading out the door, he blows me a kiss.

"Good luck," he says.

"I think you mean good-bye," I say. He just shrugs.

When he's finally gone, I wash my sheets immediately and spray perfume around the room to get rid of his scent. But even though his cologne leaves with him, the unsettling feeling in the room doesn't. It only gets worse after he leaves, when I sit at my desk chair pretending to work on yesterday's chemistry homework. I try to lose myself in facts, a strategy that usually works. But tonight it doesn't, and instead I want the unlikeliest distraction of all.

I want my mom. I want her to tell me everything is going to be okay, that I'm being paranoid for nothing. I want her to tuck me in like she never did when I was a little girl because she always had somewhere else to be. Right now, I'd even settle for her acting like her irresponsible self. Anything to make me feel less lonely. But I'm alone in the house, the victim of another hastily scrawled Post-it note. *Out tonight!!! Love, Mom.*

I remember her sobbing over a martini one night, her sooty black eye makeup running into the fine lines on her face. "The people you love and need the most never need you back," she had wailed, sloshing the contents of her drink all over my bunny pajamas. She was talking about some guy, but maybe it was the most honest advice my ten-year-old self could hear.

I look at my lamp and count backwards to stop the tears collecting in my eyes from turning into actual crying. I don't know why today is any different than any other day, why number twelve has made me question everything. I don't know what I wanted from him that he didn't give me.

So I do the only thing I know to put Juan Marco Antonio firmly in the past. I open my notebook and write a giant zero beside his name. Number twelve. I fight back momentary panic as I flip through the pages before this one. Twelve sounds awfully high. Good thing I'm done, or this notebook would run out of pages entirely. I tap out a pattern with my pen, something that starts quiet and gets increasingly louder. I don't want to write anything else, but I write everything else anyway. Everything I would never say out loud. Not to anybody.

Douche bag. Total dick. Why did I sleep with this guy? I didn't even want to.

I stare at the words until my eyes hurt. *I didn't even want to.* My handwriting doesn't even look like mine, not the neat, orderly little letters that grace my lab reports. These letters are big and loopy and out of control. What's wrong with me?

He needs a nickname, a way of being put in the past. Then I can turn the page, close the book, and forget about him, same as I have with everybody else. So I give him one that fits, one that puts the control back where it belongs: with me.

Don Wannabe.

11

The morning after Don Wannabe, I'm feeling especially on edge. I don't put on any makeup and I throw my hair up in a messy bun. I don't want anybody to notice me today. I just want to blend into the background, be part of the scenery. It helps that I have something else to think about besides Number Twelve. Today I'm meeting with the other person I'm tutoring for Students Helping Students. I'm both nervous and excited and surprised to be either. I don't know if I'm any good at teaching people about chemistry, something that comes easily to me but not to most people. I never understood how teachers like Mr. Sellers spend their whole lives trying to explain it, over and over again, like a hamster on a wheel. But it's too late to back out now.

When I swing the front door open, I don't expect to see Zach standing on the porch. I jump a foot in the air when I see his smiling face, holding two take-out cups of coffee, almost like he knew I was going to open the door at that exact moment.

"Hello, Wednesday friend," he says. "I know it's Friday and I'm breaking the rules, but I thought you could use a pick-me-up." He hands me a Styrofoam cup.

"Thanks," I say, wondering how he can be this happy so early in the morning. Besides, where did he come from? There's no evidence of a car parked nearby. I realize I not only don't know where Zach lives, but I also have no idea how he gets to school every day.

"Where are you off to?" he says as I pull the door shut. "I thought we could have breakfast."

I push up my sleeve and glance at my watch. I'm early for my tutoring session. I could probably squeeze in a session upstairs with Zach. It would certainly overshadow Don Wannabe, and I'd feel much more like myself after.

"Do you want to go upstairs?" I say. "I'm doing a tutoring thing at school in a bit, but I have time for a quickie if you're fast." I start to dig around in my purse for my house keys with my free hand, but Zach stops me. When I look up, I'm surprised at the rut between his eyebrows, like he's thinking super hard about something.

"Or we could just hang out," he says. "Maybe walk to school together." He shrugs.

I swallow the laugh rising in my throat. "Walk to school? It's, like, two miles," I say. "But come on—I'll drive us."

Zach has been in the Jeep before, but only in the backseat. He looks strange sitting up front, with his knees pressed into the dashboard. I suddenly realize how infrequently I have passengers in the Jeep. I don't know what that says about me.

"Do you usually walk to school?" I ask after I do up my seat belt. As soon as the words are out of my mouth, I want to take them back. It's none of my business, and I don't want to make Zach's business mine.

But he's already nodding and smiling like some goofy bobblehead. "Yeah. I mean, my mom drives me when she can, and sometimes I borrow her car, but I hate to put her out. Besides, all that walking does wonders for my glutes."

I smile without meaning to. I never thought I would hear Zach say the word *glutes*. Now he looks like he wants to keep talking. This happens all the time with him. I say one thing that veers out of our regular bedroom territory and he gloms onto it. I should know better.

There's one way that I know to shut him up.

I strain against my seat belt until our faces are an inch apart and press my lips onto his. I suck gently on his top lip, then his bottom one, until he stirs uncomfortably.

"Coffee," he says weakly. "It's, uh, spilling on my lap."

"Sorry," I say, pulling away and starting the car and pretending nothing weird is going on. The Zach I know wouldn't pass up a kiss from me for anything, even spilled coffee.

The Zach I know doesn't show up at my house unannounced, either. He sticks to the time and date. Or so I thought.

"So, tutoring, huh?" Zach says, taking a sip of his coffee. "That's cool. But I could never get you to tutor me."

I peel out of the driveway and back over part of the curb in the process. Zach swears under his breath. "Shit," he says. "I just burned my mouth. Has anyone ever told you you're a crazy driver?"

"No," I say, gripping the steering wheel tightly. "Just that I'm a wild ride." I laugh and expect Zach to laugh with me. Maybe he will change his mind and want to pull over somewhere and get in the backseat after all.

But he doesn't pay any attention to my sexual innuendo. "So

why won't you tutor me?" he says. "I never knew you tutored other people. It's like you're cheating on me."

I sigh exaggeratedly loudly. "You got me," I say. "I'm stepping out on you."

"Seriously," he says. "Am I a lost cause or something?"

His words hang in the air, along with the smell of spilled coffee. I know he's talking about chemistry, but is that all he's talking about?

"Of course not," I say. "But I think you have it pretty good. You get great marks in the class and don't have to do any of the work. I didn't think you cared."

"Maybe you didn't think," he says quietly.

I roll my eyes. "Don't give me grief just because you got stuck with a new lab partner. You know I'll still help you out. We're friends, remember? Friends help friends."

I don't have to look at him to know he is smiling, and just like that the vibe between us has crossed back to normal, like Zach has stepped back from whatever ledge he was teetering on.

"Can I come?" he says. I'm about to roll my eyes again and sigh, my typical reaction to his dirty jokes, but he finishes the sentence. "Can I come to your tutoring thing with you?"

"Oh," I say. "I don't think it works like that. It's more one-on-one. But I can give you one-on-one time later today, if that's what you want."

"I'll take it," he says cheerfully. "Let's go get a milkshake or something."

We drive the rest of the way in silence, punctuated only by Zach's slurping noises and my screeching brakes. I'm trying to figure out if "get a milkshake" is code for something else, but I really don't think so. Does Zach not want to sleep with me anymore? I think back to last week in the kitchen, when he told me he loves me. Maybe I shouldn't have brushed him off. I don't want to stop sleeping with Zach. He's reliable, the one person who gives me a guaranteed release from everything else in my life. I don't like this feeling, like he's right in front of me but slipping slowly away. I guess if I want things to stay the way they are, I need to meet him halfway. If he wants to get a milkshake with me, I can give him that.

My newest chemistry student is a baby-faced junior named Toby Easton. Toby wants to become a veterinarian, and with steely determination tells me that he needs at least a B plus in chemistry to get into a good undergrad program.

"This is my weak spot," he says, rubbing his forehead with his hands. "I spend more time with this textbook than I do with my girlfriend, and I got nothing to show for it."

As I try to explain monomers and polymers in terms he might understand, my mind wanders to Toby's relationship. I wonder what he means by "nothing to show for it." Does he mean crappy grades or a shitty relationship? Maybe both? If this were four months ago, I might offer Toby a different kind of help. But it's not four months ago, so classroom help is all I have to give.

When the bell rings to signal the start of classes, I'm relieved. This is even more difficult than I thought, trying to get somebody to make sense of something so straightforward. I don't get why Toby's brain just isn't processing what I'm saying. I can almost feel his eyes glazing over, and he just looks so lost. How can he be that lost when there's always a formula to follow, which means there is always a right and wrong answer?

This bothers me through the rest of the day, through my classes and lunch period and my nondate with Zach, which turns out to be just a milkshake after all, at a little place near the beach. Zach asks me what's going on when he notices that I have chewed through my straw.

"I'm just feeling off," I tell him, trying to suck the rest of my milkshake through my mangled straw. I shouldn't even still be thinking about Toby. Whenever I help somebody in the bedroom, I'm able to keep from obsessing about him. I can remove myself from that part of my brain and not let it trickle into real life. I can literally and mentally shut the page on each guy. But the one guy I'm not going to sleep with is sticking around. I'm annoyed that I can't get through to him the same way I get through to guys in my bedroom. And I'm annoyed that I even care.

"Want to take a walk on the beach?" Zach says. "We can talk about it. Or not talk."

I smile at him even though I don't mean to. The truth is, I'd rather be with Zach than be alone.

We walk mostly in silence. Zach doesn't try to grab my hand or put his arm around me but gives me my space. Usually when Zach and I aren't talking, it's because we're having sex. This is a different kind of silence. It should feel weird but it doesn't. It feels almost like we're real friends. Not just Wednesday friends.

"What're you doing this weekend?" he asks, chucking a pebble into the calm water.

"More tutoring," I say, remembering that Angela is coming over with Faye to study. Thinking about Faye in my house makes my stomach feel unsettled. I hope she doesn't mention Zach. I hope she moves on from both of us and finds some other girl to be friends with and some other guy to have a crush on.

"Can I come?" he asks, and I shake my head again, but this time I start to laugh.

"I can't get rid of you," I say.

He grins. "That's the point."

12

In addition to prayer group and regular Sunday service, Angela and Charlie are part of a youth group that meets at church every weekend. I know this because she usually asks if I want to attend. Sometimes I go, just to maintain appearances. It's too late now to tell her I'm an atheist, so I have to keep up the façade somehow. But today, I just can't make myself sit in a circle while some kid gives a sermon on something I don't believe in, surrounded by people who know those little hymnbooks front to back. I definitely can't tell Angela that church feels like a cult to me. Today's excuse is that I have to prepare for our study session this afternoon, which is partially true. I like to live up to my reputation as a chemistry superstar, and spending the other night with Juan Marco Antonio and yesterday after school with Zach didn't help.

But I can't seem to concentrate in my bedroom. My eyes keep drifting to the bed, and my mind keeps flashing to the things I have done in it. Usually I do everything in my bed. Besides sleeping and having sex, I also study in it, watch movies, read books. I have a desk but barely use it. Kim used to chastise my attachment to my bed. "Don't become one of those fatties who lay around all day and end up with bedsores," she said once, when I was holed up in my room, poring over my notes before finals. Now, when she's around to see a new guy come in or leave, her eyes flash with something resembling pride. Better a slut than a fatty with bedsores.

So I take my books to our backyard with me and recline on a lounge chair beside our neglected swimming pool. I was full of excitement as a kid when we moved here and I found out there was a pool in the backyard, but Kim and my dad found it more of a hassle than anything else. As a result, it's overgrown with algae and fallen leaves. Every so often I sit out here in my bathing suit and close my eyes and imagine I'm somewhere else, like I'm doing now, except I'm in a bra and underwear. I open my robe to let the sun warm my skin. Kim would undoubtedly tell me how terrible the sun is for causing premature wrinkles. But she's not here. I'm completely alone, until a familiar but unexpected voice breaks the silence.

"Mercy."

My eyes fly open and I pull my robe around my body as quickly as I can, almost launching myself off my lounge chair in the process. Charlie stands beside the gate, wearing dirty jeans and an amused expression.

"Charlie, what are you doing here? Aren't you supposed to be at church?" *And not sneaking up on me at my house*, I want to add.

"I could say the same thing about you," he says as he strides over. He's dragging a shovel behind him and wearing grass-stained gloves.

"You're not going to kill me and bury me with that thing, are you?" I laugh, but the sound is high pitched, not relaxed like I intended.

"Not unless you'll make roses grow," he says, putting the shovel down and crouching on the ground beside me. "Didn't your mom tell you she hired me to do some gardening for her?"

I shake my head. Kim most definitely left that detail out. A glance around our backyard would let anybody with eyes know exactly how little Kim cares about things like plants and flowers. She hasn't gone through a gardening phase in ages.

I suddenly feel like I'm going to be sick. It was almost four years ago exactly when Luke was our gardener. After that summer Kim lost interest in having somebody maintain our backyard, maybe because Luke just stopped showing up. I remember her bitching about "the unreliability of hired help" and me telling her she scares them away. Our rotating array of maids would prove that. But Kim wasn't the reason Luke left. I was.

"You okay, Mercy? You're a bit green." Charlie takes a seat on the end of my lounger. His weight makes the chair dip slightly.

"You're the one who's green," I say, attempting a gardener joke. But my voice sounds thin and weak, like the girl from four years ago has jumped back into my body and is trying to get comfortable.

"Nah. I just wanted the extra money. I'm saving up for kind of a big purchase." He flashes a smile and looks down at his hands.

"Care to elaborate?" I say.

There's something strange about this whole situation. Charlie comes from a family that's just as rich as mine, probably richer because his parents are still together and his mom actually works, unlike Kim, who just shops off my dad's monthly support checks. Charlie isn't hard up for cash, and his parents could probably buy him anything he wanted.

"Nope," he says, removing his gloves and stretching out his fingers. "We're all allowed to have one little secret." He puts a hand on my shoulder and squeezes.

I want to laugh it off, but my chest is constricted like somebody is sitting on it and not allowing me to breathe. *We're all allowed to have one little secret.* Is he trying to tell me he knows mine?

"Fine. You got me." He removes his hand from my shoulder and stands in front of me. "I'm saving up for something for Angela. I can't tell you what, but I can tell you I'll probably need your help, when the time comes."

I let myself take a small sip of air. I feel my hands start to shake, so I press them together. I'm losing it. I'm starting to think everything is about me. When I started my sessions with the virgins, I told myself I wouldn't get paranoid. Paranoia would eat away at me and drive me insane. But it has been growing inside me the whole time.

"Of course," I say. "Anything I can do to help." My voice sounds far more measured than I feel.

"Thanks, Mercy," he says, picking the shovel off the ground. "Just pretend like I'm not here. I'll be as quiet as I can."

I make myself stay in the backyard, even though all I want to do is be alone. But that would look suspicious, so I start writing chemistry notes from my lounge chair, sneaking occasional glances at Charlie. I wonder where he learned that the bare-root roses have to be planted in a spot where they'll receive at least six hours of sunlight, and how he knows that they need to be separated from competing trees or shrubs. Kim certainly didn't tell him that. The weirdest part of all is that he plants around where the roses died the last time they were planted, the summer Luke taught me about gardening. That was when I started getting interested in chemistry. I loved how plants had to follow a formula, too.

By the time Charlie finishes his work, the air feels about ten degrees hotter. He wipes his sweaty forehead on his T-shirt.

"Do you want to come in for a drink?"

The words are out of my mouth before I even have time to think them through. I don't actually want Charlie to come in for a drink. I want him to leave so that I don't have to think about gardening or Luke anymore. With Charlie digging up the garden, it's almost impossible to concentrate on things like equations and formulas and volumetric titrations. I'm hoping he will politely decline, make up some kind of excuse for having to leave. But instead he smiles broadly and follows me into the house.

I had almost forgotten about the fact that I'm wearing a bathrobe with only a bra and underwear on underneath. But in the kitchen, with my bare feet on the cold floor, it's hard to ignore.

"We have water and some kind of green concoction," I say, peering into the fridge. Kim must be on one of her juice cleanses this week.

"I'll just have water. Thanks."

I open the cabinet to retrieve a glass. When I turn around, Charlie is peeling his shirt off.

"What're you doing?" I say, clenching the glass tightly in my hand. He balls his T-shirt in one of his hands. I can't help but notice his ab muscles, the veins running down his biceps. Charlie never used to look like that. When did he get in such good shape?

"Sorry. I'm hot. And this shirt doesn't smell so good."

I pour water from a pitcher into the glass, spilling some on the counter in the process. I don't know why being alone in the kitchen with Charlie is making me this flustered. It's not like I haven't hung out with him before. But our common denominator has always been Angela. Angela is what we have in common. I only know Charlie because of her, and that's the only reason he knows me.

"Angela's coming over to study later," I say, gripping the countertop with my fingertips.

Charlie gulps down the water and cocks his head. "Do me a favor," he says. "Don't tell her I was here. You know that little secret I mentioned? Maybe it can be ours."

I chew on my bottom lip, trying to keep the surprise off my face. I already have secrets from Angela. The whole atheist thing tops the list, followed closely by the virgins. Angela doesn't know about Luke and what happened after he left. There are so many things I have kept hidden from my best friend. It's not that I don't want to share them with her. Sometimes when we're having tea together after school or taking a long walk, I imagine what she would say if I were to unload everything on her. I never go through with it, because I know exactly what she would think.

But this is different. This is voluntarily keeping something from her that shouldn't even be important. Charlie is our new gardener. I don't know why he wants it kept secret. Maybe he's embarrassed. Maybe he wants to avoid youth group on the weekend. Maybe he really is saving up his money.

"Deal," I say. Charlie extends his hand and envelops mine in a sweaty handshake. My hand feels tiny in his, like his giant fingers could reduce my bones to dust.

I wave through the window when he leaves, sauntering to his truck with his shirt still off.

Now I'm not just keeping my own secrets anymore.

13

"I don't get it," Angela says, slumping over my carefully constructed diagram. "I'm just meant to fail this class, I guess."

She really doesn't get it. Every time I start to explain something, she zones out. I can tell she's pretending to pay attention, but her mind is wandering, just like her eyes are doing around my room. Angela hasn't ever been the easiest person to help, but today she seems more distracted than usual, from the second she walked in the door and commented that something "smells different." I immediately thought she knew about Charlie, that our handshake had created some kind of scent giveaway, but then she sniffed my arm and said it was my perfume.

"I think it's obvious," Faye says. She's lying on the floor of my bedroom with her laptop open on her stomach, her hair splayed out behind her.

"You might think it's obvious, but Angela doesn't." I cast an irritated glance at her. Generally, Faye's bluntness would be a characteristic I admire, but the last thing I want is for Angela to feel even less confident about chemistry than she already does.

"No, it's not that. You keep trying to explain it to her. And you're a good teacher. But she's thinking about something else."

I look from Faye to Angela, who is trying to avoid my eyes.

"I bet I know what she's thinking about," Faye says, her mouth twitching into a smirk. "It's a boy."

I snap my fingers in front of Angela's face. "Earth to Angela," I say. "Is she right?"

Angela covers her face with her hands. "I can't concentrate on anything lately. I'm having one of those midlife crisis things."

"At seventeen? I don't think so." I soften my voice.

"I'm just, you know, so conflicted."

"About what?" I say gently. Angela sounds like she might be on the brink of tears. I have only seen Angela cry once over the course of our friendship, and that was because a teacher chewed her out for reading from cue cards during an oral presentation.

"About Charlie."

Faye plucks her computer off her stomach and rolls over. "I knew it! It's always about a boy. Boys are the source of all the pain and all the pleasure. Especially the good ones." Her voice drops into something barely louder than a whisper. My eyes flicker to her involuntarily, and she gives me a tiny smile, almost like she was testing my attention.

I tear my eyes away from her and look at Angela, who is staring at her hands. "What's up with Charlie?"

Angela spins the promise ring Charlie gave her on their anniversary around her finger, something she does when she's nervous. Or scared.

"I love Charlie. Charlie loves me. Lately, I've been having these feelings." She sighs. "You know."

"I don't know, Ange."

"I know," Faye says. "You want to spread the love around. Be with other guys. You're bored with this Charlie dude. Right?"

Angela furrows her brow. "Not right," she says. "I only want to be with Charlie. But that's the problem. I think Charlie wants to *be* with me, if you know what I mean."

I reach my hand out and grab Angela's. "He wants to sleep with you?"

Faye interjects. "Wait, you haven't slept with him yet? How long have you guys been together?"

"Two years," Angela says. "But we were going to wait until we got married. Still are. I don't know." She covers her face with her hands.

Faye's laugh sounds like a bark. A seal—that's the animal she sounds like. One of those barking seals at the zoo that never shut up. "He must be the last of a dying breed. Nowadays if you don't give it up till date three, you're going to find yourself single."

She looks directly at me when she says it, and for a second I'm afraid she knows everything, even though that would be impossible. But her gaze is completely disarming. It's full of confidence, full of certainty. It says, *I want what I want when I say I want it.* I bet most guys can't stand up to that gaze. I can just imagine Zach crumbling underneath it.

But whatever is going on with Faye has to wait. I can probably count the times Angela has gone into the details of her relationship with Charlie on one hand, including this time, and having a third person around is making this even more awkward. Especially a third person like Faye, who is distracting *me*.

"So what made you change your mind?" I say, squeezing Angela's hand softly. "About waiting until marriage. Is Charlie pushing you to sleep with him?"

Angela shrugs and fiddles with her shirtsleeves, which are way too long for her arms. Angela has never been like most girls in our grade, who wear short skirts and tank tops. She never buys clothes that fit right.

I'm about to open my mouth to defend Charlie's loyalty, but I think twice when this morning's encounter flashes through my mind. *You know that little secret I mentioned? Maybe it can be ours.*

"Do you still have yours, Mercy?" Angela says quietly. She doesn't meet my eyes as she says it. Angela has never asked me this before, but I have thought about what to say if she did. I wonder how long she has been waiting to ask this very question, how long those words have been strung together in her brain, waiting to come out.

I'm not ready to answer, but I have to. I look down at my binder and hope nobody noticed the panic that has shot through my stomach and up my throat like a ball of fire. I focus on the equation written there to steady myself. $1\ CH_4 + O_2 \rightarrow CO_2 + 2H_2O$. Logic and numbers and balance, exactly how life isn't naturally, exactly how life isn't unless you make it so. But there's no way I'm telling Angela the reality. So I reinvent the truth.

"It was last summer. A guy from that art class I took."

"You took an art class last summer?" Angela looks as surprised as if I said I killed someone last summer. I mentally want to kick myself for saying something so stupid. Not only do I have zero artistic ability, but I spent most of the summer hanging out with Angela and obviously never mentioned any art classes.

"My mom made me go twice a week," I say quickly. "She was in her 'try new things' phase."

Angela nods and I feel a pang of guilt. I'm not just a liar—I'm a good liar. And that makes it even worse.

"Anyway, there was this guy there. Luke. We went out a few times and one thing led to another, and we, you know, did it." I almost choke on his name. I haven't said it out loud for so long that it feels like a wad of poison I have to spit out.

"Why have you never mentioned him before?"

"I don't know; it just never came up. And he moved back to Nevada."

"So let me get this straight." Faye props herself up on her elbows. "A guy crossed a state line for some *art class*?"

I cast a sidelong glance at her, hoping she doesn't punch any more holes into my story.

"He was spending the summer in California with his dad," I say.

She nods, causing her hair to pool around her shoulders. "I can see his point. Nevada in the summer can get pretty dull. Even Vegas gets old. What part is he from?"

"You're from Nevada," I say slowly. Of all the states, why did I have to pick the one Faye is from? Probably because it's true. The real Luke is from Nevada, although I have no idea where he is now.

"I'm from Sparks. Born and bred," she says with an eye roll. "Your guy? Maybe I know him."

"No, Carson City," I say, feeling a sliver of relief. Maybe I can pull this off after all. "He was from a rich family. Told me they wanted to get rid of him for the summer."

"Do you still talk to him?" Angela says. Her eyes are wide with curiosity.

"No," I say, a bit too quickly. "Well, not regularly. We e-mail from time to time. I don't know if anything will come of it, though."

"A summer romance," Faye says, eyes raised to the ceiling.

"I had one of those once." She gives me a deadpan look. "I was thirteen. He bought me ice cream and we made out behind my parents' shed."

"Well, I can't believe you didn't mention him before," Angela says, and I can tell she's hurt. "You'd be the first person I would tell. Probably the only person." She glances at Faye and her face reddens slightly.

"I wanted to tell you," I say, my voice small. "I was just waiting for a good time." I want to smile to prove it, but the corners of my mouth don't want to turn up, leaving my mouth a quivering line. I didn't know Angela when I really lost my virginity, and I could never tell her the truth. But if I close my eyes and imagine things were different, I can almost visualize having a normal first time and telling my best friend about it. Almost.

"What was it like?" Angela averts her eyes. "You know, the sex part. Did it hurt?"

I look down at the lined paper again, the equation written there. I can train my mind to be a formula, too.

"A bit, I guess. I don't know. It was nice. He made it special." My throat hurts with the effort of choking out the words.

"I remember my first time," Faye says. "It was with the same boy who bought me ice cream. Two summers later."

"You were fifteen?" Angela says, her mouth hanging open.

Faye shrugs. "And that was only because he wanted to wait."

Angela shakes her head. "I'm even more behind the curve than I thought." She presses her cheek against the palm of her hand. "I don't know what to do. Virginity is a big deal. I don't just want to lose mine and regret it."

I wiggle closer to her, close enough to rub her back sympathetically, which is unusual for me and Angela. We don't have a touchy-feely friendship like a lot of girls at school, who hug and kiss and walk down the halls with their arms wrapped around each other's shoulders. But right now I just want to bury my face in her hair and tell her everything. I want to tell her virginity isn't something you just lose, like a spare key or a homework assignment. It's something you give away. Or something that gets taken away from you.

"Did you love Luke?" Angela says, leaning into my shoulder.

The question catches me off guard. I can't let her know how much this question means to me, how often I have thought about it, even after everything.

"I don't know," I say. This, at least, is honest. "Maybe I don't know what love is."

"Fifteen," she whispers, gazing at Faye. "I was still kissing my Justin Bieber posters when I was fifteen."

I wish I could tell her so many things. I wish I could tell her that there really is a Luke, and he really was from Nevada. But there was no art class, and it wasn't last summer.

And if Angela thinks fifteen is bad, I wonder what she'd think of thirteen.

14

I don't plan on sleeping with Jeremy Roth. He isn't part of my plan, and Don Wannabe really *was* supposed to be the last one. But when Angela and Faye leave, I need something to take away the edginess I'm feeling. I don't want to be alone. Jeremy didn't even find me the old-fashioned way—in person. I told myself when this started that I would never sleep with a guy who solicited me through Facebook or via text message, but that's exactly what I'm about to do.

> *Hey beautiful. I have a situation I could use some help with. Can we meet somewhere?*

The message has sat in my in-box for days, but I haven't paid any attention until now. I didn't click on it, but I didn't delete it, either. I almost didn't want Angela and Faye to go, because I knew I was going to open the message and respond favorably when they did.

"You guys could stay," I told them before Faye ushered Angela out the door. "We could order pizza or something."

Angela looked at me wistfully, like she wanted to take me up on it, but she had plans with Charlie, like a normal person in a relationship would on a Saturday night. And Faye had her own plans.

"I have a date," she said. "And I can't go out looking like this." She looked down at her perfect body in her tight jeans, which prompted Angela to roll her eyes.

When I shut the door behind them, I was equal parts sad and confused. Sad because I'm the only one without plans on a Saturday night, the only one with an evening of bad reality TV and stale microwave popcorn stretching ahead of me. Confused because all afternoon Faye seemed to be flirting with me, when the other day she was flirting with Zach. If this is her idea of playing with my head, I can play that game, too.

So I do the only thing I know will make me feel better. I message Jeremy back with my address and tell him to come over in an hour. I know he will be late, because he's in my English class and always sneaks in late and heads for a desk in the back row. Which happens to be where I sit, not because I'm late but because I hate being called on in English class, where there's no right answer and no wrong answer. I hate the murky in-between and when Mr. Bell brings up some cloudy subject like "Iago's motivations as the antihero" and expects somebody to spout out some brilliant response. "Enlighten me," is his catchphrase of choice. I wish somebody would just hit him over the head with "enlightenment" and help him see things in black and white, like they should be.

"Hello," Jeremy says, standing at my doorstep with a bottle of wine an hour later. "I thought this might be nice. I stole it from my dad's stash. The label says it's a Merlot." He says it like Mar-*lot*. Not surprising from a guy who thinks *Hamlet* is a type of deli meat.

"I don't drink," I say, leading him upstairs. Which is only partially true. I do drink occasionally, but not with guys like Jeremy and never before sex. I only had to make that mistake once to learn from it.

"That sucks," he says. "It loosens you up. Don't mind if I do, though."

He doesn't wait to see if I do mind before unscrewing the top and downing a quarter of the bottle. A few droplets leak down his chin and onto my cream-colored carpet, where they proceed to bloom like little flower petals. Jeremy doesn't notice.

"I'd watch how much of that you drink," I tell him. "Alcohol and soft dicks have a very close and personal relationship."

He laughs, a slow, overly confident laugh, a laugh in which every staccato syllable—"ha, ha, ha"—can almost be seen as well as heard.

"Wait here," I tell him as I slip into my walk-in. I have already decided what not to wear for Jeremy. Nothing light colored. He has proven that he's the kind of guy who leaves stains where he shouldn't.

But the drawer containing my black lacy negligee is suspiciously empty. I mentally catalogue where I could have left it. It's not in my laundry basket, which is the only place it would be if not in its proper drawer. I momentarily entertain the horrifying thought that Kim found it—or even worse, borrowed it—but that's impossible. I keep my closet locked unless I'm in my room. And the only time I was in my room today was—

All afternoon, with Angela and Faye. Angela would never steal something from me, which only leaves Faye. But why would she steal a negligee? She did mention going on a date, but I would assume she has her own fancy undergarments. I shrug and decide to blame Kim after all. Of the three of them, she's the least trustworthy.

"Everything okay in there?" Jeremy says. I shoot him the middle finger, almost wishing he could see it from his side of the wall. If he has this little patience now, I feel sorry for his girlfriend.

I pull out my second choice, a sheer crimson teddy, and shimmy into it. The color matches the wine.

Jeremy lets out a low whistle when he sees me, a noise I always thought was super cheesy.

"Bring that hot ass over here," he says. His shirt is already off, revealing a chest with just enough muscle. Jeremy might not be my type, but his body is. Maybe this won't be so bad after all. It might even be kind of fun.

Jeremy unbuttons his jeans and kicks them off. He has his dick in his hand and it's already hard. He's grabbing my hand, trying to make me touch it. Then he does something completely inexcusable.

He tries to push my head down.

"I don't think so," I say, springing away from his grip with trembling hands. "You don't need it."

He pouts, but only for a minute, before pushing me onto my back against my pillows. Usually I'm the one in control, but this feels different. This feels like everything is moving a bit too fast.

"Slow down, stud," I say in a tone I hope is playful. "Let's get a condom first."

I let him open the packet and roll it on. He does everything right. And once he's on top of me, he does everything right there, too. For a minute I forget I'm even supposed to be showing him how to do it. For a minute I start to feel like I'm his girlfriend and he's my boyfriend and we're just taking a study break.

I'm surprised he's still going strong when I flip him onto his back. Usually this is where they're happy to let me take control to show them what to do. But he's still leading somehow, locking his hands on my hips and grinding deeper into me. When he finishes—loudly—I look at the clock.

Jeremy lasted eight minutes. In my bedroom, that's a new record. He's panting a bit but doesn't even look all that winded. I guess some people were just meant for sex.

Either that, or Jeremy has done this before.

He turns away from me and I stare at his back, at the little red dents my fingers left. I'm definitely not going to come out and ask him. What would I say? "Are you *sure* you're a virgin?" Somehow I don't think that would go over well and would probably hurt my reputation more than his. And if he really was a virgin until eight minutes ago, I would be giving him a seriously unnecessary ego boost.

"You're not going to have any problems," I say instead, poking him in the back. "Your girlfriend is going to be very satisfied. Maybe just go a bit more gently on her."

He turns around and gives me a strange little smile. "Can we do it again? That was great. But I'd feel way more prepared if we could do it one more time."

I bite my lip. I really shouldn't. I have no reason to sleep with him again, and I should kick him out. But at the same time, it felt so good. Maybe if we do it again, I'll get off, too.

"I know how to convince you," he says and snakes down to the end of the bed. Before I know it, he's between my legs, working something I can only describe as magic with his tongue. This is definitely not the work of a virgin. Now I know he must be lying, but I'd rather he not admit it at this point. The deed has already been done, so what's wrong with doing it again?

He takes me right to the brink, to the point where we both know a second time is inevitable. And a third. A third time has never happened in my bed until now.

Neither has a guy sleeping over.

But I'm learning that there's a first time for everything.

15

I'm woken up by two things: Jeremy's morning wood poking into my back and a loud knocking on my door.

"Mercedes, honey, wake up! We have yoga in half an hour! I made you a detox tea; it's waiting in the kitchen."

A nightmare. That's my first thought. But the knocking doesn't stop. And when the knocking does let up, doorknob jiggling commences. That's when I bolt upright.

"Kim! I'll be down in a minute."

"Okay, honey, but your tea is getting cold." The voice on the other side of the door is unnaturally chipper. I groan and fall back on my pillows. *Since when do Kim and I do yoga together?* She hasn't even been home all weekend. She told me she was spending it with Fred from the bar, or was it Ted the investment banker? Maybe they're the same person. If this is one of her ideas for a bonding ritual, it couldn't have come at a more inopportune time.

"Morning, beautiful," Jeremy whispers in my ear. He has an unfortunate case of morning breath, so I turn the other way. I feel hungover, even though I had nothing to drink last night.

"You need to leave," I say, but it's muffled by my pillow. He could probably sneak out the front door easily enough—Kim is most likely in the kitchen, reading the entertainment section and drinking her disgusting detox tea, so she probably wouldn't hear him slip down the stairs. But it's risky. I can't help wondering what he told his parents. Most parents would be concerned if their teenager didn't come home at night. Maybe Jeremy and I have more in common than I thought.

"Come on," he says, stretching out his arms. "Let's have one more round, as a good-bye."

"Absolutely not," I say, rolling out of bed and gathering his clothing from the floor. I ball it up and toss it at his chest without looking at him. "Here's the plan," I continue. "I'm going out with my mom. When we get back, you won't be here. Just go out the back door and pull the screen door shut."

I sit on the side of my bed and pull on my underwear. It would be easy to flaunt Jeremy in front of Kim. She would know that I'm keeping myself busy, that I'm taking advantage of being young and thin, the two attributes in which Kim places the most value. But that would be giving her what she wants. So I'd rather slip him out the door and pretend I'm a regular teenager going to yoga class with her regular mother on a regular Sunday morning, even just for an hour.

"Don't I get any feedback?" Jeremy says. He's making no attempt to move. I feel my face get hot, but I never blush. I walk to the bathroom to splash cold water on my face. Jeremy whistles as I walk away.

When I'm safely in the bathroom with the door shut, I sit on the toilet. My body shakes and my throat swells. Worst of all, I feel hot tears prick the back of my eyelids. I never let guys sleep over. I never let guys have a third time. Not even a second time. That's not part of the plan. My system only works because it is a system, a routine with an order to it. I am reliable, or at least I used to be. My system has rules, and I just broke a big one.

I stand and wipe my eyes with the back of my hand. Jeremy won't tell anyone. He can't. That's the system. That's how it works. He won't mention this to his friends at school, because that's how rumors start. If the rumor is about me, it's also about him. And if it's about him, his girlfriend will find out. But his not mentioning our sleepover to anyone rides on my pretending nothing is out of the ordinary. I push my bangs off my face and blow my nose. I need to get my shit together and go to this fucking yoga class and get Jeremy out of the house.

When I leave the bathroom, he's fully dressed. I find a T-shirt and shorts in my dresser drawer that will suffice as yoga gear. By the time I turn around to face Jeremy, my hair is in a perky ponytail and I have a smile pasted on my face.

"Ten out of ten. Extra points for your confidence, because that's usually the thing that needs the most work. Technically flawless. That's your report card."

Jeremy grins. "I could get used to this," he says.

"You will," I say. "With your girlfriend." I find his shoes on the floor and hand them to him, suddenly aware that I don't even know his girlfriend's name. The realization hits me like a punch in the stomach. He didn't bring her up once, and I didn't ask. I was supposed to sleep with Jeremy to ensure she gets a perfect first time, and I have no idea if she even exists, or if he just sent me that message because he wanted to get in my pants. If that's the case, I'm not sure who I'm more horrified with—Jeremy or myself.

I clear my throat. Now would be the time to bring the mystery girlfriend up, but I don't even want to. I would rather not know the truth.

"See you Monday at school. Don't forget: we have that poetry thing due."

He slaps his forehead. "You're amazing," he says. "Best sex ever and saving me from failing English."

"Bye, Jeremy," I say before closing the door behind me. I rush to meet Kim downstairs, hoping that forcing myself to go through the motions quickly will clear my head of all the jumbled thoughts inside it. By the time we're in the downward dog position in a class full of women, Jeremy is the furthest thing from my mind. Almost.

"How did you get so flexible?" Kim whispers. "This position is impossible." When I shrug, she says, "You must be a yoga natural."

But when our instructor stops talking and tells us to lie in corpse pose and clear our heads, all my thoughts come rushing back. *Best sex ever.* That's what Jeremy said before I shut the door in his face. Normally, best implies having something to compare it to. And if Jeremy lied about being a virgin, how many other guys have lied to me, too? The whole point of doing this was to provide the perfect first time and to teach the guys how to give their girl- friends the perfect first time in return. But when did it stop being about that?

When did it start becoming about me?

When Kim and I are back at home, Jeremy is gone, just like I told him to be. He even made my bed and fluffed the pillows. Maybe he has hope for being a good boyfriend after all. Maybe.

I retrieve my notebook from underneath the boxes of condoms and make an entry for Jeremy. His nickname is easy. Unlucky Thirteen. The rest is harder to write, but I write it anyway. Maybe it's good for me, to put my thoughts into words. If numbers and facts are my lifeblood, maybe words can be my therapy.

We had great chemistry. But it's bothering me that it was that great. It shouldn't have been that great. I have my doubts that this guy is a virgin. But if he isn't, why wouldn't he just go sleep with somebody else? I wanted to ask. I wanted to ask about his girlfriend, but I didn't. Maybe I don't care about her as much as I thought, since I don't even know her name.

I stare at the words on the page and then at the hand that wrote them. I wasn't even thinking that, but there it is. What I didn't want to see. I sound like a monster, like somebody who doesn't care about anyone but myself. Maybe I am.

I tuck the journal back into its spot, grateful for the secrecy of my nightstand, grateful to the dark wood for concealing so many of my secrets. I walk into my bathroom and lean over the sink, taking a series of deep breaths. Then I walk down the hall to Kim's room.

I'm almost hoping Kim will want to make a day of it. After all, this is the first time she ever woke me up to attend a yoga class. Maybe she wants to spend time with me, go for brunch or take a walk through the park. Things that mothers and daughters do. But I set my expectations way too high, as usual.

"I have a mountain of work to do," she tells me as she stands in front of her giant bathroom mirror, applying way too much eyeliner to ever constitute a "mountain of work."

"What work?" I say. "You don't have a job."

My voice sounds caustic, but Kim doesn't notice. She just blinks her eyes and applies coat after coat of mascara in rapid succession. "I don't have a paid job, but I do *work*. I'm on the board for that big charity gala. You remember, the one you went to? You wore that gorgeous dress."

I roll my eyes behind her back. The event she is talking about was three years ago. I had wanted to wear a dress I found while shopping with Angela, but Kim bought me one to match hers, a size smaller than I wore. She refused to have it taken out, so I had to starve to fit into it.

"Fine," I tell her, turning to leave her room. "I'm going to spend a bunch of your hard-earned money."

"Have fun," she calls absentmindedly after me. I slam her bedroom door for good measure, but she probably doesn't notice that, either.

I always shop by myself for lingerie, and I never go to the obvious choices, like the plaza near our school or the bigger shopping center downtown. I go to an out-of-the-way mall with a swimwearlingerie section. It's more expensive than Victoria's Secret, but I don't care, since Kim is footing the bill. Besides, it just looks better. None of this neon, uber-padded crap. I don't believe in padding, not because I'm all that well-endowed but because guys are going to know what's under there when the bra comes off anyway, and why disappoint them? Nobody really looks like the Victoria's Secret Angels.

I don't even know why I'm shopping for lingerie, considering I'm done with the virgins for good now. I feel weird about ending with the number thirteen—how unlucky is that?—but if the experience with Jeremy taught me anything, it's that I have completely fallen apart. I used to love helping the guys plan a special night, and now the thought is utterly exhausting. My patience used to be my trademark, but it's conspicuously missing in action. I guess I'm shopping for lingerie because it's what I know how to shop for. Besides, I'll need a fresh collection, now that I'm done with my good deeds. A fresh start. New lingerie to take with me to MIT, where I might eventually have a normal relationship. Nothing that reminds me of anybody else.

After shopping here monthly for the past four months, I have never once run into someone I know. So today, when I hear a familiar voice as I'm holding up a pair of white lace panties, trying to determine if they're too cutesy, I almost jump out of my skin.

"Mercy," she says. It's Faye, wearing a name tag, the letters in loopy cursive so that it looks more like Fate. She's squinting, and I'm not even aware that I'm clutching the underwear to my chest until she pries them out of my hands.

"No offense, but these aren't really you," she says. "Unless you're shopping for Angela." She leans in and lowers her voice conspiratorially. "I call these first communion panties," she says. "They're like those lace dresses all the girls had to wear."

I let her put the underwear back.

"What're you doing here?" she says. "Shopping for a hot date?"

I shake my head. "No, just looking for some new pajamas." Except pajamas are the one thing this store does not sell.

Faye raises her eyebrow. "Good God, you're a terrible liar," she says. "So you have a hot date. You don't have to tell me who it's with. Just let me help you find something more you. I'm thinking green, emerald green. Something to match those big beautiful eyes of yours."

I look at the floor. Nobody has ever told me I had big beautiful eyes before. I feel a rush of affection for Faye, affection mixed with frustration. Does she use that tone of voice with everyone? Because the way she said it didn't sound like a mere compliment.

"How was your date?" I hear myself say the words before I can take them back.

She smiles at me, but it's almost a smirk. "I don't know. It's just hard to find someone you're interested in these days. Everyone's a version of somebody else."

She bends over to open a drawer full of bras. Her shirt rides up, exposing the arch of her lower back and the tattoo there, the one I noticed after the soccer game. It looks like a winged insect, maybe a butterfly.

"Dragonfly," she says without looking away from the drawer. "So typical, right? A dragonfly tramp stamp. But I really wanted to rebel against my mom, and I was dating a tattoo artist at the time."

I nod. I know exactly what she means. This sounds like the kind of thing I would have done years ago, if I thought getting a tattoo would have any impact whatsoever on Kim. But I know it wouldn't. Kim has a giant rose on her left shoulder and a heart with some guy's name on her hip. I wish I didn't know this.

Faye sorts through negligees, pushing the hangers at a rapid-fire pace. "Nope, not this one, definitely not this," she keeps saying, without giving me enough time to even see them. She pauses at a black nightgown, then pushes past it. "Too cliché," she says.

My rush of affection runs cold. I remember the missing negligee from my closet, the black lacy one, and wonder if Faye could be the thief after all. But she works in a boutique and probably gets a 50 percent discount, and I'm not exactly jumping to admit that I noticed a sole negligee missing from so many in my closet.

"This," she says loudly, stopping at a spaghetti-strap concoction that looks black at first, until she holds it in front of the light and I realize it's very dark green. "This is you."

I want to say, *You don't know me well enough to know if that's me. You don't know me well enough to recommend something for me to wear in my bedroom. You don't know me enough to form an opinion.*

But I don't say this. I say nothing and follow her to the dressing room in silence.

She got the size right—I give her that. It cups my breasts, skims my hips without being too clingy. I hate lingerie that's too tight. It's right up there with jeans that create a muffin top.

I'm just getting ready to step out of it when Faye steps in. To the dressing room. She just pushes the curtain aside and stands there, staring at me.

"You could knock first," I say, folding my arms across my chest.

"It's kind of hard to knock on a curtain," she says. "I was right, though. That's a great look for you. Whoever you're buying it for will be a lucky guy."

"I'm not buying it for anyone," I say.

"Of course you are. Nobody buys lingerie that they don't expect somebody to see. Who is it? Is it Chemistry Boy? I knew he was looking at you a lot."

Damn Zach and his stupid puppy-dog eyes. But she has a point, so I come up with a lie.

"It's a college guy," I say. "We've been out a few times. I thought I should be prepared, in case, you know." I look down at my feet.

"I've been through my share of those," Faye says, twirling a strand of hair absentmindedly around her finger. "Most times they don't live up to the illusion of a supercool college guy that you had in your head. Just to warn you. And you think they know what they're doing, but they're even worse than high school guys. Mostly the girls they slept with in high school didn't know any better, so they just kept doing the wrong thing. Except by the time they're in college, they think it's the right thing and it's harder to get them to change."

I nod, hopefully not too emphatically. She's right, and she has just reaffirmed why I do what I do. What I did. They have to learn it right the first time, because guys are impossible to change.

"Somebody ought to just tell them what they need to do from square one, huh?" Faye says. "There needs to be some kind of manual. Preferably, an interactive one." She laughs.

I give her a tight-lipped smile and start to close the curtain, but she puts her hand on the curtain to stop it. For a minute I'm not sure what she is going to do, if she is going to get in here with me and shut us both in. But she just smiles at me, a different smile than the one she uses in public. And just like that, she's gone.

I leave without buying the lingerie, even though I really like it. I don't buy it because of Faye. For whatever reason, I don't want her to think I'm buying lingerie with someone special in mind. I don't want to take it home with me, because I will think of Faye when I look at it.

"Want to come over later?" Faye says when I wave good-bye. "We could watch a movie or something. Or just bitch about guys. I'm done with work at five." She says it casually, but the invitation doesn't sound like a whim.

I nod mechanically, wondering why I feel so strange. I guess Angela is the only person I have really hung out with on a regular basis. Faye is vastly different than Angela, and I feel different around her.

"Great. I'll text you my address. See you at seven?" She winks and disappears into the dressing rooms.

Back at home, I spend an hour flat ironing my hair and choosing an outfit that is both casual and cute. I don't know why I'm nervous for an evening that involves my clothes staying on, but I'm definitely on edge. I'm so used to planning for guys, dressing and undressing for them and trying to morph myself into their dream girl. I'm so used to it that I don't really know where that girl ends and the real me begins. I suppose what it comes down to is confidence. I'm confident in that girl, the one who emerges from my walk-in wearing lingerie when I'm done getting ready. But at Faye's house, I'm not going to be that girl. I'm going to be me.

Whoever that is anymore.

16

I end up getting to Faye's ten minutes late, because her house is totally hidden from view of the street and dwarfed by bigger houses on both sides. Maybe the most surprising thing is that it's small, unlike the majority of the homes in Rancho Palos Verdes. It's plain and unassuming and doesn't suit Faye at all.

When I pull into the driveway, I take a deep breath. My heart is pounding and I shake off the feeling that I'm nervous—nervous to go into Faye's house, because that means something. This isn't about school or chemistry tutoring or some sense of obligation. Faye wants me here.

When I walk up the front steps and ring the doorbell, I hear laughter coming from inside. Faye's laugh, that seal-bark one. And another laugh that sounds familiar, too.

I don't put it together until Zach opens the door.

"Mercy," he says, stepping forward like he wants to hug me but stopping at the last moment. "You made it."

"Welcome to my humble abode," Faye says, appearing in the hallway wearing a frilly pink apron over her jeans. "Sorry if it was hard to find. Now you see why I had to get a part-time job."

Zach laughs. "I hear you. That's why I'm the guy making your sandwiches at the Submarine King."

I look at him, but he stares at the ground.

"You make sandwiches at Submarine King?" I say.

A flush creeps into his cheeks. "Yeah—you should see how much of an artist I am with lunch meat," he says, jamming his hands in his pockets.

Faye laughs again. "It's so weird," she says. "Zach and I work at the same mall and had no idea until today. I went to the food court after you left and there he was, wearing the cutest little outfit. This bright yellow hat—"

Zach's face turns full-on red. "Come on—it's not that bad," he mumbles.

"I didn't know," I say dumbly. Zach won't meet my eye, and I don't know what else to say. I know what he's probably thinking: *You didn't ask.*

"Well, let me give you the grand tour," Faye interjects. "There's not much to it." She shuffles back down the hall and beckons for me to follow. "The bathroom is upstairs, and that's the door to the garage. Which we don't use to actually park because Lydia hoards all kinds of crap in there. She never gets rid of anything. She thinks it'll all have value someday, even though it's junk."

"Who's Lydia?" I say, slipping off my shoes and following her.

"Oh. My mom," Faye says. "I just call her Lydia. She has always seemed more like a sister to me. She had me when she was fourteen."

My heart starts thumping, and the distance to the kitchen feels like walking through water, where breath is impossible to find and every inhalation feels too heavy to take in. Luckily, Faye is turned away and doesn't notice my silence or the fact that I feel like all the color has been sucked out of me.

"I'm a great cook," Faye says. "But I'm a huge slob. I think I got some of Lydia's tendencies after all."

She's not lying. The kitchen counter is cluttered with cereal boxes and stray papers and dirty pots and pans that don't fit in the overfull sink. Kim would have a conniption if she stood in this kitchen for even five minutes—a kitchen that looks actually lived in. Even though Faye and her mom didn't move here until just over a week ago and I can tell a lot of the house has yet to be unpacked, they still managed to put photos on the fridge. Kim loves her stainless steel too much to ever allow me to mar the fridge with photos and magnets.

"Is this Lydia?" I say, touching a photo of Faye with her arm slung around a blond woman's shoulders, a woman who is a carbon copy of Faye.

"Yeah. She's pretty, right? I always wanted to look just like her." Faye fills a pot with water and sets it on the stove.

"You do," I say.

There's an awkward silence, wherein I realize Faye knows I think she's pretty. I don't know why I feel weird about that.

"I want to look like her, but I don't want my life to be like hers," Faye says. "I never knew my dad. He was a loser who walked out on her when she was knocked up with me. And the only work experience she has is bartending. That's where she is now. If it weren't for the money my grandma left us, we definitely wouldn't be living here. This was our fresh start."

Faye speaks quietly, which I realize I haven't heard her do. She always has what Angela would call an "outdoor voice." But I can tell by the way she is speaking now that her voice drops when she talks about someone she loves. It's obvious that she loves and respects Lydia.

Faye clears a stack of newspapers off a chair and gestures for me to sit, then plunks a glass of water in front of me. I can't help but notice that there's already a spot cleared for Zach—how long has he been here, anyway? How much of Faye's house has he seen? Has he been in her bedroom? Her grand tour didn't extend upstairs, and I don't know if I should be relieved or offended.

And I don't know why I should feel either.

I take a long gulp of my water and watch Faye move fluidly around the mess in her kitchen, like she knows where every stack of boxes is by memory.

"I do most of the cooking," she says, using a can opener on a jar of tomato sauce. "I like to think I'm a genius at cooking on a budget by now."

"I should have offered to bring something," I say. "Like a salad. Or dessert."

Zach muffles a laugh. "You don't cook," he says.

I shoot him a withering stare. "How do you know?" I snap.

Faye looks at us and raises an eyebrow—and wisely changes the subject.

"How about you? What's your mom like? Is your dad in the picture?"

I look into my glass, hoping the right thing to say is located somewhere at the bottom. I didn't expect Faye to turn the tables on me. I'm usually good at avoiding questions like these, even with

Angela, who lets me get away with a vague "Kim's being Kim" answer. But I have a feeling this won't work on Faye.

"My dad's not in the picture," I say steadily. I can say this without anger, tears, or any emotion. My dad ceased to be a person and became more of a memory the last time I heard from him, when he sent me a "Happy Sweet Sixteen" card on my fourteenth birthday. But Kim is a different story. She's physically present but mentally absent, which is so much worse.

"Looks like the three of us have something in common," Zach says slowly. "Single moms. Deadbeat dads."

I don't look at him, but I can tell he's staring at me. I wonder what he's thinking—that as much time as we have spent in my bedroom, we're little more than strangers outside of it. I wonder if he's pissed off that I can talk to Faye but not him.

"And your mom," Faye continues, stirring pasta into the now-boiling pot of water and leaning against the oven, cocking her hip toward us. "What's she like?"

Faye definitely isn't letting me off easy. I press my hands together and think of the easiest way to sum up my mother.

"I don't know," I start slowly, looking at my hands. "She's not around enough to let me figure her out."

I don't let myself look up. I don't want to see pity on Faye's face or curiosity on Zach's. They can't think I'm weak. For a long minute nobody talks, and I'm afraid I said too much.

"Parents really fucking suck sometimes," Faye finally says. I let my eyes flicker up to her when I hear the tone in her voice. There's no pity in her eyes, no curiosity, no malice. Just a very astute observation.

"There's the truth," Zach says.

"Seriously. I mean, Lydia and I are all tight and shit, but she makes the worst life choices. She has been through so many douche bag boyfriends that I lost count, and she keeps telling me she'll never degrade herself like that again. But she still does it." Faye shakes her head.

"I know what you mean. If Kim gets one more 'cosmetic procedure,' I think she might try to attend our high school. She already dates guys young enough."

I wasn't planning on saying that, but the words spill out, clothed in sarcasm, my favorite defense mechanism. Zach chuckles, but Faye throws her head back and laughs, that seal-bark sound that I thought would get annoying the first day I met her. I was wrong.

"Watch the pasta," I yell, jumping out of my chair. "Your hair's dangerously close to the burner."

Faye grabs a fistful of her hair and bursts into another fit of laughter. "God, wouldn't that have sucked? The only thing worse than hair in your food is burnt hair in your food."

When we sit down to eat, there's an awkward silence, punctuated by the sound of forks hitting plates. I feel the need to fill the silence, like it's my fault it's even awkward in the first place.

I work up the courage to ask the question that has wiggled to the forefront of my mind. "So, it must have been hard moving high schools in last semester," I say, pushing pasta around on my plate.

Faye swallows and wipes the corner of her mouth with a napkin. "Not really," she says. "Schools are schools. They're not much different, wherever you go. Milton High is just a bigger playground."

"But why now?" My voice comes out more bluntly than I intended. Faye's shoulders stiffen, and I notice the way her grip on her fork tightens.

"We were done with Nevada. Lydia got a better job here, at a real restaurant. Not a crappy dive bar where she has to get groped by old perverts every night." She winds pasta tightly around her fork and looks at her plate, a gesture I take as the end of discussion.

Faye is done with her meal and Zach has had seconds in half

the time it takes for me to eat a quarter of mine. She filled our plates with heaping portions of pasta and tomato sauce, portions that would make Kim stick her finger down her throat before she even started. I was taught from an early age that carbohydrates were evil. "Spaghetti will make your ass expand like a balloon," Kim had told me the last time we went out to eat together. I can never eat anything around her without feeling like her eyes are on me.

Faye notices my lack of appetite. "Don't you like it?" she says. A crease has appeared between her eyebrows. I fight the urge to touch it with my finger and tell her that I love the pasta but hate eating in front of other people. Yet another way my mom has messed me up.

"I love it," I say quietly. And to prove it, I do something I haven't done for as long as I can remember: I finish the whole plate. I don't want to be under Kim's thumb when she's not around to criticize me. I can imagine her shaking her finger at me, admonishing me for not following the "one-thirds" rule she instituted when I hit puberty, where I would be praised for eating only one-third of what was on my plate and leaving the rest. But tonight, I don't care.

When I try to help Faye clear dishes, she waves me away. "This is the least I could do," she says, shoving plates into the sink and running them under water. "Your tutoring probably saved me from failing chemistry."

I feel Zach's eyes burning into me. I wait for him to make his usual joke about being a lost cause, but he doesn't. When I glance at him, he's staring at his place mat, and he doesn't look angry or upset, just sad. And that's a lot worse.

After dinner, Faye asks what movie we want to watch. Turns out, she shares my hatred of chick flicks and romantic comedies. Oddly enough, it's Zach who would rather watch some sappy love story than an action movie. Yet another thing I didn't know about him—another thing that I won't be able to forget, that will make it that much more difficult to keep our Wednesday lunch dates in their sealed little box.

"You're outnumbered," Faye says, plunking down between us on the couch and hitting the Play button. "Two against one. Not to mention, you're a huge pussy."

Zach stretches his legs out and puts his feet up on the coffee table, like this is his house. A thought rips through my mind. *He has been here before.* The idea makes my stomach feel unsettled.

"I like happy endings," he says. "I can't help it if I like when they end up together."

Now I don't know if he's talking about the movie, or us, or him and Faye. But Faye throws her head back until it's almost in my lap and laughs. "You have a lot to learn," she says. She leans into me, until our faces are only inches apart, and whispers conspiratorially. "Life doesn't have a happy ending most of the time, does it?"

I nod. My throat is dry, and for some reason I keep thinking that if I leaned forward two inches I could kiss her, find out once and for all who she's really flirting with—me or Zach. Maybe I'm making all of this up in my head because I don't have any friends besides Angela, who doesn't really like people touching her, so I don't know how regular girlfriends act. Maybe I should kiss her, right in front of Zach. Two inches would put my lips on hers. Two inches would give me an answer.

But then she pulls back and smacks her forehead. "Shit. I forgot the popcorn," she says, and she bounds off the couch, leaving me and Zach and a couch cushion that might as well be an iceberg between us.

It shouldn't feel like this.

"It just kind of happened," I say. "The tutoring. She invited herself over when I was helping Angela."

He shrugs and stares at the television, where the opening

credits are rolling. "Yeah," he says. "I guess she doesn't get boxed into one day of the week."

I blow out a breath. He's right. I like Zach the way he is in my head—simplified and predictable, my Wednesday friend. He fits perfectly there. Or at least he used to. But all these extra bits of information, all they do is add dimensions that force me to re-adjust to make room. Suddenly Zach takes up more space, and I don't have more space to give.

The smell of microwave popcorn emanates from the kitchen. My stomach roils. I can't possibly sit here through this movie, on the same couch with Zach and Faye. There might be room physically, but not mentally.

This is why I don't make friends.

"I just remembered I have a huge assignment in English that I need to finish," I say, standing up. "It's due tomorrow."

Zach knows I'm lying. He knows I never procrastinate. But he doesn't say anything, which is what I thought I wanted. A quick getaway. A painless exit. But I just feel empty as he gives me a close-lipped smile and a strange little wave good-bye.

Faye is disappointed. She's dumping what looks like the entire content of a saltshaker shaped like a cat into a huge bowl of popcorn, and she makes that face again, the one where the crease appears between her eyebrows.

"I wish you could stay," she says as she walks me down the hall.

"Me too," I say, and part of me means it.

I expect her to stop in the foyer when I put my shoes on and open the front door, but instead she follows me to my Jeep, padding down the driveway in her bare feet.

"We should do it again sometime," she says, rocking back on her heels.

"Yeah," I say, and part of me means that, too. "Thank you for dinner. It was perfect."

And then Faye does something unexpected. She reaches in to give me a hug, and I find myself smelling her hair, the same way Zach smelled mine. I don't expect it to smell the way it does, earthy and vaguely floral. When I pull away, she brushes her lips against my cheek and smiles.

I return her smile, wondering what that brush of her lips against my cheek meant, if anything. I thought I was good at reading people, even stereotyping where appropriate. But Faye is almost impossible to figure out. I can't decide if I like that about her.

I wave as I pull out of her driveway, my heart thudding in my chest. I drive home slowly for once, trying to get the jumble of thoughts in my head to form some kind of linear pattern. I'm unsure if I'm happy or sad or hopeful or disappointed or all of the above.

Maybe I should have stayed for the movie. I would have stayed for the movie if Zach weren't there. My stomach squirms when I think about what they're doing right now. I almost stop the Jeep more than once and turn around and go back.

But I can't control everything. I can't control whatever's going on at Faye's right now. Maybe she's straddling Zach right now and maybe his hands are all over her perfect denim-clad ass. Maybe his fingers are in her hair and he's running his tongue across her perfect teeth.

I don't know what I'm jealous of—the thought that she has that effect over Zach, the power that I thought only I had, or the thought that she wants him instead of me.

When I'm finally home, upstairs in my room, I pull out my journal. I need to get rid of the mishmash in my head, get it on paper. When it's on paper, I'll feel better, just like I do after the virgins. When it's in my journal, I can move on.

Tonight was weird. Maybe I'm reading too much into it. This could very well be what regular teenagers do every day. But something was weird. I felt wanted.

I stare at my own handwriting and hesitate. I almost don't want to continue, but I have to. I at least want to remember feeling this way.

I don't know what to think about Faye. There's just something about her. She's unlike anybody I've met. And when I'm with her, I feel like I don't know myself at all.
Or maybe I know myself better than ever.

17

Faye doesn't mention dinner when I see her during chemistry on Monday, but the way she puts her hand on my arm and leans her face so close to mine that our safety goggles touch makes me hyper-aware of everything she does. Angela doesn't mention her "midlife crisis," and Jeremy Roth doesn't even glance my way when we cross paths in the parking lot. Kim doesn't mention yoga or detox tea or charity events when I bump into her before school. Zach doesn't bring up tutoring or milkshakes. So it's basically back to business as usual.

Luckily, I have ample distraction, and not in the form of sexually inexperienced guys. As weird as I feel ending on Unlucky

Thirteen, maybe it's for the best. I'm not superstitious, but I'm choosing to take the number as a sign. It's time for me to really call it quits and focus on other things instead. Like this dance Angela is making me go to.

"Why the sudden interest in high school dances?" I ask when we're cleaning our beakers after class on Wednesday. "I thought you hated all that organized stuff." This much is true. Angela has always demonstrated an indifference bordering on disdain for football games, parties, and yearbook committees, which makes her attendance at Charlie's soccer game and interest in this dance very out of character.

"Charlie wants to go to this one. He says the DJ is really good."

"Fine," I say. "But why do I have to third wheel it with you?"

"You won't be third wheeling it. You should find a date, too."

"Sorry if I'm not jumping at the proposition." I reach over and pick up my backpack. Zach, my "Wednesday friend," is coming over for a lunch date. At least, he's supposed to. I haven't talked to him since the weirdness at Faye's house, and I'm not sure what to say. *I think we might like the same girl, and I might be jealous that you like her better than me?* There's just no way I can bring that up without sounding totally insane.

"Come on, Mercy. There have to be tons of guys who would be dying to go with you."

I scan the half-empty classroom, watching people filter out. Zach is still at his desk, chewing the end of his pencil thoughtfully. I could take a date. I don't need to be unattached anymore, like I did when I was being sought out by the virgins. I have no reason not to find somebody to ask. Zach would be the obvious choice, but I can't go with him. Not after I made it so clear that I didn't want to be his girlfriend. I wonder if Faye is taking a date. She would have her choice of just about anyone.

Speak of the devil. Faye barrels back into the room like a hurricane and makes a beeline for our shared desk. "Forgot my purse, again. Thank God nobody stole it," she says. "I think I have short-term memory loss. Or maybe it's your influence on me." She winks and blows a kiss before running out the door.

Angela visibly flinches. She hates when people say things like "Thank God," or her personal pet peeve, "Jesus Christ!" This time, I'm grateful she notices Faye taking the Lord's name in vain, because she didn't notice the wink or the air kiss or the smile that Faye left in her wake, the one that won't leave my lips.

Zach walks out of the room without looking at me. He makes not looking at me so much more obvious than the glances he kept throwing over his shoulder last week that I wish I had never said anything to him about it.

My phone beeps. I expect the text to be from Zach, but it's not. It's from Charlie.

I need your help with something. Can we meet today?

I mentally catalogue my itinerary for the rest of today. Second period French, third period lunch, aka quickie with Zach. I text back.

I can meet you after school. In the quad okay?

He texts back almost instantly.

Can I come over instead?

Sure.

I pause before hitting send. I wonder what's so important that Charlie has to meet me alone and if it has anything to do with his new part-time job as our gardener—or Angela's behavior on the weekend. Whatever it is, I guess I'm going to find out soon.

At lunch, Zach makes it clear that he's not interested in studying for next week's chemistry test. When he fails to undress me the second we get in the door, I entertain the horrifying thought that he's not interested in me anymore, either. He plunks down in front of the TV instead, on the leather couch Kim loves too much to ever let me sit on.

"Let's just hang out today," he says, pulling me down beside him. "Let's just chill. It's been a hectic morning. Besides, there's something I want to talk to you about." He rubs his hands together.

I jerk away from him, very aware of the unease gnawing away in my stomach. He's going to say something about movie night at Faye's house. Or maybe even let me in on some other facet of his life that I know nothing about. Suddenly I don't want him to say anything. I don't want it to be more complicated. So I do my best to clear his mind, too.

"I have a better idea," I say, straddling his lap and hiking my skirt up. Luckily, it works. He pins me down by my wrists and meets my mouth with his, and our bodies rub against Kim's precious couch before he scoops me up and carries me upstairs. It's the sweetest kind of silence, the kind where our breathing is in sync and I can forget about everything and *be in the moment*, the way Kim's yoga instructor told us to be. We can go back to how we were.

But when it's over, the spell is broken. He doesn't even wait until we get our clothes back on before asking me to the dance.

"I don't think so, Zach," I say, turning my face away from his.

"I don't see why you won't go with me," he says, slumping over me in defeat. "We have sex all the time, but you won't be seen in public with me. You didn't even want to sit on the same side of the table when we got milkshakes. And you sat ten feet away from me at Faye's."

I raise my eyebrow. "That's not true," I say. And it's not. I sat on the other side of the table because I didn't know where I was supposed to sit. But I don't tell him this, because then I would have to admit to him that going for milkshakes with him is the closest I have ever come to an actual date. And I can't tell him why I felt so uncomfortable at Faye's, either. Because then I would have to admit that I might be certifiably nuts.

"I don't even want to go to the stupid dance," I say. "But if I do, I'm going alone."

"I'm a good dancer," he says, snaking his arms around my waist and running his lips across my shoulder. "It could be great foreplay."

I kiss his cheek and pry myself out from under him. "I'm not your girlfriend, Zach."

He frowns. I hate when he makes that face.

"Fine. Maybe I'll ask another girl."

"You should," I say, locating his pants on my desk chair and tossing them to him.

"I'm serious," he says, tugging on my elbow. "I can't wait around for you forever."

I stare at the floor because I'm afraid that if I look at him, I'll see exactly how much he means it. Zach is attractive and sweet and funny and smells good. Most girls would be happy to be with him. I'm not like that. I'm happy *when* I'm with him, but I don't want to *be* with him. It would be so easy that way, so uncomplicated. Having a boyfriend would be a good way to put the virgins behind me. Monogamy, the ultimate bookend. But I can't do that to Zach. I know I would just end up hurting him. I would mess up and he would realize I'm not who he thinks I am and he would disappear.

But I also don't want him to be with anybody else, as selfish as that is.

"You know, you break my heart every Wednesday," he says. When I look up, he's smiling again, but it's not his usual smile. It's more reserved, with the corners of his mouth slightly pinched. I ignore that it's not his regular smile, because I don't want him to know how disarming this new smile is to me.

And I don't want him to know that I can even tell the difference.

"I'm sorry," I say. The syllables sound strangled. I don't even know what I'm apologizing for—the dance or the milkshake date or Faye's or everything else.

"If you say so," he says, doing up his belt. "How about you come over tonight? My mom's taking some course. I thought it would be fun for you to see my place for a change."

I try not to outwardly balk. I never go to a guy's place. Not ever. Not even Luke's, four years ago. And I'm not planning on starting now, not even with Zach. Zach might seem like Luke's polar opposite, but I learned from Luke that you can think you know a guy, only to find out too late that he's someone totally different. That he had been wearing a mask. I can't take the chance that Zach could be wearing one, too.

Besides, I have a good reason. Charlie coming over gives me an excuse that for once doesn't involve being naked with a different guy. "Can't tonight," I say. "I need to help a friend with something."

"Fine," he says with a drawn-out sigh. "But this weekend, I really might need some of your mad tutoring skills. My experiments suck." He pauses. "That is, if you could fit me in on a weekend. I don't know if you make exceptions for lost causes."

I take a deep breath. Zach is insistent on bending the rules. But it's nice to feel wanted, not wanted by a virgin who doesn't know any better but wanted by someone who does. Even though I'm emotionally guarded with him, Zach still knows me better than almost anyone else, and somehow he still wants to spend time with me.

"This weekend," I say, throwing his shirt at him. "Come over on Sunday. After dinner. My mom's making me do a yoga class with her in the afternoon." I rub my temples, wishing it wasn't true, but after Sunday's class, which Kim dubbed "a great success," I was automatically corralled into going again.

"I like the idea of you getting all bendy for me," he says, and suddenly he's normal Zach again, and I'm flooded with relief. "Now I'm not just your Wednesday friend. Even if you don't want me for a boyfriend."

I turn away from him as I put my own shirt on, not because of modesty but because I'm afraid that Zach knows me too well to see my face when he mentions that word. *Boyfriend.* I have more history with that word than anyone knows, even though the one guy I considered my boyfriend never came out and said it. So I guess I'm seventeen, with zero boyfriends but exactly fifteen guys under my belt, literally. Luke, Zach, and the thirteen virgins. I have slept with almost exactly as many people as my age.

I don't know if that's something to be proud of or horrified by, or maybe both. But since I don't want to think about it right now, I do what I do best. I spin around and grab Zach and press my mouth against his, and lose myself in the familiar contours of his body.

18

I didn't bank on Kim being home when Charlie comes over, and I definitely didn't expect to find Charlie seated at the kitchen table with her, drinking what must be her smelly detox tea and smiling broadly, like he always has tea after school with people's moms. I stand and watch them before I enter the kitchen, before they know I'm home. Kim crosses her legs and hikes her skirt up her thighs, and leans in to give Charlie a view of her propped-up cleavage. *Gross.* I never thought I'd see my mom flirt with my best friend's boyfriend, but I guess with Kim anything is possible.

"Oh, honey, we didn't hear you come in. Charlie was just telling me how insightful you are in prayer group. I never knew religion was so important to you!" To Charlie, she throws in an exaggerated wink. "I'm very spiritual myself."

I fight the urge to chuck my backpack at Kim's head. "If by spiritual, you mean you bought some power beads and read *Eat, Pray, Love*, sure you are," I say.

Charlie raises his eyebrows and laughs. Kim looks like I just slapped her across the face.

"If you don't mind, I'm going to borrow Charlie," I say, gesturing for Charlie to follow me upstairs.

"I hope this one doesn't sneak out in the middle of the night," Kim mutters under her breath before taking a swig of her tea. I shoot her the middle finger from the landing, even though she doesn't look up.

"What was all that about?" Charlie says once we're safely in my bedroom.

I was hoping he didn't hear her, but of course Kim managed to make me look bad in less than two minutes. I pull my bedroom door shut and, as an afterthought, lock it. It feels weird having Charlie in here when I do that, but Kim eavesdropping at the open door would be worse.

"Nothing," I say quickly. "Kim's used to guys pulling a runner in the night. I think she expects the same thing to happen to me."

Charlie clasps his hands together, almost like he does in prayer group, except he is wearing a very different expression. "And what exactly does your mom think we're doing in here?"

I turn my eyes to the floor. Heat is creeping up my neck, but I don't want to come across as rattled. Staring at the carpet is supposed to be a way to refocus, but instead I'm forced to see the very spot where I slept with Juan Marco Antonio. Even though Charlie could never know that—even though the room is spotless—I still feel like all the guys who have been in here must have left some sort of evidence, some presence Charlie can sense.

"Just homework," I say. "You know, the usual."

Charlie chuckles and stares at his hands. For a minute, there's a long and awkward silence, one that probably feels longer than it actually is. It's awkward because of the weekend, because we share a secret now, after years of Charlie just being Angela's boyfriend to me. Now he's more than that. He has made me, for better or worse, complicit in whatever scheme he's cooking up.

"Our anniversary is coming up soon. Two years together. So it has to be a really good gift."

I sit down on my bed, expecting Charlie to take the desk chair across from me, but instead he plants his butt on the mattress beside me. Close. I shift down and turn to face him. I notice a pair of lacy panties on the floor and push them under the bed with my toe, hoping Charlie didn't see them.

"Of course I can help," I say. But a simple text would have sufficed. And that would have avoided Charlie's interaction with Kim, and having him see the inside of my bedroom, somewhere I never imagined Charlie setting foot.

"Any initial observations?" He stretches back on my bed, a little too presumptuous for somebody who has never been in my room before.

But I don't say anything. Instead, I stand up, with the guise of rummaging around in my desk for a pen and notepad. I take a seat in my desk chair, pen poised, like I'm ready to write down any brilliant ideas.

"Two years is a long time," I say. "Something really personal. Like, maybe something engraved with your names on it? Angela loves stuff like that." I think about the promise ring, what it stands for. How often I see her spin it lately.

As if on cue, Charlie raises his hand, twirls the silver promise ring on his own finger. "I want to get her something to bring her out of her shell. She's so . . . inhibited, you know?"

I think back to the red-faced Angela who avoided my eyes over the weekend, the one who can't talk about sex with a straight face. The Angela who hates talking about anything personal—the Angela who probably befriended me because we share this in common.

"What about tickets to, like, an adventure park?"

He laughs. Charlie's laugh is slow and deliberate, like each syllable has to be earned. It strikes me how unlike Faye's laugh it is, that goddamned seal bark that you don't have to earn at all.

"This is a bit awkward, Mercy. That's why I wanted to talk about it here."

I instinctively bring my arms in front of my chest, afraid of what he's going to say next. Even though the posture does nothing defensively, it makes me feel safer somehow. Always has.

But Charlie makes no movement toward me. He stares at his hands. "I want to buy her something a bit more personal than that, but I have no idea what she would like. It's something you might know better, being a girl and all."

"Jewelry?" I ask, relaxing my posture slightly.

"Lingerie," he says. I almost laugh, until he peers up at me and I realize he is completely serious.

"I guess now I know why you didn't want to talk about it in the quad," I say with a nervous laugh.

"I'm serious, Mercy. Will you help me? I'm a guy. I'm clueless."

I nod slowly, hoping my face doesn't relay my confusion. Angela was conflicted on the weekend but said Charlie wasn't pushing her to sleep with him. As far as I know, she still wants to wait for marriage. If there's one thing I know, it's that lingerie and sex are virtually indistinguishable. And if a guy buys you lingerie, it's definitely with the intent that you're going to sleep with him. But I don't want to say any of this to Charlie, because that would be betraying Angela's confidence. I guess I'm keeping secrets on both sides of the fence.

"Great. I knew I could count on you." Charlie's face breaks into a huge smile and he stands up, wrapping me and the back of the chair in an awkward hug. I don't think Charlie has ever hugged me before, and it catches me completely off guard. He doesn't even hug Angela much in public. When his chest is pressed against mine, smothering my face, I remind myself that this is *Charlie*, Angela's Charlie, who is only asking me to shop for lingerie with him because I'm her best friend—not because I have ample experience on the subject.

We go to Victoria's Secret. I'm not taking Charlie to what, until Faye, used to be my secret spot. Faye would make the whole situation more cringeworthy than it already is, with her sexual innuendos and her perfect hair and teeth and the way she looks at me sometimes, like she knows more about me than she lets on.

"Can I help you?" asks a perky salesgirl wearing an extremely padded push-up bra under her "Tiffani" name tag.

I try not to stare at her cleavage before I start. "We're shopping for—"

"My girlfriend here," Charlie says, putting his arm around my waist. "We need something special."

When the salesgirl turns to lead us toward the nightgowns, I give Charlie a bewildered expression. He just shrugs.

"Seems less weird to me," he whispers. "Besides, you can try stuff on. You and Angie are about the same size."

I trail Charlie around the store, feeling completely lost in an environment where I usually feel completely at home. I suppose he has a point. Angela and I have almost identical builds, and he wants to buy something that fits so she doesn't have to suffer the embarrassment of taking it back. But this just seems weird. Maybe what threw me off most of all is that he called her "Angie," a nickname she once told me she despised. By that point she had been calling me "Mercy" for too long to tell her I kind of hate that nickname, too. But now, I only hate it from people who aren't Angela.

Charlie picks up a black garter belt and raises his eyebrow. I shake my head. "That's too intimidating," I say. "They're complicated." When he raises the other eyebrow, I quickly say, "I mean, they look complicated," and silently vow to not say anything else.

Lucky for us, "Tiffani" does plenty of talking, chattering excitedly as she pulls items from racks so fast I can't even tell what she's grabbing. She whips her head around and surveys me with squinting eyes. "Thirty-two B, right?"

I nod and look at the floor, wishing Charlie didn't know my bra size. Somehow Tiffani makes the scenario even more humiliating.

"Don't worry—they're the perfect size to work with," she says. "You can make them look huge with the right bra. And you know they'll never get saggy!" She looks down at her own bulging chest and giggles. "I wish mine were that size," she says in a tone of voice that implies she absolutely does not wish hers were that size.

She leaves me in the dressing room with about twenty different options. Most are tasteful, minus a very skimpy black corset that looks like something out of a bondage film. Of course that's the one Charlie wants me to try on.

"I think Angela would be scared of this," I say, waving the hanger around, willing it to disappear.

"The whole point is for her to think outside the box," he says before I pull the door shut. It crosses my mind that Charlie is the second person I've inadvertently shopped for lingerie with in less than a week. At least the first was not by choice.

Of all the lingerie I own, a corset is a new one, even for me. Forcing myself into it leaves my hair in complete disarray. Not bedroom hair. More like hurricane hair. I can barely breathe and my breasts are threatening to spill over the top. Not in a sexy way.

"Definitely not a good pick," I call to Charlie.

"Can I at least see it?" he calls back.

"Are you serious?"

"Yeah, I'm serious. I have to like it." He lowers his voice. "It's my first time, too."

My face, which was set in an expression of shock, softens. He may be unorthodox, but he has a point.

"Fine," I say. "But don't laugh." I open the door. And right away I wish I hadn't.

Charlie is facing away and turns around with his hands partially obscuring his eyes. He's peeking at first, but drops his hands—and his jaw—when he sees me. But not in the same frightened way as the more uncertain first-timers, like Evan Brown. Guys like Evan Brown don't drop their jaws because they mean to. It's an expression that isn't supposed to happen, like blowing your load ten seconds in.

And that's not how Charlie looks at me. Charlie's jaw drops deliberately, like he had complete control over it and decided to let it fall. And he says nothing, just stares at me until I feel my own face start to go red—and I never blush. Only when I start pulling the curtain back does he finally speak.

"I wish Angie would wear that."

I laugh, but it sounds like it's not coming from me. I cross my legs, grateful that at least my bottom half is covered by a pair of shorts.

"Maybe try that purple one."

I close the curtain and breathe deeply, or as deeply as I can with my lungs mostly compressed by satin and lace. Getting the corset off is even harder than getting it on, and I rip the bodice a bit in the process. I hope Tiffani doesn't notice and make me buy it.

I try on the purple one, the pink one, the long blue one. I don't show Charlie any of them, instead calling out from behind the curtain whether it's a hit or miss. My anxiety is mounting, and Charlie's enthusiasm seems to be waning. Finally, he decides on the white lacy one, even though I advised him against it.

"The most surefire way to make a girl feel more like a virgin is by putting her in bridal lingerie," I say as he pays at the checkout. "Something more neutral might be less scary for her."

He rolls his neck and shoulders, like he has spent all day at a desk job and is only now waking up.

"You're a good friend," he says. "It means a lot."

I edge away from him, hoping he won't put his arm around me and make me play his girlfriend again. "I hope so," I say, but even I can hear the wariness in my voice. *If I'm such a good friend, why do I feel like I'm betraying Angela?*

"Angie's going to love this," he says with a satisfied smile that I can't bring myself to return. Because even though Charlie thinks "Angie" will be happy, I don't think she would like any of what went on this afternoon behind her back.

19

I have a revelation the next morning in the unlikeliest place. Prayer group, which was rescheduled from yesterday because the drama geeks took over the library for their annual Shakespeare read-a-thon.

Charlie is reciting something that I'm not paying attention to, not only because I don't understand it or believe it but because the very sound of Charlie's voice today makes me think of silk, like lingerie, and Angela wearing it. It's not a mental picture I want. As I'm staring at the open Bible in my hands, trying to think about something else, my revelation happens.

I know how to help Toby Easton with polymers. The answer was right in front of me the whole time, but not in the pages of my notes where I was looking for it.

"Come over to my place after school," I tell Toby after his chemistry class lets out. "I have something to show you."

He puffs out his chubby cheeks. It's almost like he's suspicious. He couldn't possibly know about what goes on in my bedroom. Could he?

"Is that normal?" he says, fumbling with the papers in his hand. The top one bears a mark unfamiliar to me. A big red C. "I mean, I never went to a tutor's house before."

I narrow my eyes at him. "And how's that working out for you?" I say, gesturing to the C. "Five twenty-four Silverberry Run. Be there at six."

I stop at the water fountain on my way to class. My hair starts falling into the fountain, until a hand pushes it back for me. I close my eyes. For some reason I expect to see Zach when I stand up. But Charlie is there instead, wearing the same look he had on yesterday when I came out of the dressing room.

"I was thirsty," I say dumbly, wiping my mouth. My cheek feels hot where his fingers just were. I don't want his fingers there. I don't want anybody pushing my hair behind my ears for me. That was what Luke used to do. *This is what girlfriends do.*

"Hot date tonight?" Charlie says, tilting his head and pointing across the hall. I follow where he is looking and see Toby at his locker with a pudgy blond girl clinging to his neck. That must be the girlfriend who comes second to his textbook.

"No," I say brusquely, wrapping my arms across my chest. "I'm his tutor." How long has Charlie been watching me, anyway?

"I had no idea you were a tutor," Charlie says, propping his foot against the wall. "But now I can totally see it."

I nod. "Well, who knows if I'm any good at it."

Charlie leans in. "I bet you're an awesome teacher," he says.

I don't have time to react because Zach saunters up beside me and puts his hand on my shoulder.

"Hey, Mercy," he says. "I need to talk to you about something." He looks from my face to Charlie's and back to me again.

Charlie crosses his arms. He opens his mouth like he wants to say something else, but the bell rings and he heads down the hallway.

"What were you guys talking about?" Zach says, staring at his retreating back.

"Nothing," I say quickly. "Nothing important." I start walking in the opposite direction. "I'm late for class. Can we talk later?"

Zach shrugs. "Sure, I guess," he says, stopping abruptly. "Look, this might sound weird, but I don't like how Charlie looks at you. He's kind of strange, don't you think?"

I raise an eyebrow. "That's what you wanted to talk to me about? I can take care of myself, Zach." I shift my backpack strap and stare at my feet. "Besides, what's it to you? Are you jealous or something?"

Zach's face clouds over and I immediately wish I could take back what I just said. I know Zach is just looking out for me, but I don't need looking out for. I can take care of myself.

"You know, I don't think there's anything to talk about after all," he says. "See you around."

I remain planted in the hallway when he keeps walking. *See you around.* That's Zach-speak for *you're an asshole*, although he would never say that. Not even when I deserve it.

I half expect Toby Easton not to show up after school. Maybe his girlfriend isn't okay with him going to his tutor's house. Maybe he isn't okay with it. I'm grateful that Kim isn't home, because she would definitely scare him off.

It's weird having a guy over and not going through my regular routine first. I'm wearing the same jeans and T-shirt I wore to school today, with the same flimsy ponytail and stale makeup. I get ready, but in a different way. I line up everything we will need on the kitchen counter. Then I wait.

He shows up at half past, wearing the same uneasy expression he had on in the hallway at school. "I'm desperate," he says. "This class is killing me."

"You're in the right place," I say, leading him into the kitchen.

"Holy . . . ," he says when he sees the cluttered countertop, all the bottles and jars and flattened Ziploc bags. "What's all this?"

"This," I say, spreading my arms out, "is your interactive lesson in polymers."

He eyes me up with suspicion. He doesn't want to put his notebook away. He's clinging to it, to whatever he wrote down in there.

It's not a regular lab experiment, what I have set up in the kitchen. It's something more basic, and hopefully more fun. Because that's how I have been teaching people in my bedroom all this time—by going back to basics, breaking it down step by step, making it less intimidating. I figure it's worth a shot to apply this method of teaching to Toby, but in a very different way.

"During polymerization, chemical groups are lost from the monomers so that they can join together," I explain, standing behind the counter. "But you don't need to remember that yet. You just need to remember that examples of polymers are plastics and silicones. And that's what we're making. Silly putty."

Toby laughs, until he realizes I'm serious. And the more serious I get, the more relaxed he gets. He lets go of his notebook and follows my instructions. His attention isn't focused on writing and remembering things, just listening to each direction. He obediently shakes the glue solution and adds food coloring and makes the borax solution without flinching. By the time we end up with small plastic bags full of sticky globs, Toby looks like he's actually having fun. I watch him stretch the putty and rub it between his fingers.

"It kind of makes sense," he says. "The chemical properties of the putty change because of the amounts of the ingredients we used." He shrugs. "Right?"

"Right," I say, breaking into a smile. It worked.

"Thanks, Mercedes," he says. "You really saved my life."

I freeze midmotion, with my hand gripped around a wad of putty. *You really saved my life.* Somebody else said those very words to me not so long ago, after I helped him. Evan Brown.

I don't want to think about Evan right now. I busy myself cleaning up the mess on the counter before Kim gets home and thinks I'm in the process of building a bomb or something. Toby looks genuinely grateful when he leaves, and there's something familiar building in my chest. Pride. The same pride I used to feel when somebody left my bedroom. But this is better. This is, in chemistry terms, an undiluted solution. Not a temporary high, but something better. There's no residual doubt, no lingering what-ifs.

I don't know if I'm proud of Toby or of myself, or both. And if I'm proud of myself, it might be the very first time.

20

After the kitchen is clean, I know I should start my home economics assignment, the one I haven't even chosen a topic for yet. But instead of opening my textbook, I open an old photo album instead. It's filled with pictures of me and Angela. A few from the time we told her parents we were going to the grade-nine dance but really went to get burgers and milkshakes instead. A bunch from two summers ago at the beach, when Angela was afraid to go in the water because she was convinced a shark was going to grab her leg. One from the time we went camping and tried unsuccessfully to pitch a tent because Angela forgot the instruction manual at home.

In all of the pictures, we're smiling, laughing, carefree. And it makes me realize that nothing has been that way lately. We're both more serious, more withdrawn. Every time I look at Angela, she's distracted, like she's miles away. And maybe she would say the same thing about me.

I try to justify what Charlie told me. That he's planning a surprise, that he just wants Angela to come out of her shell. But that's the thing about Angela. She has always had a shell. It's her armor, the protective barrier to guard her softness. It's part of her. And if I know that, Charlie should, too.

I promised him I would keep his plans a secret, and I meant it. But my loyalty is to my best friend.

So I put the photo album away and grab my keys to the Jeep and pull out of the driveway, making one quick stop before ringing Angela's doorbell.

When she opens the door, she looks surprised to see me, which makes me feel awful. I used to drop by unannounced all the time. But not anymore.

"Mercy," she says, pulling the door open. "What's up?"

I shrug, hopping from one foot to the other, hoping she can't sense my nervousness.

"I was studying and got hungry," I say, holding out the plastic bag I'm carrying. "And it's been awhile since we did this, don't you think?"

Her face breaks into a smile when she looks in the bag. "Chocolate chips," she says. "You know, I could use a study break, too."

I follow her into the kitchen and hop onto one of the barstools at the counter. I watch her pull out a cookie sheet, one that doesn't bear the burnt residue of our previous cookie-making efforts like the ones in Kim's kitchen.

"Let's do it right this time," she says, and that makes me feel even guiltier because I want to make everything right. My friendship with Angela. The distance between us.

"Well, following the recipe is a start," I say. "Don't turn the oven up too high. That's what ruined it last time."

I wonder if she's thinking what I'm thinking, that last time was a long time ago.

"Let's not forget the brown sugar, either," she says. "And you got vanilla extract. This is totally going to end well."

By the time we start measuring ingredients and mixing them together in a giant bowl, I have all but forgotten my actual reason for coming here. It feels like old times, talking and laughing as we eat more of the chocolate chips than we put in the batter, Angela chastising me for making the blobs of dough on the cookie sheet too big.

After the first batch goes in the oven, the kitchen counter is a mess of flour and sugar granules, and Angela's face is pink and shiny as she sets the timer for ten minutes. I don't want to bring Charlie up. I don't want anything to ruin this.

But I know it's now or never.

"So, how are things going with Charlie?" I ask, licking batter off the back of a spoon.

Angela takes off her oven mitts and slumps over the counter. "Good, I guess." She cocks her head quizzically. "Why?"

I put the spoon down and sit up straight. "I don't know," I say, and the rest of the words dissolve like sugar on my tongue. *Because we went lingerie shopping for you last night. He picked out this white lacy thing that you'd hate and he has some big plan and I'm really worried.*

Angela raises an eyebrow. "I know what you're thinking," she says, and I wish for once she did, because that would make this a whole lot easier.

"What?" I ask.

She stares at her hands, where she is rolling a bit of leftover dough between her fingers. "You're thinking about what I said in your bedroom, about how I was confused. But I'm not anymore."

My heart thuds erratically. "You're not?"

She shakes her head and wisps of hair fall out from behind her ears. "No, I've made up my mind. I'm not sleeping with Charlie until we get married. No matter what."

"Does he know that?" I blurt out.

She looks up. "Well, I haven't said anything, but he'll just have to understand. I always said I'd wait, and I'm not changing my mind."

I grip the counter with my fingertips. I wish I could just be relieved, but I'm scared. Scared of how Charlie will react when Angela doesn't want to put that lingerie on.

"That's good," I say. "I mean, sex is a big deal. You can't go back, once it happens. So you have to be totally sure."

"Like you were with Luke," she says, and I nod quickly without meeting her eyes. A silent lie but maybe the biggest one I have ever told.

"Charlie's planning something," I say weakly. "For your anniversary. I don't know what exactly, but he has some big romantic thing planned. He asked for my help. I just didn't want you to be surprised."

I don't know how Angela will react to that, and this is why it's so hard telling the truth. People don't have a standard reaction. People aren't a chemistry experiment you can tinker with until the proportions are just right.

People are terrifying that way.

"Thank you," she says, touching my wrist lightly. "You know how much I hate surprises. At least if I know one's coming, I can prepare myself."

When I glance up, she's smiling and I almost want to laugh because it's true. Angela does hate surprises. She hated the surprise birthday party her parents threw for her when she turned sixteen and she hates surprise endings in movies and she hates pop quizzes even more than the rest of us. Everyone who knows Angela knows that.

Charlie should know that.

After a few more minutes, the timer starts to beep, and Angela spins around and opens the oven.

"Don't get too excited, but these look really promising!" she says. "Quick—pass me the oven mitts before they burn."

After putting the cookie sheet on a cooling rack, Angela plucks one cookie off and breaks it in half.

"Here goes nothing," she says, passing one half to me.

We bite into them at the exact same time and stare at each other, both waiting for a reaction.

"They're perfect," Angela says, nodding repeatedly. "After all this time, we finally got it right."

I manage a smile. We finally got it right.

Maybe I finally got it right, too.

21

"You're wearing that? To the dance? How do you expect a guy to look at you, let alone want to see you again?" Kim cocks her hip and smirks. I stare at her, in her too-tight top and too-low jeans, and wish I could wring her too-lifted neck.

"What's wrong with it?" I say, dropping my arms to my sides. I had hoped Kim would be home before I left, but now I'm really wishing she wasn't.

"What's wrong with it? You look like a tomboy. Those jeans are so . . . baggy." She says *baggy* like it's the most despicable word in the whole English language. To Kim, it probably is. Baggy pants, baggy eyes—anything baggy is the enemy.

"Maybe I am a tomboy," I say, plucking a ChapStick from the

pocket of my baggy pants and applying it. Kim hates ChapStick almost as much as baggy pants, because ChapStick does not make a statement.

"You have such a nice figure, honey. That no-carb diet really suits you." She leans forward and smooths my hair down. "You should show it off."

"Thanks for the tip, Kim," I say, fighting the urge to tell her all about the giant plate of pasta I ate at Faye's. To add to the look of sheer horror on her face, I grab a hoodie instead of my usual leather jacket and delight in the fact that her eyebrows move a fraction farther than I thought her Botox would allow.

"Don't get too drunk," she shouts after me. "Call me if you need a ride."

"But it's Friday night," I holler back at her from the driveway. "Won't you be drunk in an hour?"

Angela doesn't say anything about my outfit when I show up at the dance, just like I knew she wouldn't. Sweet, considerate Angela. I feel a swell of affection toward her.

"I got you a glass of punch," she shouts over the music. "It's not alcoholic. Don't worry."

"I'm more worried that it's not," I say, but she doesn't hear me. She's waving through the thickening crowd at somebody wearing all black with one of those ridiculous fedoras that everyone at Milton High has started donning lately.

It's Charlie. When I see that it's him, I'm glad I wore a hoodie and old jeans. Is it my imagination, or is he staring at me like he knows what I look like without clothes on? I guess he practically does. I raise my hand to my cheek, where he touched it yesterday. I suddenly want to tell Angela about that. But what would I say, that her boyfriend's hand happened to graze my face? Maybe I made the whole thing up in my head.

"This DJ is sick," is all he says. Angela nods excitedly. I don't say anything because I think the DJ is terrible. I'm not thinking about the music anyway. I know Charlie and Angela have their big anniversary coming up, and mental pictures of Angela in the white negligee keep creeping into my head. Except in my mental pictures she is trying to hide.

Angela wants to dance. She has mastered that whole "dance like nobody's watching" cliché, complete with overemphatic moves that aren't at all in sync with the rhythm. I sway back and forth, focusing on my feet, very aware of all the people who might be in this crowded gym at this very moment, people I don't want to make eye contact with. Particularly guys who came into my bedroom for their first time. When I started with the virgins, one of my rules was to not make appearances at student events, especially ones where alcohol may be involved. People get mouthy when they're drunk and say things they regret the next morning. But I'm apparently breaking my own rules all over the place this week.

"I'm glad your horizontal moves are better than these," a low voice says directly into my ear. Zach. My stomach does a little flip and I realize I'm glad he is here and I'm glad he is alone. I whip around so we're face-to-face.

"Shut up," I say. "I never said I was a good dancer."

He reaches out like he wants to touch me but tucks his hands behind his back instead. "Look, there's something I should tell you," he begins, but whatever he is saying gets drowned out by the pulsating music.

I lean in to hear the rest, close enough to feel the sweat through his shirt. But he pushes me back. I cock my head in confusion. "What's going on, Zach?" I yell.

He says one word. Only one syllable. I don't hear it, but I see how his mouth forms it.

Faye. And when I turn around, she's behind me, dancing with her eyes closed, snaking her arms in the air. Yesterday by the water fountain, Zach wanted to tell me something and I wouldn't listen.

I wonder if it would have stung any less.

"I'm so glad you're here," Faye says when she opens her eyes. She shimmies closer to me, until our faces are almost touching. "I hope you don't mind. I was going to ask, but I didn't see you yesterday."

"Mind what?" I shout over the music that seems to be getting louder, the whole gym pulsating.

"That Zach asked me to the dance."

I nod repeatedly, some sort of hybrid of nodding and bobbing my head to the beat. I glance over at Zach. He's staring right at me with his hands tucked deep in his pockets, the one person not dancing. I think back to what he said on our last lunch date. *I can't wait around for you forever.* I guess he meant it, but forever came a lot sooner than I thought.

"Why should I mind?" I yell, tearing my eyes away from him. "I don't like Zach. Zach doesn't like me. We're not even friends."

Suddenly she grabs my wrist, pulls me out of the circle of bodies, through other circles of bodies, until we're out of the gym, where she pushes her hair off her forehead and fans her face with her hand.

"I needed a breather," she says when we spill into the hall. "It's way too hot in there."

"You're still yelling," I say.

"Sorry," she says, lowering her voice. "But yeah, Zach asked me after school. I said yes because nobody else asked me." She leans over the water fountain, holding her hair in one hand. I squeeze my eyes shut.

I wonder if Zach knew he was going to ask Faye before I even turned him down. It's hard to think of Faye as somebody's consolation prize. I don't know if I should be flattered or shocked, but I don't feel either. I just want to leave, since it's too late to rewind time to change my mind about coming in the first place. Or to rewind time and accept Zach's offer. The thing is, I don't know if I'm more upset about Zach wanting to go with Faye, or Faye wanting to go with Zach. It's too confusing to think about in a place this full of people.

"Are you sure this is okay?" Faye says. Her hand is suddenly on my wrist, cool and steady. "Because you don't look like it's okay."

I stare at her hand, her thin fingers encircled by chunky turquoise rings. I wonder what it would be like to hold that hand. "It's fine," I say, forcing my mouth into a smile. "But this dance kind of sucks."

She wipes her mouth. "Kind of? This is hopping compared to my old school. The fact that you guys have actual punch at a dance is so retro. I thought that only happened in the movies."

"That punch could definitely use some spiking," I say, even though I wouldn't drink the punch either way, alcoholic or not, knowing how many idiot freshmen have probably spit in it by now.

"Lucky for us, I brought provisions," Faye says. "I did learn a thing or two from my old school." She grabs my hand and marches me down the hallway to a girls' bathroom, which is filled with freshmen jockeying for mirror space to apply lipstick and eyeliner. But Faye doesn't want mirror space. She pulls me right into a stall with her, which probably garners some strange looks.

"Vodka behind the toilet," she says as she unearths a flask and sits cross-legged on the floor. "Works every time. Nobody checks back there."

"Shouldn't you be with your date?" I say nervously, crouching down beside her. Faye takes a few calculated sips and holds the mickey out for me. I haven't drunk hard liquor since my first year of high school, when it was my only distraction from everything going on. I used alcohol to center myself, because it was the only thing that worked back then. I suppose now's as good a time as any to find out if it'll still work.

I take the mickey and press it to my lips, then tilt it down my throat. It burns going down and almost makes me gag. I forgot how unpleasant taking shots is, especially when the vodka is cheap and hasn't been chilled in the freezer. At least Kim taught me some important life lessons.

"Nah, I needed a break from him. He's sweet but so touchy-feely. I don't like that. You know?" She takes another sip of the vodka and puckers her lips.

I nod. I do know. I've told Zach multiple times that he needs to check his "affectionate tendencies" at the door. I lost track of the times he tried to wrap me in a hug behind my locker door or "accidentally" brush my hand during chemistry. But if anyone should be receptive of that kind of touching, it's Faye, who always seems to have her hand on my wrist or her arm around my shoulder, and I have only known her for two weeks.

"I like this better," she says, leaning against the wall and stretching her legs out.

"What? Hanging out in the bathroom with me?"

She shrugs and her mouth twitches into a little smile, which turns into a grimace when she takes another shot.

"School dances have such a forced festive feeling, like everyone has to act a certain way. When you're in the bathroom, that's when shit gets real."

I sputter on my next shot of vodka and almost spit it out. "Shit gets real. Literally." I start to laugh, harder than I have laughed in a very long time. At first, Faye looks at me with a bewildered expression, then starts to laugh, too, and the whole bathroom is filled with our laughter, my regular one and her seal-bark one.

"You cackle like a hyena," she says, which just makes me laugh harder, until there are tears in my eyes.

"You're drunk," she says after I regain my composure enough to have another shot.

"I'm so not," I say, wiping a tear off my cheek. "I'm just happy, you know?"

She tilts her head and peers at me intently, like she's seeing me for the first time. Her smile turns into a full-lipped frown, but even her frown is beautiful.

"You're not, though," she says. "Happy. Maybe you're drunk happy, but it's not the same."

"Why did you really transfer to our school?" I ask. Drinking makes me blunt, a fact I suddenly remember.

"Who were you lingerie shopping for?" she asks, equally as blunt.

By the time I get to my feet in the stall, I'm having more than a little bit of trouble standing, but I don't know if it's just the booze or the restlessness creeping through every inch of me. "This place is too small for me," I say, attempting to swirl my arms around but smacking them into the metal door instead.

Faye stands up, too, and puts her hands on my shoulders. "We're in a bathroom stall," she says. "Of course it's too small, silly."

"Not the stall," I say. "This whole place. School. The city. California."

She curls her bottom lip into a pout. "California's too small for you? That's too bad, because I was just starting to like it here."

"I'm getting out," I say. "I'm going to MIT. I'm going to wear a parka in the winter. I might even make a snow angel. I'll be just another number." I sing the last part, expecting it to sound better out loud than it does.

Faye closes the inch between us. "Snow angels are vastly overrated," she says. "And you could never be just a number." I'm close enough to smell her lip gloss, something fruity and sweet. My heart slams against my ribs. She's going to kiss me, right here in the bathroom. I was right. I wasn't making it all up in my head. She likes me. She wants me.

I pull away, my head spinning. The scene is all too familiar, and I suddenly realize this is the very stall where I tucked my Cons up onto the toilet seat and eavesdropped on Jillian talking to Annalise.

I fumble with the latch and step out of the stall, and that's where the night starts to get fuzzy for me. I got jostled through a crowd, through a forest of sweaty hands and fingers. I danced, but I don't know who I danced with. Somebody asked my name. Somebody else asked for my number. Somebody picked me up, gripping my waist tightly. Hands, hot hands, under my shirt. But when I wake up in a bed that isn't mine under an unfamiliar blue duvet in a strange room with no idea what time it is, I realize that I don't remember much at all.

22

"You," Zach says, handing me a glass of clear liquid that I sure hope isn't vodka, "are the cheapest drunk I have ever seen."

I strain to crack my eyes open. The contact lenses I left in are more or less congealed to my eyelids. Zach, wearing an expression somewhere between amused and concerned, is standing in front of ugly plaid curtains.

"Where am I?" As soon as I open my mouth, I regret it. I can taste the unmistakable musk of puke, puke mixed with something acidic that can only be vodka.

"You're at my house," he says, putting two Advil in my hand. "Sorry about the mess. I wasn't expecting to have a girl over. Much less the dancing queen of Milton High."

Fear washes over me, along with a new wave of nausea. "What do you mean, dancing queen? I don't even dance."

He sits on the edge of the bed. I turn away from him so he won't smell my horrendous breath.

"You danced last night," he says. "You wouldn't stop. Not even when I tried to get you to leave."

I flop back down on the pillow. "Oh. My. God. Please tell me nobody saw." I clap my hand over my mouth as I remember a more important question to ask. "Who was I dancing with?"

He raises an eyebrow. "Not me, if that's what you mean."

I rub my mouth with my hand. "Who?" I say, but it comes out muffled.

"There was one guy who kept trying to spin you around. But he wasn't around for too long. Then Charlie tried to pick you up." He narrows his eyes.

"What do you mean Charlie tried to pick me up?"

Zach presses his palms together. "I mean pick you up. As in, lift you in the air. It was kind of weird. That's when I told him I could take it from there, and that's how you ended up here."

"Maybe he was just trying to help," I say.

Zach shrugs, and I can tell he doesn't think so. "Well, I think it made you sick," he says. "But nobody saw you throw up except me and Faye."

I bite my cheek to stave off a new wave of nausea. "Did I ruin your date?"

He shakes his head. "Nah, she understood," he says. "She was worried about you. Helped me get you out to my mom's car. She felt really bad about getting you so wasted."

I squint my already half-closed eyes. Zach smooths my bangs off my forehead and applies a cold cloth. I should tell him to stop, that I don't need to be taken care of. But it feels good and I don't want him to stop.

"I called your mom," Zach says. "I found her number in your cell phone. I let her know you crashed here."

"You called Kim?" I pull the washcloth over my eyes. Zach probably thinks he did the right thing, but now Kim's going to take this minor screwup and lord it over me.

"Don't worry. I told her you were taking care of a friend." He pushes the cloth off my face.

"Why would you do that?" I ask.

"Because you would do the same for me." He shakes his head and laughs. "Actually, she was pretty funny. She told you to enjoy your one-night stand."

I feign a smile, but the effort hurts. Could Kim be more embarrassing?

Zach leans back onto the pillow beside me and closes his eyes. I know he has dozed off when I hear him snoring lightly. I never knew Zach snored. All the time he has spent in my bed, and I always kicked him out before he could fall asleep and make himself comfortable.

I sit up gingerly, trying to take my mind off my spinning head and lurching stomach by focusing on Zach's room. Zach's *bedroom*. I haven't been in any boy's bedroom, not even Luke's. Luke never invited me over. He said it was because he hated his dad, but now I don't know what to believe. I used to imagine what it looked like, what I would look like in it.

I never pictured Zach's, but if I had it probably wouldn't have looked like this. His room is small and cluttered, with clothes strewn everywhere and books piled high on a messy desk. Our massive chemistry textbook is at the top, perched perilously atop books half its size. A pang of guilt shoots through me.

I swing one leg over the bed, then the other, and rise wobbly to my feet. I shuffle over to the desk, putting one hand on it to steady myself. *Breathe, Mercedes. You're not going to throw up again.*

My phone number is tacked to a corkboard on the wall. Mercedes Ayres. I recognize my own handwriting, my neat little lettering. I remember giving him that little slip of paper after our first Wednesday date, after I couldn't believe I had slept with somebody I barely knew. It was so unlike me. I made it happen. I controlled the situation. I controlled *him*.

My stomach lurches and I run to the hall with my hand covering my mouth. Thankfully, the bathroom is right across from Zach's room and I make it to the toilet in time. There isn't much in my stomach to throw up, but what does come up is acidic and runny brown in color, like diluted coffee. Kneeling on the porcelain floor, I watch it splash in the toilet bowl and float on the water's surface before flushing the mess down. When the water comes back up, it's clear again. I wish it were that easy to make every kind of mess go away.

"Are you okay?" Zach's voice comes from outside the door, accompanied by a gentle knock. "Can I get you something?"

"I'm fine," I say, trying to sound brighter than I feel. I run water in the sink, trying to stave off the tears pricking at my eyelids. I don't know why I feel like crying. Maybe because I'm embarrassed, or maybe because this situation never would have happened at my house. I feel like it has been a million years since Kim ever took care of me. She doesn't try, and I don't think I would let her if she did. It would just end badly.

Just like this will end badly, too. I can't let Zach take care of me, either. He's not my boyfriend, and he shouldn't have to wipe up a drunk girl's puke and clean up the messes that spring up in her wake.

He deserves better.

Before I come out of the bathroom, I splash water on my face and put toothpaste on my finger to rub around the inside of my mouth. I paste on a smile before pushing Zach's bedroom door open. For the first time, I notice he's wearing flannel pajamas. I've never seen Zach in pajamas, and it feels intimate somehow, like I have crossed a line.

"I should go," I say, locating my purse on a nightstand beside Zach's bed. "I need to be getting home."

"You should stay for breakfast," he says. "My mom's making French toast."

I try not to outwardly balk. "Your mom?"

Zach blushes. "She always makes us French toast on Saturdays, before she goes to work."

I rub my temples. "She knows I'm here?"

"Yeah," he says. "I mean, I couldn't exactly get you into the house without her knowing. You were pretty loud."

I sit on the side of Zach's bed. This must be what rock bottom feels like. The ultimate humiliation. I wish I could take a giant eraser and wipe out the last twenty-four hours. I wish I could go back in time and stay home from the dance like I should have done anyway.

"I can't meet your mom," I say, dropping my head in my hands. "I'm a mess. I look like shit. And I probably smell terrible."

Zach sits down beside me and wraps an arm around my shoulders. "You couldn't smell terrible if you tried," he says. "And you look great. My mom's cool—trust me. She has been wanting to meet you anyway."

I grip my jeans-clad thighs with my hands. Zach's mom wants to meet me. What has he told her about me? I can't exactly imagine that conversation. *Hey Mom, there's this girl I bang on Wednesdays. She's a real peach. The type I really want to bring home for Sunday dinner. No, she's not my girlfriend. Funny story there . . .*

Zach leans in, close enough that his breath tickles my ear. "Seriously, Mercy. This is no big deal."

He's wrong. This is a big deal. I haven't met anybody's parents. Not even Luke's. But I don't have much of a choice. I'm trapped in Zach's room, and short of escaping out the window, the only way out is French toast and awkward small talk.

So I take a deep breath and follow Zach down the hall.

The first thing I notice about Mrs. Sutton is that she has actual gray hairs. Kim claims that she has never found a single one on her own head, which I know is bullshit, but any actual gray hairs would be promptly bleached into oblivion.

The second thing I notice about Mrs. Sutton is that her hug doesn't hurt. She's soft and plump and wraps me in an embrace that doesn't involve bony elbows or protruding collarbones or rock-hard breast implants. And her smile isn't fake. It's open and loving and I know she probably smiles like that at everybody, but it feels like that smile was meant just for me. I feel myself defrost a bit just being around her.

She doesn't mention my hangover. She doesn't ask if I'm Zach's girlfriend or how we met. She serves me a giant slab of bread dunked in eggs, fried, and topped with sticky maple syrup that she claims is a "family secret." I can't even remember the last time I had anything for breakfast besides black coffee. Probably around the same time I last had a real family breakfast with Kim and my dad, around the age of eight. Even then, Kim encouraged me to limit my portion sizes and to have egg whites instead of yolks.

Zach's mom encourages me to have seconds and sifts icing sugar over the top of each slice of bread. I eat hungrily, greedily, using the bread to sop up every last bit of syrup from my plate. I'm completely out of control.

"That was delicious, Mrs. Sutton," I say when I'm finished. "Thank you so much."

"Please, call me Julia," she says, her eyes crinkling at the corners.

"Julia," I repeat. Zach clears our plates and starts piling them in the sink.

Before Julia leaves for work, she gives me another hug and tells me I'm welcome anytime. I almost don't want to let her go. Maybe this is what it feels like to have a mother who cares. Maybe it's not carbohydrates that I'm starved for, but actual affection.

When Julia is gone, I realize I should go, too. I can't hide out at Zach's house the whole day. I need to face reality, my own reality, with my problems I don't know how to fix and my mother I don't know how to love. I run back to Zach's room to grab my hoodie, and, as an afterthought, I check the pockets. The right-hand pocket contains a little piece of lined paper. Written on it is a name—Rafe Lawrence—and a phone number, along with a note.

In case you forgot our conversation—see you Sunday at nine, your place.

I did forget the conversation, but it's coming back to me now, in flashes and bright colors. Rafe pulling me out of a throng of dancing bodies, shouting over the music, asking for a favor. Me telling him I'd be glad to help him out. I guess it slipped my mind that I'm done with the virgins. Plus, Zach is coming over on Sunday for tutoring. I'll have to find a way to let Rafe down without pissing him off.

A buzzing noise makes me jump, and I whip around. It's Zach's phone, vibrating like crazy on his dresser. I don't know why, but I walk over and pick it up.

There are three text messages displayed on the screen, all from Faye.

Is she okay? Honestly, I'm worried about her.
Do you think we did the right thing, not bringing her to her
own house?
Call me later and we can figure out what to do.

I stare at the screen. My cheeks are hot with humiliation. I feel like a little kid who did something bad, who hurt the people around me. A stupid kid who ruined something that people were probably looking forward to. A pathetic, hopeless kid who needs to be taken care of.

I'm somebody who hurts people. How many times can I hurt Zach and Faye without them turning their backs on me and realizing that their lives are better off without me? Maybe that's what Faye meant by *we can figure out what to do*. They're figuring out how to get rid of me.

I turn Zach's phone back over.

I'll make it easy for them.

23

Our yoga instructor tells us to "clear our heads." He says this a number of times, along with "sweat out your negative thoughts" and his favorite slogan, "be in the moment." When I look to my right, Kim has her eyes clenched shut and the stupidest expression on her face. I think she was going for serene but fell short and ended up somewhere near constipated.

I've got so much to clear from my head, but it's going to take a lot more than a yoga class. Guilt and sadness and frustration. I hate the way I left Zach's house, with a perfunctory hug and an awkward thank you. I hate that he let me leave.

Mostly I hate what I did last night, when I typed out a message I didn't want to send.

Sure—my place at nine. See you then.

I sent it to Rafe Lawrence.

To Zach, I sent a message letting him know I was too sick to tutor him. I waited for him to send a rant back, to let me know that he was over it. But he didn't. He sent back a sad face and offered to bring me soup, and I felt lower than I ever thought possible. I wanted to take it back, but it was too late. I had already committed to Rafe. Maybe it was the wrong choice, but it was my choice.

Rafe will be the last one.

I position myself in downward dog, breathing through the rush of blood to my head. I know who Rafe is from his visibility on the school theater scene. He isn't somebody I would have pegged as a virgin, but sometimes it's the ones you least expect who surprise you. Angela dragged me to see Milton High's production of *Grease* last year because she is absolutely obsessed with the movie and complained afterward that Rafe was too "smarmy" to be a convincing Danny Zuko. I nodded my assent but secretly disagreed, thinking he was just smarmy enough.

"How about dinner tonight?" Kim says when we're toweling off after class. I narrow my eyes at her. When I got back from spending the morning at Zach's house, Kim wasn't even home. I figured she would show at least an iota of parental concern after I failed to come home after the dance, but I was wrong. She didn't even leave a note, but I did hear her stagger in at some wee hour of the morning, laughing and telling her male companion to shut up. I don't want to have dinner with Kim tonight. Why should I care if she doesn't?

"I have a date," I say, stepping into my sweatpants. "He's coming over at nine."

I watch her face for any expression of shock, surprise, anger, anything, but she's paying close attention to a hangnail instead.

"Well, dinner would be at five," Kim says, sweeping her hair into a ponytail. "Plenty of time. Part of my new diet plan is not eating anything after seven o'clock."

She rattles on about a new vegan restaurant she wants to try, even though she's not a vegan. Pretending to eat healthy is Kim's flavor of the month, similar to the short-lived juice fast and shorter-lived abstinence from alcohol. And Kim's not a secret fad dieter, either. She makes it known to everybody—friends and strangers alike—that she's "on the Zone" or "giving up meat." She likes the attention more than the actual idea of giving anything up.

"Fine," I say with a sigh. I don't have the strength to argue with Kim today.

"You won't regret it," Kim says. "This restaurant is the place to see and be seen."

I roll my eyes. That's exactly the kind of thing Kim would say.

In actuality, the restaurant is completely bohemian which I can tell Kim wasn't expecting. In a sea of long dresses, short hair, and Birkenstocks, Kim is totally out of place in her tube top and towering high heels. She glances around nervously. "You'd think people who eat this clean would want to show off the results," she whispers when our waitress—a tiny girl in a billowing muumuu—shows us to our table.

The menu reads more like a gardening guide than something found at a restaurant. I let Kim order for me because I know she will get her way regardless, and there's nothing I could order that wouldn't make her shoot me a judgmental side eye anyway. I commit myself to hating this place on principle, with its obnoxiously green décor and references to nature. I think of Charlie, with his gardening gloves and shovel and his big secret planned for Angela, and whatever appetite I came in with all but disappears.

"What do you think?" Kim asks, after watching me force down a wheatgrass shot.

"I think this is why grass is in the ground," I say, wiping my mouth. "Not fit for human consumption." I almost want to add, *I have swallowed worse*, just to see her reaction.

"So, there's a reason I asked you to dinner," Kim says, pushing her sprout salad around on her plate.

Oh no. The last time she started a sentence that way, she wanted to let me know she had decided to move her twenty-year-old boyfriend into the house. Luckily, that phase didn't last even as long as the juice fast.

I take a bite of my grilled pear sandwich, the only thing that looked remotely edible on the menu. I spit it out. It's not.

"It's your father," she says. "He wants to spend some time with you. Says he wants a 'second chance.'" She puts *second chance* in air quotes.

I push my plate away, still tasting charred pear in my mouth.

"Second? Try tenth. I'm not falling for it. Don't let him bullshit you, Kim."

"Look, Mercedes. I think this time is different. He actually called me, instead of sending an e-mail at some ungodly hour. He admitted what happened between us was his fault."

I narrow my eyes. "What do you mean, his fault? Who else would be at fault for driving away in his stupid car?" I sound angrier than I actually am. I came to terms with growing up without a dad long ago, but the one memory that still hurts me is my dad waving from that stupid red Mercedes as he pulled out of our driveway. It's probably the clearest memory I have from my childhood, period. I hate how that one gets to stick in my mind and that I can't do anything to banish it or swap it out for something happier.

Kim clasps her hands together and studies the remains of her mangled salad. "This is very awkward," she says. "I didn't want you to find out about this until you were an adult, but you're seventeen now. I guess now is as good a time as any."

She stops talking and stares at me. Kim is almost as famous for her dramatic pauses during conversations as she is for her fad diets.

"Your father didn't just up and leave us. It wasn't that simple. We both had our problems, and we both gave in to our vices."

I shrug. "So dad was a drunk?" I do remember lots of liquor bottles adorning our kitchen when I was little, but I always assumed it was Kim doing most of the drinking.

She looks down at her hands. "No, honey. He wasn't a drunk. He was"—she drops her voice down to a hush so that I have to lean across the table to hear her—"unable to look beyond a small mistake."

Now it's my turn to stare. "What do you mean, a small mistake?"

Kim closes her eyes and massages her temples, an awkward motion due to the excessive length of her nails. "We both made mistakes. Your father made his share. He spent too much time at work, sank all of his money into his stupid car collection. He didn't pay attention to me." When she opens her eyes, I'm surprised that they're rimmed in red.

"What are you trying to say, Kim?" My voice gets louder without me meaning it to.

"I'm saying that I slipped. Just once, but once was enough for him to leave. He couldn't trust me anymore."

The wheatgrass shot—or something else—churns in my stomach, threatening to come up. "Wait a minute. You cheated on Dad?"

Kim nods almost imperceptibly. My head starts spinning. She never elaborated on why he left, and since she was always so reluctant to talk about it, I never brought it up, either. She managed to bad-mouth him in almost every way possible, from his propensity to throw money away to his absences at family functions. I always assumed if anyone had cheated, it was him.

"Why didn't you tell me before?" I spit out.

She begins quietly. "I knew you'd be inclined to blame me. But he was even more at fault. He told me he only married me because I got pregnant with you, that he wasn't ready to be a dad. He even said I tricked him into sticking around."

"So you're saying I was a mistake?" I grip the table, hoping that steadying my body will also steady all of the ugly thoughts clamoring for space in my head. *I'm a mistake. I wasn't wanted.* Kim was twenty-eight when she had me. Old enough to know better, twice as old as Lydia was when she had Faye. I can just imagine her lying to my dad, telling him she was on the Pill when she secretly stopped taking it. She only wanted me to keep a man around—a man she cheated on. What a giant crock of shit.

"Of course not, honey. You're the best thing that ever happened to me." Kim reaches across the table for my hands, which I swiftly hide in my lap.

"So you cheated on Dad," I say slowly, trying to comprehend the words as they come out of my mouth. "You cheated on him and pushed him away."

"You make it sound so simple," Kim says, her hands still outstretched. "It was once. I was lonely, so I went to the bar and met someone who made me feel good about myself. He actually complimented me. I didn't realize how depressed I had been."

I grit my teeth. "So some guy at a bar feeds you a line and you throw away your marriage for it? Great decision, Kim. Well done."

"That's not what it was like," Kim says, raising her voice. People are probably staring at us, transfixed by our family drama, but I don't let my eyes stray from Kim's face. "Your dad checked out of the marriage way before it happened. He told me he wasn't attracted to me. He told me he wanted to leave."

"So where do I fit into all of this?" I say, my voice quivering. "Dad wanted to divorce me, too?"

Kim wipes her eyes with her napkin. "He wasn't ready to be a father," she says slowly. "He never got there. And I think when things went bad, you reminded him too much of me. He couldn't be around you because it was too painful for him."

I stand up, my chair scraping the floor. "He was wrong," I say. "I'm nothing like you."

"Don't go, sweetie," Kim says, gesturing for me to sit down. "Please don't go. I never stopped loving your father, just like I'll always love you."

"You have a weird way of showing it," I say, grabbing my purse. "And in a few months I'll be out of your hair completely. So it'll be like your mistake never happened."

I have never cried in public, and I don't plan on starting now. I focus on the ground and bite my lip as I weave through tables on my way out the door. But since I'm not looking up, I bump right into somebody.

"I'm sorry," I say instinctively. When I look up to see who I hit, I feel like I have been punched in the stomach. It's Jillian Landry, holding hands with Tommy Hudson. The first.

"Mercedes," Jillian says sweetly. "It's totally my fault. I never watch where I'm going." She laughs, a sound as airy as wind chimes. She lets go of Tommy's hand. "Babe, this is the brilliant tutor I was telling you about. The one who's helping me pass chemistry."

Tommy opens his mouth and closes it again, like a fish gaping for air. Finally he manages a cursory hello. Obviously he didn't know that the same girl who helped him is helping his girlfriend in a very different way. I see the fear flash across his eyes, the momentary panic that I'll blow his cover and ruin his life.

"See you on Wednesday," Jillian says, but her words are muted, like somebody turned the volume way down. I bite the inside of my cheeks and wave good-bye. My hand feels like lead.

When I'm outside the restaurant, I break into a run, sucking in giant breaths of air that turn into heaving sobs. My purse slaps against my waist and my lungs feel like they're about to capsize, but I don't stop running until I'm home.

24

I pace around my bedroom until Rafe is scheduled to arrive, but I'm not sure if I'm listening more for the sound of the doorbell ringing or the sound of Kim's key in the lock. When nine thirty comes and goes, I don't hear either. Maybe Kim is drowning her sorrows at the bar, telling her life troubles to some idiot who doesn't know any better. She's probably sitting in a dark corner there now, waiting for some drunk guy to feed her a line. How pathetic. And maybe Rafe forgot about our date or decided he wasn't interested in me after the vodka wore off. Also pathetic.

I stare at my phone, hoping to see a missed message from Zach or Faye. I haven't heard from either of them today. Maybe they have given up, and I don't blame them. If they could see me now, they'd no doubt run the other way.

I'm wearing black stilettos, fishnet tights, and a negligee the color of midnight. I loaded up on the makeup, rimming my eyes in kohl and painting my lips in that red Kim said didn't suit me. I don't look like myself, or even any version of myself that I would recognize. I'm edgy and very aware that if Rafe doesn't show up, I don't know how I will get rid of the edginess and stop it from eating away at me.

Doorbell. Key in the lock. Doorbell. Key in the lock. I strain my ears, unsure of which sound I actually want to hear.

And at nine forty-five, the doorbell rings. Rafe's eyes bug out when I open the door, which was exactly the reaction I needed from somebody tonight. I force a smile but couldn't feel further from carefree.

"I thought I wanted to wait," he says when we're locked in my bedroom and I'm straddling his waist and unbuttoning his shirt. "But really, I figure nothing in life is worth waiting for. Especially something that's going to give you pleasure."

I grab his face with my hands and pull him toward me. The motion catches him off guard. I want him to react, to turn into something feral, to flip me on my back. But he just sits there, letting me writhe on his lap until I finally tell him to take his pants off.

"Wow," he says, his voice raising at least an octave. "This is all happening so fast. Wow."

I resist the urge to roll my eyes as I maneuver myself underneath him. "You've got to use your arms to hold yourself up," I say, struggling for breath as he positions himself on top of me. "You can't just flop on top of me like a dead fish."

"Don't flop like a dead fish. Got it." I can tell he's concentrating intently by his furrowed brow and the way he bites his lip. When he finally enters me, he moans in pleasure and flops like a dead fish all over again. I feel absolutely nothing besides a mounting sense of irritation.

Why does somebody get to have such strong, capable arms but have no idea how to use them? I blow out a breath as I wait for him to finish. Rafe is exactly the type for whom instructions of any sort are lost instantly, because he has his own way of doing things.

My irritation turns to guilt when I think about Zach. Zach's way of doing things. Zach is great in bed and does everything right without being told.

Zach is also great out of bed. The kind of guy who takes care of a drunk girl who didn't even want to be his friend. The kind who wants to bring you soup when you're sick. The kind who doesn't suspect you of faking sick when really you're blowing him off to sleep with a guy you don't even want to sleep with.

I feel sick. This is why I didn't want anybody to get close. This is why I don't want a boyfriend. This is why I don't *have* a boyfriend.

So why do I feel like such a cheater?

When Rafe finally rolls off me, I pull my sheets over my body, a gesture that doesn't mean much. Rafe isn't looking at me anyway. He steps back into his jeans and starts laughing, a sound that starts out as a nervous giggle and ends in a sound resembling a roar.

"What's so funny?" I say.

"I really owe you," he says.

"You don't owe me anything, Rafe. I hope you learned something. Pay it forward to your girlfriend. Pass it on."

This is the part where I would usually initiate a conversation about how and where he planned to do the deed with her, about how he intended to make it special and memorable. This is the part I used to like the most. Tonight, I can't even fathom dealing with it.

"No, I owe you. You saved my life!" Rafe gesticulates wildly with his hands.

"I wouldn't go that far, Rafe. It's just sex." My mounting irritation reaches a pinnacle. I want nothing more than for Rafe to leave me alone. And I want nothing more than for people to stop telling me I'm saving their lives.

"It's not just sex. I'm free now."

I pull the sheet over my head, expecting some spiel about how sex is the body's utmost expression of freedom, or the human body's highest art form. One of the other drama nerds, Joaquin—aka the Preacher—gave me a similar spiel a couple months ago. He even had tears in his eyes, although with drama geeks you never know if those tears are real or fake.

"I'm glad you feel that way." I roll over, hoping he will take his cue to leave. But he doesn't.

"You don't understand. And maybe I shouldn't tell you this, but I'm feeling so open right now. My girlfriend—Caroline—she's absolutely psychotic. I tried breaking up with her at least a dozen times. I tried everything. I stopped calling, I blew her off, I even changed my Facebook relationship status."

I push my bangs off my face and pull the sheet down. "What are you talking about?" Despite my calm exterior, budding fear is replacing my previous irritation. I didn't stalk Rafe on Facebook before he came over like I normally would, since I figured I already had him pegged as the musical superstar, Milton High's Danny Zuko. I'm going to be seriously pissed if my own stereotyping bites me in the ass and I just slept with this idiot for no reason at all.

"I'm talking about life! We only get one life, and it's too short to spend with somebody you don't love. But Caroline couldn't get that through her thick head. She told me the only way she'd ever leave me is if I cheated on her. And that's where you come in."

I bolt upright. "Wait a second. You used me as a cop-out so your girlfriend would dump you? Grow a pair, Rafe. That's pathetic. And she won't find out anyway."

He shakes his head. "No, you're wrong. She *will* find out. These things always get out, sooner or later."

"No, they don't," I say, pointing my finger at him. "Nobody has ever complained about their girlfriend finding out. Not ever. You guys don't tell, because if you do you're screwing over yourself and all your friends. And the girls don't know about it because nobody talks. That's why it works."

He pulls on his shirt. I bite the inside of my cheek hard enough to draw blood. I cannot let Rafe know how unsettled I feel.

"I know you think you have a flawless system," Rafe says, crossing his arms. "But if it was flawless, I wouldn't be here. I'm here because I'm banking on it being flawed. I'm here because someday, hopefully not too far down the line, the virgins at Milton won't be the only ones who know about you."

"That's not a very nice thing to say, Rafe. Can you imagine how many relationships that would ruin?"

He shrugs. "Not my problem. I'm an actor, not a fucking philanderer. I'm looking out for number one here."

I point at the door. "You're welcome to leave now. And I think you mean you aren't a fucking philanthropist, not philanderer. Because you are the exact definition of a fucking philanderer. And number one? You don't even rank in the top ten."

He gives me a sweet smile on the way out, making me wish I were close enough to slap him in the face.

"Mercedes. I hope you don't hold any ill will toward me, because I'm forever grateful to you. I'll probably mention you in my wedding speech, once I find the right girl. But the right girl sure as hell isn't Caroline."

When he's gone, I leap out of bed and wash my sheets immediately, wanting to disinfect myself from anything that has been in contact with Rafe. I almost can't believe that his dick was inside me, and I can't believe I wasted number fourteen on such a complete loser. And at this moment, I don't care about numbers at all. I'm done paying it forward. *Really* done this time. It's sad that Rafe took the last spot, but this is getting too weird for me. The virgins were supposed to make me feel in control, but I feel the complete opposite, like control has gone careening away from me. I should have just stopped at Evan Brown like I planned to, because that was when things started going downhill fast.

I shut out the lights and try to fall asleep. Kim still isn't home, and the fact that it's after ten thirty means there's a good chance she's pulling an all-nighter somewhere, with someone. Rafe's words echo in my mind. *These things always get out, sooner or later.*

I pick up my cell phone. No new messages. I should have spent tonight helping Zach with his chemistry homework. That's what a real friend would have done. I wonder what he would think if he knew what I was actually doing tonight.

Pressure is building behind my eyes, but I refuse to cry over somebody as stupid as Rafe Lawrence. So I pull out my notebook and press down as hard as I can with my pen, so hard that it makes an indent on the next page. Not that it matters, since Rafe's entry is the last one I'll ever write. Rafe Lawrence, number fourteen. I don't bother to rate him, because he doesn't even deserve a zero. Instead, he gets a rant.

CREEPY LYING ASSHOLE. Of all of them, I wish I could take this one back.

My eyes burn. The tears want to come, but I won't let them. Then I write down the worst thing of all, something I didn't even know was true until I stare at it on the paper.

He made me feel like nothing. Like I was the most pathetic person in the whole universe. Maybe I am.

A lone tear falls onto the page. I scratch it out furiously with my pen, creating a big black blob. Then I scrawl a name for Rafe across the bottom of the page.

The Bad Actor.

25

On Wednesday, I drive to school hoping Zach still wants a lunch date. We haven't broken a Wednesday in as long as I can remember. I *need* this lunch date to happen. Zach is honest and thoughtful and has no ulterior motives. He is everything Rafe Lawrence is not, and I hate that Rafe Lawrence is the last person I had sex with.

But when I enter the chemistry lab, I realize it's not going to happen. Zach got to class early—and Zach never gets to class early. He's always the last one to waltz in, usually right after the bell rings. Today, he is sitting in my spot, and he certainly isn't catching up on homework. He's whispering in Faye's ear, with his hand sneaking up her thigh, inching toward the crease in her jeans. I know this move on Zach. This is the move Zach pulls out when he really wants to get laid.

I stand at the door, unsure if I should make my presence known or turn around and come back later. Zach is moving one hand through Faye's hair, pushing it behind the nape of her neck. That move is one Zach doesn't make very often. That is the move he makes when he actually likes a girl. I remember the first time he did that to me. It was one of our first times having sex. I avoided making eye contact and made a joke, something about keeping his hands where I could see them. Faye doesn't do that. She smiles, a megawatt smile I can see from across the room. Up close, it must render Zach powerless.

"Mercy!" Angela comes up behind me and makes me jump about half a foot. Zach removes his hand from behind Faye's ear and they both look at me. Faye bites her lip and looks down. Zach avoids eye contact and vacates my spot.

"Oh," Angela says, looking at them with wide eyes. "Sorry— didn't mean to interrupt you guys." She starts talking about the last assignment, how she still doesn't understand how iodine plus ammonia is supposed to create nitrogen triiodide. I'm not really listening.

I'm grateful that most of the class consists of Mr. Sellers rattling on and on. We're supposed to be taking notes, but I can't seem to focus on anything except Zach and Faye. Faye and Zach. I don't love Zach. I had so many chances to be his girlfriend, and I never took him up on it. He has every right to whisper in Faye's ear or even stick his tongue down her throat. I just got too comfortable with our arrangement. I never really gave much thought to what would happen if something—or somebody—got in the way of it. And just because Faye invited me to her house and maybe almost kissed me in a bathroom stall, that doesn't mean she likes me as anything more than a friend. She's obviously into guys, just like I am.

I don't know what to do once chemistry is over. I don't want to go to my other classes, or sit in the cafeteria at lunch and possibly have to see Faye and Zach there together. I don't want to make small talk with Angela or avoid the weirdness that bubbles up in my stomach when Charlie is around. I don't have an appetite, and I'm suddenly very aware of the gnawing sensation in my gut.

Loneliness.

I'm about to blow off the rest of the day, to skip a class for the first time ever, even though the thought fills me with anxiety. I haven't gotten my acceptance letter from MIT yet, and while the dean of admissions won't know that I blew off a day of classes, I still don't feel right about doing it. I walk down the hall slowly, like I'm afraid I'll get caught.

My breath catches in my throat when I see Faye standing at her locker. I'm hoping she hasn't seen me, and I speed up my pace a bit, until we make eye contact in the little magnetized mirror she has on her locker door. Even without seeing her mouth I know she's smiling.

"Mercy," she says, beckoning me over. "I wanted to talk to you."

I lean up beside her, letting my eyes shift to the contents of her locker. She hasn't even been at Milton High very long, but her locker is already a mess of books and papers and about a thousand lip glosses. Tacked under her mirror is a bright pink Post-it note with a familiar phone number and address written on it. Mine. Zach's is nowhere to be seen.

Faye presses the palms of her hands together. She's uncomfortable. "Look, nothing is going on," she says. "We're just friends. Zach told me you guys used to see each other a bit. I wouldn't want to come between anything." I sense some hesitation in her voice, something she's not saying.

I shift my backpack from one shoulder to the other. Faye used the past tense. *You guys used to see each other.* Implying used to but don't anymore. I guess I expected too much of Zach to tell me himself. But that's Zach. He never finishes what he starts, being the type to have a new hobby every week and a slew of unfinished projects in his wake.

But none of this is Faye's fault. "It's perfectly fine," I say, plastering on a big smile. "I'm not interested in Zach at all. There's nothing to come between."

Faye shuts her locker door. "This is none of my business, but I'm not sure if I believe you. Besides, I don't know if I'd be that into him. He's not my usual type."

I know what she means. When I first met Zach, before I even started with the first-timers, I never thought he was the type of guy I would sleep with. I had only ever slept with one guy when Zach was assigned as my lab partner, and Zach was nothing like Luke. But that was ultimately what made Zach attractive to me. He was *nothing* like Luke. He was goofy and clumsy and passive and said sorry all of the time, even when things weren't his fault. I didn't know guys like him existed.

So I thought I would conduct my own experiment outside of the classroom. I asked him to have lunch with me and brought him back to my house and waited for him to follow me up to my bedroom. He was so timid that I thought I had made a mistake, until I pressed him against the wall and kissed him and he kissed me back. He was so good at kissing that I knew he had done it before. And since he was that good at kissing, I couldn't help but wonder what else he was good at.

He didn't want to go all the way that day. He wanted to take me on a real date, get to know me first. But I didn't let him. I started taking my clothes off and watched his eyes go as wide as dinner plates and I knew I had him. He followed my lead, made me feel wanted, made me feel good. He never asked for more than I wanted to give him.

We never did eat lunch that day, but our Wednesday lunchtime dates were solidified.

I remember thinking, *I could get used to this.* And I did.

"Well, maybe you should give him a chance." I start walking down the hall, and she follows. I don't know why I said it. I don't like the idea of Faye and Zach together, and she has given me every chance to be honest with her. But maybe it's for the best. Faye is sweet and pretty and nice and thoughtful. Everything I'm not. She would probably make Zach happy. She would be able to give him what I can't.

I'm deep in thought when we turn a corner and I smack right into Charlie, hard enough for my purse to fall off my shoulder and hit the ground. The impact sends its contents spewing out. Pens, tampons, my planner, keys. And of course, three condoms. A Ribbed, an Ultra Thin, and a Magnum, which Charlie picks up first, stifling a smile.

Faye and I crouch down to collect my stuff. Of all the people I didn't want to see the contents of my purse, Charlie would be vying for number one. I don't want Charlie to know I carry condoms around, even though I don't think he would say anything to Angela. *We're all allowed to have one little secret.* That was what he said in the backyard. He has been over since then, clipping and pruning and digging up the garden, but I have stayed out of the backyard and watched him from my bedroom instead. I don't want him to keep digging into my life, because he might find something he doesn't want to know.

Charlie hands me the condom. "Somebody's prepared," he says, but he's not smiling anymore.

Faye isn't so subtle. "What were you planning to do today?" she says.

"Those have just been in there forever," I say, snatching my purse back from her. I nod at Charlie and give him a tight-lipped smile.

"I texted you," he says as Faye and I keep walking. "It's, you know, important." He smiles again before turning the other way.

When we're in the home economics classroom, Faye looks at me with a furrowed brow. "Look, this is kind of a weird thing to say, but Angela's boyfriend totally looked down your shirt when you bent over. I think he has a thing for you. And he's texting you now?"

I narrow my eyes. First Zach, now Faye. Just like after the dance, the text message exchange. *Honestly, I'm worried about her.*

They shouldn't be.

"Charlie did not look down my shirt," I snap. "And he's texting me about something to do with Angela. Something that's really none of your business."

Faye takes off her cardigan and hangs it off the back of the chair. Without it, her cleavage is on full display. If Charlie was looking at anyone, it would be her, and I really couldn't blame him.

"*Meow*," she says, but I can tell she's hurt. "Somebody has serious PMS. Guess I won't ask you to borrow one of those condoms."

"Take them all," I say, plucking the foil wrappers from my purse and tossing them on her binder. "Although, I'm sure Mrs. Hill has plenty she would happily give you."

Faye laughs. A normal person would probably shove them out of sight, but she just leaves them there, prompting some strange looks from our classmates.

"Oh, and Faye? The correct question would have been to ask me to give one to you. Borrowing implies that you'll give it back. Please don't."

She bursts out laughing. "You're a bitch. But I like that about you." But the air between us bristles with things unsaid. I don't want to think about Faye putting one of those condoms on Zach, but it's not like I can say that, because I would sound completely nuts.

I move into my seat beside Angela, but Angela doesn't show up. I check my cell phone for missed messages but only see a new one from Charlie.

I want to move up the date. Planning something special for Angela for next weekend. Meet at your place after school?

I text back before I can say no or make him meet me somewhere at school instead. He probably wants to make sure Angela won't run into us. Maybe she talked to him by now and he knows sex is off the agenda. Maybe he took back the lingerie.

Sure. See you there.

He texts back a winking smiley face, which I always thought was the flirtatious smiley—I recognize it from Zach's side of our pre- and posthookup text message conversations, which generally veered into very graphic territory.

Somebody plunks down beside me, but it's not Angela. It's Zach.

"Shouldn't you be sitting beside your girlfriend?" I say before I can stop myself.

"I don't have a girlfriend," he whispers over Mrs. Hill's rambling lecture about estrogen and ovaries. "But I do need a favor."

"What kind of favor?" I whisper back. "I'm guessing not a sexual one."

"I need you to tutor me tonight," he says. "For real. I'm drowning, and I need help. Are you in or out?"

A wave of relief rushes over me. I nod, suddenly feeling ten pounds lighter. Faye won't be using those condoms on Zach tonight if he's with me instead.

"Come over tonight," I say. "You, me, and my very good notes."

His face breaks into a smile. "Thank you, thank you, thank you," he says. "You—"

"Please don't say I saved your life," I whisper.

"That's yet to be determined," he says with a wink.

I face the board and suddenly remember that I'm supposed to meet Jillian after school. She has a test tomorrow, and I'm supposed to quiz her with the flash cards I made last night, all of the questions I made up to test her knowledge on stoichiometry. I message Charlie back.

Make it an hour after school—I have tutoring first.

My phone vibrates in my purse almost instantly.

Sure. This won't take all night.

I write in the margin of my binder, where I'm supposed to be taking notes on whatever Mrs. Hill is talking about. Instead I scribble a note to Zach.

Can you come over at seven?

His arm hovers over the paper a long time, but when he pushes the notebook back, there are only three words. Three words and one winking smiley face.

Seven is perfect. ;)

I'm still smiling when I meet Jillian in the chemistry room when the final bell rings. She notices.

"You're happy about something," she says, after botching her second attempt at balancing redox reactions.

I shrug. I'm thinking about Zach. Zach, who still wants my help, even though I have turned him down so many times. He keeps forgiving me.

I wonder what else he would forgive me for.

I glance at the giant clock on the wall before making a diagram on a scrap of graph paper. I have to meet Charlie in half an hour, but I'm not leaving until Jillian understands this. I owe her that much.

"Just remember this," I say, tapping my pencil against the page. "The equation has to be separated first into two half reactions. Each half reaction is balanced separately before the equations are added together to give a balanced overall reaction."

I draw out a formula for each half reaction. The reduction portion and the oxidation portion. All Jillian has to do is follow the formula. Why is it so hard for her, when it's so black and white to me?

"I guess it's just a balancing act," she says, rubbing her temples. "Like everything in life. Right?" She looks up at me, like she's expecting an answer.

"Right," I say, even though my stomach starts to feel queasy when I say it. I feel like a total fraud. I don't know anything about balance. I know everything about numbers, but I can't read people to save my life. Maybe Zach is with Faye right now. Maybe when he comes to my house he'll smell like her. Maybe when I'm done tutoring him he will be done with me, and Faye will, too. They'll be happy together, and I'll be on the outside, looking in.

"You know, you're a good teacher," she says when we're done, after she passes the quiz I made for her and packs up the flash cards so she can study them at home tonight. "Much better than Mr. Sellers. You could do his job way better than he does it."

I laugh, but it sounds empty. For some reason I think about Tommy. *Why me? Why Jillian?*

"I'm going to pass this test," she says, clutching her textbooks to her chest, as if all the wisdom in there will transfer into her. "I need a seventy in this class. And I'm going to get it, thanks to you."

I give her a tight-lipped smile. It hits me, how important numbers are to everybody. Jillian needs a seventy. I lost my own virginity at age thirteen. I slept with fourteen guys. Charlie wants to celebrate two years with Angela. The Bad Actor deserved less than zero.

But the only number that's important to me right now is seven.

Seven is perfect.

26

Charlie beats me home. He's sitting on the porch, with his backpack at his feet, smoking a cigarette. I'm not surprised that he got here first, since I'm fifteen minutes late. What's disarming is the cigarette. Charlie is supposed to be adamantly against smoking, at least according to Angela. I wonder how many other secrets he is keeping from her.

"You don't smoke," I say as I unlock the door to let us in.

"I wanted to try it." He stands up and hefts his bag over his shoulder.

"Well, you can't bring it in the house," I say. "Kim would have a conniption. She's strictly anti-nicotine this week. You should have caught her in her chain-smoker phase."

"Bummer," Charlie says, snuffing out the cigarette with his shoe.

I lead him into the kitchen, wishing I could shut the door on him instead. I don't want him in my house. But I have no reason to keep him out.

"Where's your mom?" he says.

"No idea. Probably Pilates. Or maybe the bar." I laugh bitterly and pour a glass of water. "Want anything to drink?"

He looks at his wrist, even though he's not wearing a watch. "Well, it must be five o'clock by now. And that means the bar's open."

"You want an actual drink? Now?" I cross my arms. This isn't like Charlie at all.

He shrugs. "Why not now?"

I lean over the counter on my forearms. "I thought you wanted me to help you with something you're making Angela."

He leans in closer. "I do. But I was hoping to be inspired before I got started."

I look at his face. He appears earnest enough, with the corners of his lips curling into a small smile. Whatever he's planning, he's nervous about it, and I guess alcohol does take the edge off.

And even though I want no part of his plan anymore, it's too late to go back.

"I don't think that's a good idea," I say. But Charlie reaches behind me, shoves my knee out of the way with his, and opens the cabinet where Kim keeps her liquor stash.

"Don't be so uptight," he says, grabbing a bottle of something amber colored.

"How did you know where to find that?" I say as he opens the cupboard where our glassware is stored. It's unnerving exactly how well Charlie knows his way around this kitchen.

"Your mom's pretty cool. Some moms offer you lemonade after you do their yard work. Yours offers me a long island iced tea."

I roll my eyes. "Fine," I say. "But let's go upstairs." As strange as Charlie raiding Kim's liquor cabinet is, it would be far worse to have Kim come home and find Charlie in the kitchen. She would undoubtedly suck him into a stupid conversation and likely pepper it with sexual innuendos. Charlie's eighteen—fully legal—so I'm sure Kim has hit on him at least once.

"You're the boss," he says as we walk up the stairs. I walk quicker than usual. I know that my skirt is short and I don't want to know if Charlie can see up it.

When we're in my room, I sit cross-legged in my desk chair to avoid the awkwardness that ensued when we both sat on the bed last time.

"Why do you hate your mom?" Charlie says, unscrewing the lid and taking a swig straight from the bottle.

"Excuse me?" I say, taken aback by his bluntness.

"You just seem to really hate her," he says, sitting on the edge of my duvet. "She's really pretty cool, for a mom."

"No offense, but I'd rather not talk about Kim," I say, gripping the armrests of my chair. "We're here to talk about you and Angela." I resist the urge to add, *And you know absolutely nothing about our fucked-up family situation, so don't pretend you do.*

"She just wants you to be happy," he says, raising the bottle to his lips again. "She wants you to find a boyfriend."

I narrow my eyes at him. "Kim told you that? Why would she talk about that with you?"

He shrugs. "We talk about a lot of things. She says you haven't found anyone special yet. She told me she gets her hopes up whenever someone new comes over."

I stare at my fingers, clamped on the armrests. I'm gripping them so tightly that my knuckles are turning white. I knew Kim was a terrible parent, but I didn't think she would stoop as low as discussing my love life with my best friend's boyfriend. I guess I was wrong.

"She's full of shit," I say through gritted teeth. "If someone new comes over, it's one of hers."

Charlie holds one hand up in a gesture of surrender. "Whoa, chill out. I didn't mean anything. Don't shoot the messenger."

I relax my grip and force my mouth into a smile. "Well, enough about Kim's stupid fantasies. Now, let's get to whatever you're planning for Angela."

"We are getting to it," he says. "It's kind of a big deal."

"I'm sure she will love it, whatever it is," I say. "Just don't put too much pressure on yourself. Don't stress out. I'm sure it'll be something she will never forget." I'm saying the words but not really meaning them.

Charlie does another shot of rum and shakes his head. "How do you do that?"

"Do what?"

He puts the bottle on the floor and stretches his arms over his head. His neck makes a cracking sound. "You'd never guess it, but I know it's true."

I pull my knees against my chest. "I think you've had enough to drink, Charlie. I don't even know what you're saying. I get that you're nervous about . . . whatever it is you're nervous about, but you're not going to find any answers at the bottom of that bottle."

He nods like I have just said something incredibly profound. Then he stands up and does a lap around my bed. "You're right. I'm sorry. No more rum for Charlie."

I glance at the clock on my nightstand. It's almost five. Zach is coming at seven. I wish I would have told him to come earlier. I suddenly want any excuse to get rid of Charlie. Not to mention, the way he is referring to himself in the third person is creeping me out.

"So, Miss Mercy, where do I find the answers?" He throws his arms into an exaggerated shrug.

"In here," I say, half-sarcastically, pointing to my heart. I expect him to laugh, to call me out on being a smart-ass. Anything except what he actually does.

He tries to kiss me.

He's in my face so quickly that I don't have time to move out of his way. I turn my head just in time so that his lips make contact with my cheek instead of my mouth. The smell of the rum on his breath makes my stomach lurch, and I use my hands to push him backwards. Except my swivel chair catches on something on the carpet and gets stuck, giving him another chance to push himself onto me. This time I almost flip out of the chair in my attempt to stave him off.

"Charlie, what the fuck are you doing?"

He's breathing heavy and starts to laugh, which makes me even more confused and pissed off. I should have insisted we meet at school. This never would have happened there.

"Don't fight it," he says, coming closer. "There's this thing between us. It's just getting stronger."

"What thing? There's nothing here besides a mutual love for Angela." I get out of my chair and point at the door. "I think you should go. You're drunk."

"Angela." Charlie rubs his hand against his chin, like he's thinking deeply. "Angela wants so much. Angela wants to wait until we're married. And apparently Angela's best friend Mercy thinks it's important to be sure." He glares at me, and I realize he knows I talked to Angela.

He knows, and he's pissed.

"You can't just change her mind," I say, crossing my arms over my chest. "And you shouldn't want to. She's your girlfriend. You're supposed to respect her. And if you leave now, I won't tell her about any of this." I hope he doesn't realize that this is a complete lie. I absolutely intend to tell Angela everything about what just happened the second Charlie finally gets out of my bedroom.

He mock gasps. "If I leave now? Are you threatening me?"

I nod. "If you want to take it as a threat, be my guest. But get out now. Before I throw you out myself."

"You won't do that," he says. "There's something you need to do for me first."

"And what might that be?"

He sits down on my bed and pats the empty space next to him. "I want you to give me my first time. From what I hear, you're good at it."

27

Of all the things I thought Charlie might say—that he was drunk, that he was nervous, that he was sorry for scaring me—*that* wasn't one of them. My throat constricts, like my heart has leapt into it and blocked the air supply from the rest of my body. I can hear my own heartbeat in my ears, loud and panicked, like a fire alarm going off inside of me.

But I don't give Charlie the satisfaction of my panic. I go with my first instinct instead—playing dumb to find out how much he really knows.

"I'm not sleeping with you, Charlie. I don't know where you got that idea, but get it out of your head."

He stretches his legs out and pats the comforter. "So this is where the magic happens. I have to say, when I heard about what you do, I didn't believe it. But I found out for myself." He grins, a maniacal smile that makes me feel like I'm going to be sick.

"What do you mean, found out for yourself?" I fall into my swivel chair because I'm afraid my legs might give out at any second.

"Well, you don't just take these things at face value. Rumors are rumors. And locker-room talk is, well, locker-room talk. But I overheard Connor Reid in there one day, telling a couple dudes how he finally banged his girlfriend. With your help."

I cross my arms in front of my chest, fighting off a fresh wave of panic. Connor Reid, number four, aka the Screamer. Except when I slept with him, he didn't play soccer. He played baseball, so I thought he was safe. Exactly how long has Charlie known about me?

I stare icily. "So what? So some guy has a fantasy about me. Big deal."

Charlie shakes his head. He's still smiling, that shit-eating grin. "That's what I thought, too. But I had some questions, so I followed up. Turns out, you have a huge following, and not just in one so-cial circle, either. I figured *that* many people couldn't all be liars. So I did my homework."

"And?" My voice sounds a lot shakier than I wish it did.

"And you definitely live up to your reputation." He crawls up my comforter to my pillows. I get increasingly nauseous as I watch him rifle through the clutter on my nightstand, where my laptop is sitting. When he spreads out his palm to show me, he's holding a little silver and black orb.

"A webcam." He curls his fingers around the orb. "I had to see for myself, so I had a friend set it up. I think you know him inti-mately. He might have wanted to blindfold you? And God, was there ever a lot to see."

I chew on the inside of my cheek to keep myself from throwing up. "You're joking. That's not a webcam. It's a trick."

Charlie looks down at his hand and starts ticking names off his fingers. "After Juan, there was Jeremy Roth, twice. Or was it three times? And that Zach guy, but I already suspected you were doing it with him. And you finished with Rafe Lawrence. I loved that look the best. All black and those red lips." He smacks his own lips together.

My eyes dart between the webcam and Charlie's smirking face. I'm very aware that I'm trapped in here, trapped in my own bedroom with Charlie and all his knowledge about what has transpired in this very room. Charlie can probably read the shock all over my face, and maybe the panic there, too. So I try a new tactic. Honesty.

"What do you want, Charlie? You want me to admit it?"

He taps his fingers on my nightstand. "I want you to do the same for me that you did for them. Those are my terms. If you don't comply, I'll show that video to everybody, and the whole school will know exactly what you've been doing with their boyfriends and writing in that little book of yours."

"But why?" I say, my voice rising. "Why do you even care what I do or who I do it with?"

"You brought this on yourself," he says, clicking his tongue against his teeth. "At first, I just wanted to know if it was true. But then you had to go and blow my whole surprise. She knows I have something planned. She made it clear she's not giving it up until we're married, so I figured, why not come to you? You're obviously ready and willing."

My face is burning, but I try not to outwardly react, despite the way my heart is ramming against my rib cage. If he isn't lying and there is a video, I will most definitely have to change schools. But that is a much better prospect than betraying my best friend. That is something I would never do.

When I don't say anything, he throws his head back and laughs. The sound makes my skin crawl.

"I just don't get it," he says. "Why would somebody who gets laid as much as you do want to stop me from getting any? What's in it for you?" He narrows his eyes. "Or maybe you wanted this all along. For my first time to be with you."

"I'm not sleeping with you, Charlie," I say steadily. "Blackmail isn't going to work on me." Somehow my voice comes out sounding much stronger than I feel.

He rubs his jawline with his hand and shakes his head. At first he doesn't say anything, and I hope he realizes exactly how ridiculous his plan really is. But then he looks up, and the meanness in his eyes leaves no question in my mind.

"I was afraid you'd say that," he says, and he's on me before I have time to react. When I try to wiggle out of the chair, he pushes it against the wall and traps me there. His knee is pressed against my chest, and he's groping my breasts roughly with his hand.

"I know what you like," he says. "In your words, a firm, decisive touch. Except I like to touch a bit harder than that." He braces his hands on my shoulders. I scrabble with my free hand and manage to claw him across the face with my fingernails, deep enough to draw blood.

"You bitch." He puts his fingers to his cheek and stares at the blood, like it's somebody else's. I use the distraction to try to knee him in the groin, but he just pulls me closer to him.

"You know you want to," he says. "I see how you look at me. Stop fighting it."

My heart is pounding and I want to scream, to hit him again, to run away. My mind races. *Go for his vulnerable spots. Knees. Throat. Nose. Eyes.* But I'm paralyzed, trapped in my own fear like a fly tangled in a web. I squeeze my eyes shut, waiting for it. Waiting for whatever he's going to do.

But he lets go of me and drops his arms at his sides. I crack my eyes open. *Run. Run. Run, Mercedes.*

I don't run. I'm not in control, just like I wasn't in control four years ago with Luke. I'm the same thirteen-year-old, the one who acted like she was going on twenty.

Charlie leans in close and I duck my head and cower. His hot breath curdles in my ear.

"Don't even think about telling anyone," he whispers. "You tell anyone, and I will destroy you. Everybody will see that video. And I'll have to tell Angela how you seduced me, too."

My breath catches in my throat. I can't breathe. I can't function. I brace myself. But he backs away from me. Each step feels like a million miles. It's not until he's at the door that I realize he's leaving. The second he's out of my room, my body starts listening to my mind and I lock the door and crumple to the floor with my hands wrapped around my knees. Protective stance, the kind they showed us in case of earthquakes.

I hear him clomping down the stairs, the sound of his boots thudding as he hits the landing. Then I hear the door slam.

My hands start to shake uncontrollably. The sound of my own heartbeat is everywhere, the sound track to my failure. Thump, thump. *Coward. Weakling.* Thump, thump. *Victim. Liar.* I told myself that nobody would ever control me, not after Luke. But here I am, in a heap on the floor all over again. Nothing has changed. I haven't changed.

I don't know how long I sit there for, if it's seconds or hours. I sit on the floor until I hear the front door open. My body clenches up when I think it could be Charlie, but the *clack-clack-clack* on the tile floor could only come from Kim's stiletto heels.

I should get up and march downstairs and tell Kim everything.

But what would I tell her? She wouldn't believe me anyway. She would probably be on Charlie's side. I can just picture Charlie flexing his muscles and telling her his side of the story. *She seduced me. Invited me up to her bedroom. What could I say?*

I should call Angela. Angela needs to know.

This time I get up on quivering legs. My cell phone is on my desk, and I vaguely remember it was buzzing earlier, but I don't make a move to reach it. I collapse on my bed instead and stare up at the ceiling, like I have so many times before, but this time is different. This time I see all the cracks, the spiderweb forming in one corner. The maid really should get rid of that.

I can't tell Angela, because if I tell Angela, the whole story will come out. I'll have to tell her why Charlie threatened to destroy me. And I don't know whose side she would be on. I don't know if she would believe me. Charlie is her perfect boyfriend, the one who is willing to wait until marriage. The wholesome, caring guy who gave her the promise ring. The soccer star, the jock with a heart of gold.

And I'm the girl who slept with everybody's boyfriends.

Nobody will believe me.

All this time I thought I was in control, keeping the upper hand for myself, calling the shots, playing by my rules. But I haven't been, not really. Because I had the chance to fight back and I froze. A deer in the headlights, just like I was with Luke.

My body goes from feeling light and insubstantial, like I'm not really here at all, to feeling like a boulder has settled in the pit of my stomach, its jagged edges extending everywhere. It was different with Luke. I was different with Luke.

Was I?

But maybe I would have deserved it all the same. I let fourteen people at our school into my bedroom for the same thing Charlie wanted from me: a first time. Did I honestly think he wouldn't find out, sooner or later?

Nothing happened. Nothing happened. I'm safe.

But I can't get rid of this mess so easily. I can't push it into some dark place in the back of my head and forget about it. I tried to do that with Luke, to cover it up. To bury it. And instead it almost just happened all over again, like a sick version of déjà vu.

This time, I can't pretend nothing happened.

28

"Knock knock, knock knock." The voice is accompanied by a *rap-rap-rap* on my door. For the first ten seconds I'm awake, I think it's just another normal day, albeit one I overslept for. But then everything comes flooding back to me. Charlie. His hands on my shoulders. His breath in my ear.

His threat.

"Knock knock, Mercedes. You're late."

Since when does Kim even know what time I'm supposed to be at school? Since when does Kim know anything about me?

Kim starts jangling my doorknob, and I'm grateful I locked it. I can just imagine her impatient, bony hand, with all her bracelets knocking against the knob.

"Honey, you shouldn't be locking me out. And you're going to be late for school."

I open my mouth to shout something at her—probably would have been profanity—but nausea comes up instead. I reach for the garbage can beside my bed just in time to throw up into it. I wait for Kim to yell through the door, probably something about bulimia ruining your tooth enamel. But thankfully the knocking and jangling ceases and I hear her footsteps walking away.

I stand up slowly. My head hurts. I instinctively grab my cell phone, even though I'm scared to see what's waiting for me. Seven missed calls and nine text messages, all from Zach. Shit. *Zach.* Our study date, the one I had been promising him for so long. I read the messages through eyes blurry with tears.

Hey, I'm coming over a bit early. Hope that's okay! If it's not okay, I'm bringing Chinese food so hopefully that will change your mind.

Hey, I'm in your driveway. Your Jeep is here so I know you're home. I'm knocking. Want to let me in?

Okay, now I'm going to eat your egg roll. Can't you hear your doorbell?

You did mean tonight, right? Not some other night? I knew I should write stuff down.

Okay, now I'm sitting on your porch because I'm getting kind of worried.

I have called enough times to officially be considered a stalker. Please call me if you get this.

This is strange—Angela's boyfriend just left your house. Is there something I should know?

I'm still here, waiting.

I'm leaving now. I guess I'll see you around.

I don't call him back, even though my fingers hover over the keypad on my phone. I have lied about so much, kept so much of my life a secret that there's no way Zach could possibly understand. If he knew the truth, he would never want to talk to me again. And I couldn't really blame him.

I turn my phone off instead.

I consider staying home today, coming up with a mystery illness. But what would I do, and where would I go? So I stand up slowly and shuffle to my bathroom and run the shower water, even though I don't plan on getting in it. The thought of standing up to wash my hair and rinse out the shampoo is much too complicated, and I can't afford the time it would take to blow dry and style it after. So I run the water while I sit on the toilet.

The only thing worse than going to school today would be not going to school today. And there's Angela. Angela is the reason I have to go to school today. I set my jaw in determination and stare at my face in the mirror, willing myself to look stronger than I feel. This isn't about me anymore. I have to tell Angela exactly what Charlie did.

And that also means telling her why.

At the last minute, I don't leave my room in the grungy sweatpants and oversized T-shirt I planned on wearing to school. I chose that outfit because I can't stand the thought of anybody looking at me the way Charlie did last night. But hiding under layers of unwashed, unattractive clothing would just draw more attention to me. Charlie would have won. And putting on a smile is just about the hardest thing I have ever done, but I make myself do it. Just like I make myself put on a tight blouse, one with a neckline high enough to cover the circular marks his fingers left on my collarbones.

Just like I make myself strut down the hallway, collect my books from my locker, and stay awake for first period, even though my head feels too heavy for my body to hold up and people seem to be passing by in slow motion, like they're part of an alternate reality. Luckily it's not chemistry, because I don't think I could have kept the smile on if Zach and Faye were around. Thinking of Zach makes me want to inexplicably break down. I have a burning urge to tell him everything. Maybe I inherited more from Kim than her eyes and cheekbones. Maybe I'm a cheat and a liar, too, somebody who doesn't make relationships better but ruins people's lives. Maybe I was felled by my own system.

Maybe I got what I deserved.

I don't see Angela until lunch, in the cafeteria. And she's not alone. Charlie is across the table from her, holding her hand, watching her bite into her peanut butter sandwich. Angela always has a peanut butter sandwich for lunch, for as long as I have known her. I used to find her lack of desire for variety annoying, but not today. She needs to be protected. But I can't protect her here. I'll have to get her alone first, and that involves making Charlie feel like there's no chance I will tell her anything. The only way to do that is to pretend like nothing happened. I take a deep, shuddering breath. Even though the cafeteria is brightly lit and full of idle chatter, Charlie makes me want to drop my lunch tray in the garbage and run.

But I can't run. I can't turn my back on Angela. Not now, not when she needs me most. So I move forward, one tiny step at a time.

I walk past other people and other tables, keeping my eyes focused on Angela's sandwich. My lunch tray shakes in my hand and the table seems a million miles away, but I make it there, on legs that feel more and more wobbly with each step. Angela and Charlie haven't looked up and seen me yet, which is probably the only thing that keeps me going. I don't think I could deal with Charlie's smirk, that expression of victory he is probably wearing.

I force my lips into a smile as I approach the table. *Pretend like nothing happened.*

"God, I just had the worst quiz in English class. Mr. Bell has such a narrow mind. He could not get on board with my theory about Ophelia." I plunk down beside Angela.

"Don't say that," Angela says, shaking her head.

"I'm sorry, but Mr. Bell does have an exceedingly narrow mind."

"No, don't say God like that." She gives me her best "admonishing" look, which isn't very admonishing at all. Angela isn't a disciplinary type, which is one of the many reasons I love her so much. She's just too honest to be anything but herself. Her mouth twitches into a smile. I focus on that smile.

"What was your theory about Ophelia?" Charlie says.

His voice makes the hair on the back of my neck stand up, and I can feel goose bumps form on my forearms. Angela is happily nibbling her sandwich, oblivious to the sinister tone in his voice that I can't help but notice. I force myself to look at him and force myself not to rip deeper into the red marks on his cheek and watch them bleed. I wonder how he explained that to Angela.

"My theory about Ophelia was that she wasn't crazy at all. Some people are just better liars than others." I bite into my apple and make myself swallow, even though the motion feels like choking on glass.

"Whatever," Charlie says. He picks Angela's hand up off the table and kisses it. "I got to get to the library to study," he says. "But I have a feeling I'm going to ace this test. For some reason, I slept great." He hops out of his chair and blows a kiss to Angela. She doesn't notice when he turns around the second time, but I do. That look was reserved for me, a look that says *I am watching you, so don't step out of line.*

"What happened to Charlie's face?" I ask when he's gone.

"Oh. He got into a fight with his cat, and the cat won."

I nod. What a pathetic excuse. Apparently I'm the cat now. Except I don't feel like I won.

"Listen, Angela, can we meet after school? I was hoping we could do something." I figure "do something" sounds more legitimate than "we have to talk," which would only scare her.

She tears bits of crust from her sandwich and drops them onto the Saran wrap. "I would, but I have a dinner thing with Charlie."

I pick at my cuticle skin under the table. It's a nervous habit, one I always revert back to when some area of my life is out of control. Angela knows this, so I don't let her see me do it.

"Tomorrow, then? You could come over and we could piss Kim off by ordering greasy takeout and watching movies on her big screen."

Angela shrugs. "That sounds fun. But tomorrow is out, too. Charlie wants me to go to his little brother's soccer game with him."

Charlie has really covered his bases. He knows I won't cause a scene in the cafeteria, because Angela hates nothing more than a public scene that draws attention to her. So he made sure to take up all of her free time, just in case I got any ideas.

Except I don't know how I can go two days without telling Angela. I have to see her before whatever Charlie has planned goes down. What I'm most worried about is Charlie moving up the date, deciding he can't take the chance of waiting until the weekend. I have to work harder.

I rip a broken nail off under the table. A sharp flash of pain, followed by slippery warmth, confirms that my finger is bleeding. "How about we do breakfast before school?" I say. "That could be fun."

Angela looks at me like I'm deranged. "Since when is getting up even earlier fun? Besides, we have prayer group in the morning."

I shrug. "I don't know. I guess I just wanted to try something new."

Angela looks up from her now-crustless peanut butter sand-wich. Her eyes are wide and concerned. "What's up, Mercy? You're hiding something."

I sigh. It's supposed to be just that—a sigh, something noncha-lant. Except it gets stuck in my throat and turns into a trembling breath that threatens to bring tears out with it.

Angela stretches her hand across the table. "I know you're pick-ing your fingers under there. Something's up. You know you can talk to me about whatever it is."

I can't bring myself to look her in the eye because I know if I do, I'll cry. And the most embarrassing thing you can do at Milton High—a thousand times worse than getting drunk at the school dance—is cry in the cafeteria.

"Fine, let's do breakfast tomorrow," she says. "Pick me up at seven?"

I shake my head. "I'll be there at six thirty."

When we go our separate ways—me to French class to conju-gate verbs, Angela to English to deal with the close-minded Mr. Bell—I make a detour in the bathroom, where I lock myself in a stall and throw up. What comes up is a vile yellow color, the tex-ture of which I almost choke on. I try to swallow after I flush the toilet, but my mouth feels like it's stuffed with a mixture of cotton balls and razor blades. Afterward I sit on the floor beside the toilet. I feel dizzy and sick, almost like a hangover, except so much worse.

"You know, bulimia doesn't look good on you," I hear a voice say. I recognize the shoes under the stall beside me. They're pointy toed, with little spikes around the heels.

They belong to Faye.

"Are you going to tell me why you're avoiding me? Or are you going to make me guess?" I hear her pull her pants down and start to pee.

"I'm sick," I say flatly. An excuse that's corroborated by the fact that I'm puking in the ladies' room.

"Too sick to say hi to your friend? And you blew Zach off last night. He's really upset." She stands up, flushes the toilet.

"I'm sorry," I choke out. "I felt terrible. I went to bed really early."

"Alone?"

My stomach lurches again, but this time I keep the vomit from coming back up. "What's that supposed to mean?"

Her voice drops. "Look. Zach told me he saw Charlie leave your house. I won't judge you, if that's what you're worried about. Just tell me what's going on. I'm your friend. And friends worry."

I can just imagine her standing in the next stall, leaning against the toilet paper dispenser, maybe scrolling through her text messages or investigating her manicure. I can't see her right now because I'm terrified of what she will see on my face. She's going to see a liar, somebody who doesn't want anyone to know what happened last night. I don't want to be that liar.

So I do the only thing I know how to. I chase her away.

"I can't deal with your interrogation right now. I'm sick. I just want to be by myself." Even I'm surprised by the meanness in my voice. I didn't intend for the words to come out that way, but I don't want to talk to Faye about what happened. Not now, in separate bathroom stalls, and not ever.

But if she is offended, she doesn't show it. "Fine, suit yourself. But I'm around. You know, if you *don't* want to be by yourself." Her heels clack on the floor as she leaves.

When I'm alone, I wipe the corners of my mouth with toilet paper and flush the toilet again for good measure before leaving the stall. When I'm at the sink, the bathroom door swings open, and I start to duck into the stall. It must be Faye coming back. She wants answers. But she won't get the ones she's looking for. She'll see everything on my face, the guilt and the lies.

"Mercedes."

It's not Faye. It's someone I want to see even less. Jillian Landry.

"Hi, Jillian," I say weakly. My stomach makes a loud growling sound, like there's a wild animal stuck in there, trying to get out.

"The test went well," Jillian says. "I have a good feeling about it. Especially the section on . . ."

She keeps talking, but I'm not hearing her. She's trying to make eye contact, and I can't do that. I picture Charlie's hands on my shoulders, how his fingers could have done anything to me. Choked me. Ripped my clothes off. I think about how I couldn't seem to breathe, the way my body defeated me by not fighting back hard. I can't care about Jillian's test right now. The good I did for her means nothing.

"That's great," I say. "Really great." I grab the sink, hoping I won't throw up into it, and wait for her to retreat into a stall before darting out of the bathroom. I don't have to look at her to know that her face is full of concern. Concern for me. I don't deserve it.

Before I'm even in the hallway I decide I can't handle the rest of my classes today. I'm gripped by dread at the idea of venturing into the hallway at all, for fear that I'll run into one of the people I have slept with. I don't want to be seen by anybody who has any sort of intimate knowledge of me. I feel fragile, like if somebody looked at me the wrong way I might shatter into a million pieces and never be whole again.

I wait for the bell to ring, signaling the end of lunch hour, when I know I'll have a clear getaway. I don't even bother stopping at my locker for my coat and books. My vision is blurry with tears, and all I want to do is make it to the double doors without crying or seeing anybody I know.

But I see him anyway, coming out of the library. *Don't turn around*, I will him. *Please don't turn around.*

Zach turns toward me. It's enough to make the first tears fall from my eyes. There's no malice in his face, no rage. He's not angry. I wish he were. I could figure out a way to handle angry.

He's not even sad, either.

He turns around like he hasn't seen me at all.

I want to chase after him and fix it, but it's too late. He turns a corner and he's gone and I don't even know what he was in the library studying for because that's something a friend would know and I'm not a good friend.

I break into a run in the parking lot and lock my doors when I get in the Jeep, even though I know nobody is around. I don't even bother buckling my seat belt before speeding home. I don't remember getting there, just the way the cars all blurred into one rainbow of color and sweat beaded in my hair and my thoughts raced a million miles an hour. Maybe this is how Kim felt the night she got her DUI. Scared, frustrated, and out of control.

When I'm in my bedroom, I lock the door firmly behind me. I don't know what I plan on doing in here until it hits me, and my stomach lurches precipitously. What Charlie said yesterday. *If you don't comply, I'll show that video to everybody, and the whole school will know exactly what you've been doing with their boyfriends and writing in that little book of yours.* When he said it, I just focused on the threat, the nasty tone in his voice that let me know he meant it. But now all I hear is the second part. *Writing in that little book of yours.* Charlie must have the book, the one I wrote all their names in. And that's the worst thing of all. There's as much of me in those pages as there is of the guys. I think back to the notes I started writing, the fleshed-out entries. My thoughts. My insecurities. The ratings I gave. Everything.

I wrack my room in search of the book, rifling through drawers and rummaging under piles of clothes. Charlie took it. Charlie has it. I know that he has it, but I keep looking, grabbing other books off my bookshelves and watching them bounce off the carpet. Charlie took it, but that doesn't stop me from hoping to see that pearly white cover peeking out. If I can find the book, I can destroy it myself. If I can find the book, I can convince myself that everything will be okay.

I keep searching until the sun sets outside my window, until little rivers of sweat and tears are running down my face. I won't leave this room without finding the book. Even if that means I have to stay here forever.

The doorbell rings and I sink into a heap on the carpet. With any luck, whoever is down there will just go away.

But I'm starting to think nothing goes away, no matter how deep you try to bury it.

29

I won't go to the door. I *won't* go to the door. I have never been scared to go to my own door before. But I'm very aware that I'm alone in the house. Alone and vulnerable. And whoever is at the door won't stop ringing the bell. It echoes through the foyer, loud and demanding, making its way into my room. Charlie is supposed to be with Angela tonight. But what if he planted that as a ruse to get me away from Angela? What if he wants to come back?

I shake my head. "No," I say to nobody at all. Charlie wouldn't make up fake plans. But after yesterday, I really don't know Charlie at all.

I edge slowly down the stairs, my hands balled into fists so tight that my nails dig into my palms. My heart is pounding as I step into the foyer and up to the door. Just do it. Make whoever it is go away. If Charlie is ringing the bell, the door is locked. If the door is locked, I'm the only one who can let him in.

I suck in a deep breath and peek quickly from behind the curtains. I so expect to see Charlie there, wearing that smirk that was smeared across his face at lunch, that I have to blink to register the two bodies that are actually there.

Kim and my dad. The same dad I haven't seen or heard from in over three years has materialized on this very doorstep. And I realize they didn't ring the doorbell on purpose. They rang the doorbell by accident, because Kim's back pressed against it when my dad pressed against her. My parents, making out on the doorstep. Now it all makes sense. This is why Kim brought him up at dinner and why she finally told me the truth about why he left. They're getting back together, or she wants them to.

I tiptoe away from the door, even though they can't hear me and they're way too engrossed in each other to see me through the curtain. I can't handle this right now. I can't handle the uncertainty. I can't take the chance that my dad might be here to see me. He can't see me like this, his wild-eyed broken daughter. I won't let that happen. So I steal out the back door. I'm not even sure where I'm going at first until it suddenly makes perfect sense.

I can't wait until breakfast to tell Angela. I can't stay here worrying that Charlie will make a move sooner, that he thinks I'm too much of a loose cannon to keep his disgusting secret.

And since Kim or my dad definitely can't know I'm home, I take off on foot, in flip-flops and sweatpants, the grungy outfit I didn't let myself wear to school. Angela's house is only about five blocks away. I rehearse what I'm going to say in my head. *Your boyfriend is a creep. Your boyfriend isn't who he pretends to be.*

I can't fall to pieces. Angela is vulnerable, and we can't both be vulnerable, so I have to be bold.

Angela. I have something to tell you.

But when I knock on her door, my whole rehearsed spiel goes out of my head. The words are stopped on their way out of my mouth because of who answers the door. Charlie. Something resembling panic flashes across his face, and I feel a brief surge of power that doesn't last. He notices and knows the power is back to him. His panic turns to a smug smile, and I shrink into myself and have to talk myself into standing still when all I want to do is run as far away from him as I can get.

"Well?" he says, wrapping his hand around the doorknob. "If you're here to tell Angela our little secret, you're too late. It's already done."

"What?" I try to push past him into the house, not knowing what I would say to Angela if it's true and not knowing what I would say if it wasn't true. But Charlie blocks me with his body, puts his hands on my shoulders to shove me back out the door. When I reach up with my hand to pry myself out of his grip, he squeezes tighter, making me wince in pain.

"Don't you think you've done enough damage?" he whispers. "Don't make it worse."

I'm about to knee him in the groin when Angela's mom comes up behind him. I have met Angela's mom several times during the course of our friendship, and my lasting impression of her is that she is the complete opposite of Kim. Meaning, she's a typical mom, the kind who makes wholesome family dinners and wears skirts that don't stop midthigh and doesn't get drunk during the day. Basically, she's Angela, thirty years from now.

"Mercedes," she says. "How lovely to see you! We just started eating, if you want to join us."

"Yes, join us," Charlie says, his voice syrupy sweet. "I was just about to make a big announcement."

I cock my head to the side in confusion and try to protest—as much as I need to tell Angela, I don't need to tell her in front of her mom and her whole family—but Angela's mom is already ushering me inside.

"We have missed having you around," she says.

I feel even smaller than I did when I knocked on the door. She's right. The night I dropped by to make cookies was the only time over the past couple months I have been here at all. I made the virgins my priority, gave a bunch of people I barely know more attention than my best friend.

I don't know how I let that happen.

Angela is sitting at the table, twirling spaghetti around on her fork. She breaks into a big smile when she sees me. *Charlie lied. She doesn't know.*

"Mercy! Nobody told me you were coming." She looks at Charlie. "Was this your idea?"

Charlie looks at me and winks, which makes my stomach lurch. "Of course," he says. "I wanted everybody you love around when I say what I want to say." He pulls out Angela's mom's chair for her and goes to do the same for me, but I back up against the wall.

"I'll stand," I say.

"Suit yourself. But you might want to be sitting for this." He goes to his spot at the head of the table, across from Angela's dad, who is basically Angela in male form, right down to the wispy blond hair and button nose.

Charlie picks up his glass, which looks like it's filled with wine but is most likely apple juice.

"As you all know, Angela and I graduate from high school this year. I'm already eighteen, and our two-year anniversary is this weekend. Angela and I have been together long enough to know that we're right for each other, and we want this to last forever."

He rummages around in his back pocket. I put my hands

against the wall to steady myself. The bastard is going to propose. Sure enough, he unearths a small black box.

"Angela, it's not much, but we can upgrade it when I get a job and can provide for you. Which I fully intend to do." He kneels beside her chair and puts one hand on her wrist.

"Angela, will you marry me?"

30

Angela drops her fork on her plate. The clattering it makes is the only sound in the room. I put one hand over my mouth to stop myself from throwing up and keep the other hand against the wall to make sure I don't keel over. I look to Angela's mom, expecting her to protest, expecting her to say something about the fact that high school students don't just get engaged, even after two years together, even if they are prayer-group junkies.

But she doesn't protest. She claps her hands together and makes an excited little noise somewhere between a squeal and a giggle. Angela's dad even gets up and pats Charlie on the back and shakes his hand. The same hand that just dug into my collarbone minutes ago.

I slide down the wall, my head spinning. From the floor, I can see Angela's hands clasped in her lap. She still hasn't said anything. Maybe she will say no. Angela has always been practical. She knows she's young and inexperienced.

But Charlie talks for her. "Of course, it'll be a long engagement," he says to her dad. "We're in no rush. We're both committed to our postsecondary education plans. But I want Angela, and both of you, to know how serious I am about her."

I watch Charlie take Angela's hand from her lap. Angela's mom puts her hands to her mouth. The misty look in her eyes tells me that Charlie must have slipped the ring on Angela's finger.

And just like that, my best friend is engaged at seventeen, to the guy who tried to make me have sex with him last night. It's like one of those weird dreams where I'm watching a completely insane scene unfold and I'm the only one who knows what's really going on. I'm an intruder on what would be a memorable family scene, something everyone in the room would want to remember for years to come. Would, if the guy who popped the question wasn't a demented sociopath disguised as a Bible-thumper.

I don't so much announce that I'm leaving as I just get up and walk out the door. I can fake a lot of things, but I can't fake happy for Angela, and I can't be in the same room with all these people stuck in Charlie's lies. Mostly I just can't be around Charlie. He won. It's like he wanted me here, to prove it to me. I unknowingly made his night exactly what he wanted.

"Mercy, what's the matter?" Angela calls from the porch when I'm halfway down the driveway. My hood is pulled over my head, and I was hoping in all her excitement that she wouldn't notice me leave. No such luck. Angela is just too good of a friend. A good enough friend to stick with me for years without actually knowing anything about me.

A huge part of me wishes I didn't have to tell her anything. I wish I could let her enjoy her moment. I wish Charlie wasn't the kind of guy who tries to blackmail a girl's best friend. But Angela is a good friend, and for once I'll be a good friend, too.

She catches up to me at the end of the driveway. Her face is full of concern. When Angela gets concerned, she wears it all above her eyebrows, where two tiny dimples always appear. It's the same face she makes when she can't figure out a formula in chemistry and the same face she makes when somebody (usually me) takes the Lord's name in vain. Except this is a bigger problem, and I'm pretty sure those dimples are going to turn into craters.

"You're crying," she says, and I guess she's right, although I hadn't given much thought to it. "You never cry. And you never wear sweatpants out in public. Whatever it is, you can tell me."

I wipe my eyes with the sleeve of my sweatshirt. "Angela, this is something you really don't want to hear, especially not tonight."

"I don't care. Tell me anyway. That's what best friends do." Her lower lip is trembling, like she wants to cry, too.

It really sucks that I love her more than ever right now. We have never actually said to each other that we're best friends. It's one of those things that has never been formally acknowledged, because it just is. Some people don't need to put a label on relationships. As best friends, Angela and I were those people. Until tonight.

"It's about Charlie," I say, fixating on the ground.

"What about Charlie?" she says. "You knew about this?"

I shake my head and wrap my arms around myself. "No, I didn't know about this. It's about Charlie last night."

"What happened last night?" Angela bounces back and forth, from one foot to the other.

I shoot a cursory glance at the front door, which Angela left a crack open. I half expect to see Charlie's face peeping through, with that evil expression that is permanently etched into my head. The sinister look he gave me as he pushed me against the wall. But through the window I can see he is occupied with Angela's parents. A happy little scene around the dining room table, like a Hallmark card. Except I don't think Hallmark makes a congratulatory engagement card for people like Charlie.

"Charlie came over to my house last night."

"Oh. Why?"

I force myself to look her in the eye. "Well, you know that surprise I was telling you about before? The one he asked for my help with?"

She nods repeatedly, to the point where she starts to resemble a bobblehead. "Yeah, it was definitely a surprise," she says with a small laugh.

You hate surprises, I want to say.

"He never said anything about this," I say instead. "It was something else. For your anniversary." I press my sleeve-covered hands together. "God. That's not important."

"Don't say 'God,'" Angela says.

I start to laugh, even though tears are still trickling out the sides of my eyes. "God, Angela, I'll try not to, but there's really no easy way to tell you that Charlie tried to make me have sex with him."

I didn't expect it all to come out like that, like vomit after a night of drinking that you have to expel from your body. As soon as I say it, silence hangs in the air. Nothing moves, not even Angela's nodding head.

I open my mouth to elaborate, but she beats me to it. "Excuse me? What the hell are you talking about?"

Angela has never said *hell*, not as long as I have known her and probably not before that, either. This is bad.

"Charlie came to my house last night," I say, panic rising in my throat. "He wanted me to have sex with him. We were alone in my bedroom, and he threatened me."

It's the first time I have said what happened out loud, and the gravity of it makes it hard to breathe. And if I'm having a hard time breathing, Angela is, too. She puts her hands on her knees and tucks her head down, like we were taught to do in home economics if we ever felt like we were going to faint.

I glance at the window, where Charlie is now staring back at me. He knows what's going on, and that means I have less than a minute left to tell Angela everything.

"Look, I wanted to tell you earlier today. I wanted to tell you right after it happened, but I was in shock. I don't know what to do, but he wanted to have sex with you on your anniversary, and I couldn't let that happen because you need to know what a disgusting sack of shit he really is."

The words pour out of my mouth in an upward crescendo, starting fast and ending loud and angry. I didn't plan on getting that angry, but that's how it happens. My hands ball into fists, fists I desperately want to punch Charlie with.

Angela blinks repeatedly. "But why would he do that?" Her voice is shaking.

I take a deep breath. Now my throat is closing up, and I'm running out of time because Charlie is sprinting down the driveway.

"What did you do to her?" he says, wrapping his arm around Angela's bent-over body. He looks incensed. I take a step back even though I want to stand my ground.

"It's not what I did to her. It's what you wanted to do with me. Now she knows all about it." I wipe my cheek with my sleeve and try to appear more defiant than I feel.

I expect Charlie to play dumb, since it's not like he can punch me in the face with Angela standing here. But he surprises me.

"Mercedes, I wasn't going to say anything. I didn't want to ruin your friendship with Angela."

"What the hell are you talking about? She knows everything, Charlie. It's over."

Charlie whispers something in Angela's ear, something I can't hear. She covers her face with her hands and cries. Then she does something I really didn't want to see her do. She cries into his shoulder.

"I think we both agree that Angela deserves to know the truth," he says. "I wanted to tell her sooner, but like I said, I didn't want to ruin her opinion of you. She always thought so highly of you."

I throw my hands in the air. "Stop fucking around. Give it up. You're a disgusting pig, Charlie."

He kisses the top of Angela's head and gives me a sickeningly smug little half smile that she can't see.

"Now that you've given me no choice, I have to tell her." He unfolds Angela from his arms and stoops down to her height so that he's level with her eyes. He even wipes away her tears.

"Your best friend Mercedes here isn't exactly who she says she is."

Angela doesn't say anything. Her eyes dart from Charlie to me, and back to Charlie, until he cups her face in his hands and forces her to focus on him.

"You deserve so much better than her, Angie. I don't think you know much about Mercedes at all."

Angela is still looking at Charlie but speaks to me. "What's he talking about, Mercy?"

Charlie answers. "I'm talking about what goes on in Mercy's bedroom."

I grit my teeth. "Don't call me that."

"What? Mercy?" he says. "That's what you asked me to call you last night. You were begging for me to say your name. Asked me to pretend you were Angela."

He can't think she's going to doubt me. She can't believe him, now that the truth is out. She can't look into his eyes and believe him. *Can she?*

I take a deep breath. "Before or after you came onto me? Because I didn't have time to say much of anything."

Angela is crying silently. I want to reach out and hold her, but Charlie blocks me with his body. "Sweet Angie, it seems that Mercy here has been keeping a secret from you. Mercy has made the rounds of the student population, and last night she tried to seduce me. Even wore a slutty outfit for the occasion. Of course, I didn't let her have me. I'm saving me for you."

I can't see Angela's face behind her hair and Charlie's arm, but I can only imagine how deep those dimples in her forehead are. I start to get dizzy, like any second now I might fall flat onto the concrete and lose consciousness. But I can't do that. I remember who I came here for. Angela. Of course Charlie will put up a fight, but he won't win. He can't win.

"It's not true," I stammer. "He came over to scare me. To blackmail me into sleeping with him. Do you really think a cat did that to his face?" I pull my neckline down to reveal the red marks on my collarbones. "Here. Look what he did."

Angela pulls away from Charlie. My heart leaps. *I got to her.* She believes me. But Charlie starts talking again before she even gets a word out.

"That at least is true. My cat didn't scratch my face. She did, when I turned her down. She went crazy on me." He smothers Angela's face in his chest. "And whatever marks she's talking about, she did to herself. The girl likes it rough, at least according to her."

"You're fucking insane," I say. "You're actually fucking insane. You're a pathological liar. He's a pathological liar, Angela. Don't listen to him."

She says something into Charlie's chest, but it's not loud enough for me to hear. Until she pries her head away, and her face is red and contorted with tears and rage.

"I don't know who to believe," she says. "I don't believe that Mercy slept with anyone at our school. She never seemed interested in anyone. It makes no sense."

I could just lie, work with whatever momentum I have. The pendulum seems to have swung my way, but I'm not taking that route. If Angela is supposed to know the truth, she has to know all of it.

But Charlie gets there first, and he has proof, in the form of a little book he pulls out of his back pocket. My notebook, the one Angela got me. The one that was missing from my bedroom. I want to throw up, knowing he has been literally sitting on it probably the whole day. I want to lurch at him and grab it and run as far away as I can, but I'm frozen. Just like last night, I can't move to save my own life.

"Let's see. September 12. Tommy Hudson. Someone started the school year off with a bang. September 30, William Malcolm. The Biter. Ouch," he says, shaking his head. "October 11, Patrick Myles, the Nervous Giggler. October 23, Connor Reid, the Screamer." He flips through the pages. "Somebody has been a very busy girl."

Angela's lip is trembling. "What's he talking about, Mercy? Tommy Hudson is in my homeroom. He's been with Jillian since grade school."

I hang my head. I knew what Charlie was capable of, but somehow I never thought he was capable of this, too. Or maybe I didn't know how the things I have done sound out loud. They don't sound like good deeds at all.

"She sleeps with these guys, Angie. She seduces them. She lures them into her bedroom. She takes their virginity. She ruins their lives."

Angela backs away from both of us. She holds out her hand. "Give me the book," she says in a voice I don't recognize.

"Angela, what's in that book—"

She cuts me off. I don't know what I would have said anyway.

"Gus Teller. Chase Redgrave. Bobby Lewis." She thumbs through the pages. I can see her face get redder and redder. "Evan Brown." She looks up at me. "Evan Brown? I know him. He came to prayer group before. He talked about how much he loved his girlfriend and how they were waiting for marriage."

I look down at my feet again. I do remember Evan saying that, but I guess he changed his mind.

"Do you have anything to say for yourself? Or have you really been leading a double life all this time? I thought you were committed to the Lord?"

"I'm not religious, Angela," I say, scuffing the sidewalk with my flip-flop, willing my voice not to break. "I'm not religious, and I have slept with those guys. As hard as it is, I can admit I lied about all that. But Charlie coming onto me is true."

"It's not true," Charlie says. "Why do you think Mercy made such a big deal of talking to you about me? Do you really think she was being a friend? She was jealous. She didn't want you to have me because she wanted me for herself."

The most maddening part about hearing him speak is that his voice doesn't change at all, doesn't get frustrated, doesn't get mad. His voice has the consistency of silk, where mine keeps cracking.

"She used sex to break couples apart. And she wanted to do the same to us."

Angela glances from Charlie to me and back again. Somehow I know this is a decisive moment, her time to figure out where she stands. Finally she flings the little white book onto the ground and brings her gaze up. To me. Except it's not a gaze but a full-on glare, her facial features screwed up in rage.

"You should leave," she says. "And you probably shouldn't come to prayer group anymore." She turns and runs toward the house. I can see her parents in the window, surveying the action with concerned expressions. Whatever they think is happening out here, this I'm sure they'd never fathom.

I stoop down to grab the book, but Charlie beats me there. "I'm going to hold onto this," he says.

"Fuck you," I say through gritted teeth. Never before have I felt so much like I wanted to kill somebody.

"If you would have, none of this would have happened," he says with that infuriating wink. I lunge to grab the book, but he sidesteps me.

"You should have known I would never let her side with you. Angela's everything to me. And I'm always going to be everything to her."

"If Angela's everything to you, why did you want to have sex with me?"

He shrugs casually, like I asked him if he wants pizza or Chinese food for dinner and he can't make up his mind. "Because you got in my way. You went behind my back. I figured you owed me for fucking things up. But now, I'm glad I didn't waste my first time on you. I have other plans for it."

I clench my jaw. "It's not going to work," I spit out. "Angela will figure everything out. She won't believe you."

He raises an eyebrow. "Did you miss that part? She already does."

I stretch out my hand. I'm not sure what I plan to do with it. Maybe hit him, or scratch him across the other cheek. But he grabs it in midair and pulls me close to his face.

He drops his voice to a whisper. "They say you never forget your first time. I won't forget mine with Angela next weekend. Her parents are going away. It'll be just the two of us." He squeezes my wrist so hard that it hurts, then abruptly lets go.

"You think you're ruined now, Mercy? Wait until you see what I do next. All you had to do was keep your mouth shut. But I guess I should have known you're not very good at that."

"You're not going to get away with it," I say under my breath. I don't know if he heard me, or if I meant for him to. But he gets even closer, close enough for me to feel his hot breath on my ear.

"Oh, and Mercy? When I'm riding Angela, I'm going to be thinking about you."

I swing my arm back and punch him as hard as I can in the face. I have never punched anyone before, but judging from the blood on his lip and my stinging knuckles, I probably did it okay.

"Bad kitty," he says, licking the blood off his lip and winking at me before running to the house.

I stand at the end of the driveway for a long time, until Angela's mom looks out with a frown and closes the blinds. I think about what's being said inside of the house, if anything. I consider what Angela's mom and dad think of her problem friend, the one who made her cry on the night of her engagement. But mostly I think about what Charlie is saying to her, what poison he is whispering into her ear. And what might be going on in her bedroom right now.

Bad kitty. That's what Charlie said. I bite my lip hard enough to draw blood and savor the metallic taste in my mouth.

If Charlie wants to think of me as just another pussy, he's dead wrong. Because I'm going to be the one cat that has more than nine lives.

31

I don't go home. I can't go home, not knowing whether Kim and my dad might be in the house. Neither of them knows me at all, but if I show up at home with a face raw from crying, they're going to pretend they know me and want to know the source of my tears.

There's nowhere for me to go, so I walk around the neighborhood for hours, until my feet are sore and my legs are sore and the air starts to hurt my lungs with every inhale. I talk myself out of going to Zach's house about a hundred times. Julia would probably give me one of her soft hugs, ask me what's wrong, and make me hot cocoa. But then I'd have to tell Zach what I did, and I don't think he would forgive me. I don't want to keep lying to Zach. I'm going to lose him either way, and I can't lose him tonight.

So I go somewhere else, somewhere I have purposely avoided since the summer before grade nine. It's a playground, small and orderly, filled with screaming kids and their parents during the day but completely silent at night. I feel my breath catch in my throat as I see the big red slide come into view. Bits and pieces of memory flash before me. Luke pressing me against that slide, the way his breath smelled before he kissed me, a mixture of Cool Mint gum and beer and weed. I tried so hard to erase every detail of Luke, to bury them beneath every other detail of everybody else who came after him. I thought in time the memories would fade, but standing here now, I might as well be thirteen again, desperate for the boy I love to love me back.

I sit on a swing in the darkness, digging my toes into the sand. My stomach makes a grumbling noise that echoes in the silence. I should be hungry or thirsty or tired, but I know I couldn't eat or sleep.

You think you're ruined now, Mercy? Wait until you see what I do next.

Charlie's voice comes from every direction, even though I know it's just in my head. He doesn't know where I am. But I can still hear it, just like I can almost feel his hands pushing me against the wall, his fingers digging into my shoulders.

I jump off the swing and drag my feet through the sand. *You tell anyone, and I will destroy you.* I break into a run. *This is what girlfriends do.* I keep running when I get to the edge of the park. I shouldn't have come here, not tonight, maybe not ever. I run home feeling like Charlie is behind me, so close that I can hear his breath in my ear.

When I'm home, I dash up the stairs and through my bedroom and lock myself in my bathroom. My bathroom is safe. I haven't slept with anyone in here. In here, nobody can touch me. I make a bed of towels in the bathtub and that's where I wake up. But even though I can lock people out, I can't keep them from burrowing into my head. Charlie. Luke. The virgins. Everybody I have given a piece of myself to.

I seriously consider staying in here all day. Charlie will be at school, fixing me with that smile. He already won. There's nothing else I can say to change that. Faye will be there, with her big eyes full of concern. Zach will ignore me. Angela won't talk to me or even look at me.

But I can see her, and that's better than not seeing her, not knowing what's going on.

I steer clear of prayer group—which isn't hard to do, considering they're tucked away in a back corner of the library—and make a beeline for my locker. But this isn't your average beeline. I'm very aware of the eyes on me. Almost every single person I pass gives me a second look. This is not natural, not for eight a.m. when most of us have barely woken up.

And when it's not natural, that means it's not good.

I duck into the bathroom, where I'm met with a cloud of perfume and giggling girls who vacate as soon as I come in. I survey myself in the mirror, turn in a full circle. My skirt isn't tucked into my underwear. I don't have toilet paper hanging down the back of my leg. I haven't put on eye shadow as blush, and lipstick isn't on my teeth. My boobs aren't hanging out. Despite the purple half-moons under my eyes, I look normal. Which must mean whatever is going on is internal, which is even worse.

I hide in a stall, the handicap one that nobody ever uses. Hiding in a stall is always the best place to hear gossip. I learned that by accident when senior year started. And today, it proves itself as true once again.

"She's going to have to change schools," a voice says. I don't recognize the body it is attached to. And when the rumors spread to people you don't even recognize, that's when you know somebody has been hard at work.

"I still can't believe she did Isabella's boyfriend," the other voice says. "I wouldn't have believed it unless I saw it myself. And I sure did."

"I have to say, that was a lot of Rafe Lawrence before breakfast," a third voice chimes in. "More of Rafe Lawrence than I ever wanted to see."

"I don't know," the first voice says. "I say Caroline is lucky. I had no idea what Rafe is working with. I guess it's true what they say about guys with big hands."

"Like you even noticed his hands," the second girl says. "Anyway, I don't think Caroline's so lucky now that she knows what Rafe was doing behind her back."

"Speaking of backs," the third girl says. "Can you believe what Mercedes can do with hers?"

"I wish I could bend like that," the first girl says. "I can't believe I had her written off as a prayer-group nerd."

Suddenly I'm glad I'm sitting on a toilet, because I feel like I'm about to be sick in one.

The webcam Charlie said he placed in my room. The video he threatened to release, if I told anyone. I told. He must have shown it. Which means he worked fast, and the whole school has probably seen every single part of me.

"I can't believe Jeremy Roth went down on her. Anna always said he'd never go down on her. Thought it was gross. I guess it wasn't gross with Mercedes."

The first girl lowers her voice. "I just never imagined any of that from Mercedes. She was always so quiet. I talked to her once."

This is a lie. I'm almost positive I have never talked to her in my life.

"What did she say?" the second girl says. Her voice is so hushed and serious that I almost want to laugh. Laugh or throw up.

"She said, 'Get a life, you dumb cunt.'" A new voice enters the mix. I'd know it anywhere.

Faye.

The girls disappear in a cloud of hushed voices and too much perfume.

Faye chooses the stall beside me. When she flushes, I make the mistake of half sniffling, half crying into my hand.

"I know you're in there, Mercedes," Faye says. "I can see your dirty Converse shoes. You really should get a new pair."

"Did you see it?" I croak. "If you saw it, you probably saw a lot more of me. You probably shouldn't be seen talking to me. And I should probably switch schools."

"That's the thing," Faye says, stopping right outside the stall door and rapping on the metal with her fist.

"What's the thing?" I say, pushing my shoe against the toilet paper dispenser, making no move to let her in.

"I never was any good at doing what people tell me."

And like that, her head appears under the stall door, followed by her body. She pulls herself in and wipes her hands on her jeans.

I raise my eyebrows. "You know how disgusting that floor is?" I say. "Janitorial service at this school leaves a lot to be desired."

She cocks her head and puts her hands on her hips. She looks like what I imagine a stern parent would look like, not that I know from experience. I wonder if she got that posture from Lydia.

"First of all, you didn't let me in, so I had no choice."

I shrug. "And what's second of all?"

"Second of all?" She puts her hand under my chin and tilts my face up and shakes her head. "I debated telling you this, because I didn't want you to think less of me. But I've actually been there."

I look away from her prying eyes. "You've been there?" I say.

"You've been in the same situation? Come on . . ." My voice trails off. "Did somebody send you here to spy on me?" I whisper, defeated.

She puts her hands on her hips. "Seriously? You and Zach are the only people I like at this school. And I think you need a friend right about now." She smiles, that heartbreakingly sweet smile she flashed in home economics on that first day.

She crouches down and puts her hands on my knees. "Look. I saw the video. Everybody saw the video. I already knew you were lying about Zach. And so what? You had sex with some guys. Who hasn't?"

I shake my head. "I didn't just have sex with some guys. I had sex with some guys who had girlfriends." I swallow against a hard lump in my throat.

"Look, Mercy. I've been the other woman. I got myself in a mess. I ran from my problem, and you sure as hell aren't going to run from yours. That only makes it worse. So you're not going to hide in here for the rest of senior year. You're coming with me, and we're going to walk down this hall like nothing fucking happened. You got me?"

I want to hug her, to bury my face in that beautiful hair of hers and sob into her and ask her why she's committing social suicide by being my friend when it would be so easy to be my enemy. But if I let myself be weak, I might never leave this bath-room stall.

"How can I look them in the eye?" I squeak out. "I never wanted anyone to get hurt. They were never supposed to know. I thought I was helping." Suddenly, saying it out loud, I hear how pathetic it sounds, how completely ridiculous. I wasn't helping anyone, my-self least of all.

"How do you look people in the eye after that?" I whisper.

Faye smiles and laughs, that goddamned seal-bark laugh. Right now, it sounds like music. She extends her hand to help me up.

"Who says you have to look them in the eye? Pick a spot on the wall and stare at that instead."

I sling my bag over my shoulder. "Where'd you learn that?"

"I told you, I made mistakes, too," she says. "We didn't really move here because Lydia got a better job. Let's just say I'm pretty good at being Girl Most Hated by now." She grabs my hand and squeezes it in hers.

And this is how we make it to chemistry. I take Faye's advice, staring past the laughing and glaring faces, faces of everyone who has seen me naked. I tune out the jeers, the excited chatter, the judgemental expressions. I ignore the screeching cries of "SLUT!" the people trying to shove their cell phones in my face. I grip Faye's hand so hard that I probably almost break bones. And when class ends, she's there to hold my hand and carry my books for me, like an old-school boyfriend from the fifties. And I have never been so grateful for anybody in my life.

But even Faye can't save me from the girl who comes out of nowhere and hits me in the face.

Her face is a twisted mask of fury. I don't recognize her, but she recognizes me. And hates me.

"You bitch!" she screams.

My face is stinging from where she hit me, and I reel into what I think is a bank of lockers but is actually another girl, who yanks on my hair so hard that a chunk of it must come out of my scalp. Faye lets go of my hand and pushes the second girl backward with surprising force for somebody who can't weigh more than ninety pounds. The second girl topples over and Faye pins her down. The first girl is on me again, until a strong pair of hands picks her kicking and screaming off the ground.

I recognize his smell before I see his face. It's Zach. He's not ignoring me. I haven't lost him.

"Everybody needs to calm the fuck down!" he shouts.

I have never heard Zach speak with such authority before. I remember when I first met him, telling him he needs to stop being so shy. I guess he finally took my advice, at the best possible time.

But nobody else seems overly intimidated. A pack of other girls, a few of whom are vaguely familiar, are advancing on me, all of them wearing the same angry expressions, some of them fluttering pieces of white paper in their hands and pointing at what I recognize as my own handwriting. As they get closer, their faces come into view. I recognize Laura, my onetime elementary school friend, and Britney from French class, whose mouth is twisted in a scowl. They're like a pack of wolves, advancing on their kill. I have never seen a fight in the halls of Milton High in all of my years here, and now I'm lying in the thick of one.

One that I caused.

My eyes dart to the periphery of the pack, where Jillian Landry stands by herself, her mouth open in shock. She doesn't look mad. She's not crying, either. She just looks heartbroken, which is the worst of all to see. I did that to her. Maybe I deserve to be left to the wolves.

"Back off, before I get Principal Goldfarb," Zach says, extending his arms to keep the pack at bay. "Don't think I won't do it. You all want detention before prom?"

One of the girls starts wailing. "My boyfriend Connor was supposed to take me to prom!" She bursts into tears. "Until that little skank took him away from me!" Her friends put their arms around her and make murmuring sounds. I know they are burning holes into my head with their hateful glares.

Zach glances from me to Faye. "Run," he says. "Meet me back at the place we meet on Wednesdays."

Faye grabs my hand. The pack lets us go, calling out after us. I hear a slew of colorful names. SLUT. HOME WRECKER. WHORE. BOYFRIEND THIEF. TRAMP. Once we're in my Jeep—Faye wisely doesn't let me drive when she sees my hands shaking over the wheel—we speed out of the parking lot and back to my house. Only when we're in my bedroom with the door locked do I let myself actually breathe.

I flop backward on my bed, feeling like all the energy has been sucked out of me. I'm dizzy and nauseous, but there's one thing I have to say, one thing Faye has to know.

"I never slept with Charlie. I never tried to seduce him, like he's probably telling everyone. He planned the whole thing. He wanted to ruin my life."

Faye sits on the bed and takes my hand. "I know," she says.

She believes me. Maybe Zach will, too. I think of his text messages from that night. *See you around.* And the way he ignored me in the hallway like I was nothing to him.

"He'll come around," Faye says, smoothing my hair off my face. "He just needs time."

I don't know how somebody who has known me for such a short time can already read my mind.

Zach knocks on the door five minutes later. "I barely made it out alive," he says, standing with his arms crossed in front of us. "It's fucking mayhem back there." He clears his throat. "And I think you owe me an explanation as to why my bare ass is all over the Internet."

He hates me. I knew it. I sit up too fast and everything starts spinning. Zach puts his hand on my shoulder and my heart leaps, like if he can still bear to touch me he might forgive me. His familiar scent, that touch I'd know anywhere. The boy who just wanted to be my boyfriend. Maybe I should have just let him, and none of this would have happened.

"Where should I start?" I whisper.

"At the beginning," Zach says. "Wherever that is."

I grab his hand, the one that's resting on my shoulder. I wait for his fingers to clutch mine in response, but they don't.

I take a deep breath and recall one piece of advice from Kim. The only piece that ever held weight with me. *Always lift your chin up high when you did something wrong. Because you might know you did something wrong, but nobody else has to.*

With my chin up, I tell them everything.

32

I tell them about the virgins, and I don't mince details. I tell them numbers. I tell them about my white notebook. I tell them what has been really going on in my bedroom all this time. And finally, I tell them about Charlie. I can't get through that part with my chin up. When I get to Charlie, I start to cry, which is ridiculous. Nothing happened. I know nothing happened, but that doesn't change what could have happened.

Zach's hands ball into fists, and he sets his lips in a thin line, which makes them appear almost colorless. "I knew it," he says. "I knew there was something about the way he looked at you."

Faye, who is sitting cross-legged beside me, covers her face with her hands. "He thinks he can get away with it, with ruining all those people's relationships. They need to know the truth."

"What truth?" I say. "I'm the one who ruined those relationships. He's just the messenger. He told me he would ruin me if I told, and now he has. Angela won't talk to me again."

"Somebody has to put him in his place," Zach says, gritting his teeth. For a second I think he's going to punch the wall, but he stops just short of it. "I can't believe this."

"Please promise me you won't do anything," I say, standing up and grabbing Zach's hands. "I'm going to handle this. I'll figure it out."

Zach pulls his hands away and stares at his knuckles.

"We could tell the truth," Faye says. "That he tried to seduce you. People will have to believe it." She looks from me to Zach, who doesn't meet her eyes.

My heart sinks. An awkward silence ensues. "Do you even believe me?"

He doesn't say anything at first, and I think I'll die if he doesn't believe me. I'll disappear, cease to exist. But I know what I am. I'm a bad friend, a slut, a liar. I lied about tutoring. I lied about being sick. Zach has no reason to believe me now.

"I should have punched him in the face when I saw him leaving your house," Zach says. "The guy looked so fucking happy. But you know what I felt when I saw him?"

I shake my head.

"Envy. I felt sick with it. You know what he did when he saw me standing there like a moron in your driveway? He winked at me. I wanted to pound him. But I didn't, because I remembered what you said before. That I was jealous of him. And I was."

Faye stands up quickly and makes up some excuse about making us some lunch. She slips out of the room before I can even grab onto her, cleave to her like an anchor in this mess.

Now it's just me and Zach. I want him to touch me. I want him to hug me, because I know I would feel safe in his arms. But this isn't just about me. This is about him, about the only guy who liked me for me. The one who ended up getting hurt.

"I'm sorry," I say, but it sounds hollow, and I know it doesn't mean anything.

"All this time, I knew you were holding something back from me. You always kept me at a distance. It all makes sense now, but I wish it didn't. I thought there was a chance for you and me. That if I didn't leave you alone you eventually wouldn't want me to." Zach stares at the wall, the carpet, my bed. Everywhere but at me.

I can tell he's trying not to cry, and that makes me want to cry.

"I didn't want to hurt you," I mumble, and it sounds ridiculous out loud, like the dumbest thing I could say.

"It would have hurt a lot less if you would have just told me you were hooking up with other guys," he says, raking his hands through his hair like he wants to pull it out. "It would have made more sense. Of course I had to be on Wednesdays, because all the other days were taken."

I deserved that. I deserved that, but it still feels like a slap in the face. My cheeks burn and my eyes sting and my teeth start to chatter.

"Look, I'm sorry," he says, pressing his fingers against his forehead. "I didn't mean it like that. I believe you about Charlie, and if I could break his nose right now I would. But I'm not sure if I can be around you."

My breath catches in my throat. The air is stuck in my lungs. I'm about to lose Zach. He's slipping away.

I already lost him.

"I have to go," he says, and when he takes his hand away from his face, his eyes are red. "I need some space to think."

He walks toward the door.

"Wait," I choke out. "Zach, wait."

He stops but doesn't turn around.

"I need to know you're still my friend. We're friends, right?"

He turns his head ever so slightly. *Come back*, I will him. *Come back, and I won't hurt you again.*

"I thought you didn't want to be friends," he says, and just like that he's gone.

I collapse on the carpet. Zach has been all over this room. He has been in here more than anybody else besides me. I had so many chances to make him feel like I wanted him here. So many times I could have reached over and put my arm around him, or let him put his arms around me like I knew he wanted to. But I was in control. I called the shots. I told him when to arrive, when to leave. I set the boundaries. *Don't kiss me like that. It's too intimate. Don't try to hold my hand. I don't need a back massage; let's just get down to business.*

I thought it was easier that way. But it doesn't feel easy now.

When Faye comes back upstairs, she's holding two mugs of what smells like Kim's detox tea.

"You realize there's no food in your house, right?" she says, sitting on the carpet beside me and handing me one of the mugs. The smell makes me gag, and I bite the inside of my cheek so that I don't throw up all over Faye.

"Zach hates me," I say.

Faye wraps her arm around me, and I breathe in her scent. She cradles my head like I'm a little kid, and I let her. I know I look pathetic, but I don't care.

"He doesn't hate you," she says. "He's just upset. He needs some time to deal with it."

"Is that what he told you?"

"He didn't have to," Faye says, running my hair between her fingers. "His world just got shook up a bit—that's all. Give him space. He'll come back."

I want to believe her, but I don't.

For some reason that old adage flashes into my head. *You made your bed, now you have to lie in it.* I start to laugh, softly, until tears start leaking out of my eyes. Faye brushes her thumb across each of my cheeks.

"You must have been so scared," she murmurs. "Being alone with Charlie. I can't even imagine."

I fight the overwhelming urge to tell her everything. Why I'm such a basket case, even though nothing happened. Even though he didn't get what he wanted. I want to cry into her shoulder and tell her every single thing about me. She might understand. She might get it.

But she might not, and I can't take that chance.

"You should go back," I say, sitting up quickly. "I should probably be alone. Don't skip math. You know you have that test." This much is true. Faye was stressed out about her algebra test last week and told anyone who would listen that she would "never use that crap in real life."

"I don't care," she says, raising her chin defiantly. "You're more important."

I shake my head. "No, I should be by myself. I have some things to work out."

She nods and unwraps her arm from around my body. "Whatever you need," she says, squeezing my hand. "I'll call you after school. Let me know if you need anything. I'll drop it all in a heartbeat."

When she's gone, I think about her words. I roll them over and over again in my head and feel nothing. *I'll drop it all in a heartbeat.* I thought hearing those words from Faye would mean more.

I thought retreating into her, having her arms around me would mean more. But it's not enough. Not enough to make me feel safe and not enough to make me feel like myself.

There's only one person who could make me feel that way, and he's not speaking to me.

I sit down at my desk and open my chemistry notebook. I'll lose myself in logic, just like I always do. Formulas and numbers and equations that have to balance.

But it doesn't work this time. Every number makes me think of another way I screwed up, another person I screwed over. The virgins were all numbers to me. Number one. Number five. Number ten. The ratings I assigned all meant something, too. Seven point five. Eight. Six. It was my system. And now I'm alone in it, the one cog left in the machinery.

I'm startled by the sound of a key turning in the front door. My blood turns to ice in my veins and I grip the pen in my hand tightly. *It's Charlie. It must be Charlie.* I leap up and lock my bedroom door and slide down the wall.

"Honey, what are you doing home?" Kim's voice drifts up the stairs. For a second I consider playing dumb, but she has already seen the Jeep in the driveway. She knows I'm home.

"I'm doing an independent study project," I call back, thinking that should be enough to get rid of her.

"I wasn't born yesterday," she says, knocking on my door. "Come on—let me in. I have something for you."

I open the door slowly. "Fine," I say.

She surveys my face. I can tell from the way her eyebrows lift slightly that she's surprised. I know what she probably thinks, that I'm hungover and trying to get out of classes. I must look the part. I know my face is puffy and my eyes are red rimmed and my hair is a greasy mess.

"This came for you," she says, handing me a manila envelope. My stomach drops and I cover my mouth because I'm afraid I'm going to be sick.

Kim mistakes the gesture for surprise. "It's from MIT," she says. "Aren't you going to open it?"

It's a big envelope, a big envelope with some weight to it. I don't even need to open it to know it's an acceptance letter, the one I have been waiting so long for, the letter accompanied by course catalogues and information on residence and brochures starring smiling students. One day ago I would have been filled with excitement to open this. One day ago I would have been filled with pride. I would have called Angela and she would have jumped up and down on the other side of the phone. But Charlie took that away from me, too. I know my eyes are getting wet and glassy, and I wish Kim would leave, but she's just standing there, waiting for me. I take the envelope and walk over to my bed.

"Oh, sweetie," she says. "I should have the camera. This is a big moment."

My fingers feel numb as I open the envelope. My breath hitches in my throat when I read the first sentence, even though I knew what it would say. It's more real, seeing it in print.

Dear Mercedes,

On behalf of the Admissions Committee, it is my pleasure to offer you admission to the MIT Class of 2016.

"You got in," Kim says, sitting down beside me and squeezing my hand. "You got in. You got everything you wanted."

She means it in a nice way. She's proud of me. I can tell by the way her hand is trembling slightly and the flush in her cheeks. But she's so wrong. I didn't get anything I wanted. Maybe what I deserve and what I want are two very different things.

"We should celebrate," she says. "A fancy dinner, some drinks. Something special. We won't get to do that kind of thing once you're in that other city."

"Massachusetts," I snap, surprised at the venom in my voice. "It's called Massachusetts, and it's a state, Kim. And I don't want to celebrate. I have work to do."

Her hand goes limp on mine. I hurt her. But really, what did she expect? Kim's priorities have long been established, and I'm at the bottom of the totem pole. Now she can know what that feels like.

"I get it," Kim says. "You have work to do. Schoolwork should come first."

I resist the urge to roll my eyes. Kim's choosing now, of all times, to get preachy about schoolwork?

"You should make sure you're at school tomorrow," she says, standing up and taking a step toward the door.

"I'll be there," I say, pasting on what I hope is a convincing smile before noticing the familiar black leather bag around her shoulder. "What are you doing with my purse, Kim?"

"I found it downstairs, thrown beside the door," she says, dangling it in front of me. "This is a Prada bag. Take better care of it."

I snatch the bag from her grip and shut the door in her face. I can tell she's lingering outside, debating whether or not to force some stupid plans on me. But there's no way I'm caving in. Whatever is left of the little girl inside me, the one who used to cry herself to sleep when she heard her parents fight, is pulling at my shirttail, telling me to open the door and collapse in Kim's arms and spill everything. But that little girl has been gone a long time, and I'm not listening to her now, not when I need logic on my side more than ever.

I'm very aware that my purse is vibrating, so I locate my phone inside it. I'm stupid enough to expect a text from Faye, checking up on me. Instead, there are twenty-seven new messages, all from unknown numbers, all a variation of the same theme.

I HATE YOU
I hope you get herpes
You're going to pay for this
Don't show ur face in school skanky bitch
You can run but you can't hide. Videos are forever
I HOPE YOU DIE
We are going to make your life such hell

I slump down on my bed and drop my phone on my nightstand, where it lands with a clatter and continues vibrating periodically. I want to turn it off, but I can't bring myself to. The truth is, I deserve all of those words. I plan to have a good cry and fall asleep on a pillow wet with my own tears, but sleep doesn't come to me. Something else comes to me instead. Something I remembered Angela saying, back when we first met and she didn't have a cell phone. I had helped her pick one out. She ended up getting one identical to mine, probably because I knew how to use it and could show her.

"I'm so bad with technology," she had said. "I miss when people wrote letters. I feel like the world just moves too fast for me to keep up."

It's a long shot, but any shot is one worth taking right now. So I write Angela a letter, by hand, telling her everything. I tell her things I have never told anybody, things from before we met, things I haven't fully admitted to myself. I tell her the whole story about what happened with Luke, even though I don't understand it any better myself when it's down on paper. I don't know how to end it. *Your friend, Mercy* seems presumptuous, since I don't think we're friends at all anymore. *Sincerely* is much too formal. *Love* is much too gushy.

So I end it with honesty. "I don't expect you to forgive me, but I hope you can understand someday."

33

Faye calls me when I'm huddled in a heap on the floor, trying to sleep. I tried sleeping in my bed but just kept imagining different guys beside me, blocking me off from any source of oxygen.

"I have to tell you something," Faye says. "I went to the website."

I suck in a breath, feeling like I might choke on the air. I squirm and clutch the edges of the duvet. Faye has seen everything. How can she be on my side after that?

"He posted your journal entries. All of them. I just thought you should know that."

All of them. All of those words. I imagine them lined up like ammunition, ready to take shots at the names within those pages. The nicknames, the ratings. All of the worst things I thought about myself. I can't go to school on Monday. I can't go ever again. I can't face those people. The knowledge that my journal is out there is the worst kind of naked. They haven't just seen my outsides, but my insides, too.

Faye is silent on the other end. She's pissed off, having second thoughts about me. Maybe she never even had first thoughts. Then I remember what I wrote about Faye, the entry I scribbled when I came home from her house, the words I used to preserve whatever I felt about her.

There's just something about her.

"Do you hate me?" I ask. My voice sounds clotted and mangled, and I realize I'm crying.

"God, Mercy. Of course not. I could never hate you."

"You must think I'm a monster," I say, pressing my face into the carpet, letting my tears leak out the side of my eyes.

"You're not a monster," she says. "You thought you were helping those guys. I get it."

"I can't go back to school," I say. "I just can't face them."

"You can, and you will," she says. "I'll be there. So will Zach."

For a long while nobody says anything. I can hear her breathing on the other end, and that's enough for me, to just know she is there.

"I'll meet you in the parking lot on Monday," Faye says. "You won't have to face anybody alone."

"You're too good to me," I say. "I don't deserve it."

"Well," she says softly, "there's something about you, too."

I can hear the smile in her voice. It gets me through the night, through the panicky nightmares that force me to wake up in a film of sweat.

Faye is there Monday morning, just like she said, before I even get out of my car. She insists on walking into school with me, like she can protect me. But she can't protect me from the message scrawled in permanent marker on my locker, waiting for me.

WHORE.

I don't even try to wipe it off. I just leave it there. Maybe I can switch lockers. Or maybe it doesn't matter. Everybody knows what I am anyway, and it won't make a difference. This way at least people know the truth. It's honest.

Faye makes me eat lunch in the cafeteria, even though all I want to do is lock myself in a bathroom stall. It's weird, with just the two of us and no Zach. I wonder what he's doing right now, if he's somewhere in the sea of faces. I dart my eyes around, careful not to make direct contact with anybody. Several tables over, Rafe Lawrence is standing on his chair, gesticulating wildly. The people around him keep laughing and looking our way.

"Ignore them," Faye says, biting into a cheeseburger. "He's an idiot."

I push food around my plate. I couldn't bring myself to eat it if I tried.

Something smacks the side of my head, and when I move my hand to feel what hit me, my hair is wet and goopy and Faye is on her feet, shooting her middle finger in the air. I know hundreds of eyes are on me, waiting for me to cry because a pudding cup just hit me in the head. I know what they're all thinking. *Cry, bitch. Cry. Let us all see it.*

"In five years, none of this will matter," Faye says, wiping my hair with a napkin. "Nobody will remember this."

Yes, they will. In five years people will still remember who ruined their lives.

When I get back to my locker after lunch, a familiar form is hunched over it, biting his lip. Zach. He's scrubbing the permanent marker, or trying to.

"Hey," I whisper.

He keeps scrubbing furiously, his hand moving in a frantic circular motion.

"It won't budge," he says with a sigh. "I'm sorry. I did my best." He starts blacking in the letters with more marker, eventually encasing the whole ugly word. I watch him and I know this is why he wasn't in the cafeteria, that he spent his lunch hour trying to rub away everything I did. I want to tell him that it doesn't matter, that what's underneath will still be there no matter how hard he tries to make it go away.

"You don't need to do that," I tell him, putting my hand on his shoulder. People are watching us. I know what they're thinking. *Now he's cleaning her locker. I wonder what she's giving him.* I don't want people to see Zach like that.

He flinches under my touch. "Yeah, I do," he mumbles. "This is what friends do."

My relief is so immense that I almost can't keep myself standing up. *This is what friends do.* This is what Zach thinks friends do. And all this time I didn't want to be his friend. All this time, and I was pushing somebody away who I really never wanted to get rid of.

Somebody who wants to protect me.

But Zach can't protect me all the time. He can't save me from the girl who pushes my head down at the water fountain, causing my lips to mash against the porcelain. He can't save me in French class, when Laura and Britney tell Mrs. Palmateer that they can't be in the same small group as me anymore because of "personal differences." He can't save me from the glare Gus Teller gives me, the one I feel even after he walks away. The Crier. What was I thinking, writing them down?

Worst of all, he can't save me from the fear that Charlie is lurking around every corner, reveling in the hell he caused.

"I know it doesn't seem like it now, but this will blow over," Faye says as we walk to my car after school. But I know she's trying to convince herself.

Toby Easton messages me to let me know he can't make our tutoring session. He says a "family thing" came up. I know better. He doesn't want a tutor whom everybody has seen naked. He's a nice person, too kind to tell me to fuck off like the rest of the student body. Somehow losing Toby's respect hurts worse than almost everything else.

My only solace is the MIT acceptance letter. I carry it around in my purse with me, and when I'm alone, I pull it out and read it. I read it until it's almost etched into my head, until I use it to erase all of the insults, all of the dirty glares and pudding cups flung my way. I use it to remind myself that I'm getting a fresh start. Nobody at MIT will know who I am. Nobody will know what I did. They won't see the video or read the pages of my notebook. I'll be another face in the crowd. A number, like I told Faye.

You stood out as one of the most talented and promising students in the most competitive applicant pool in the history of the Institute.

It's almost funny. Somebody at MIT thinks I'm talented and promising. Try telling that to anybody at this school right now, when the only word used to describe me would be the one on my locker. I guess I underestimated the power of words, at least until now. The words in my notebook, the ones I never thought anybody else would see, the ones that did the kind of damage I never thought possible. The words I wrote in the letter to Angela, if she ever reads them.

I don't see Angela until Wednesday when she's getting out of her mom's car in front of the school. Angela is the only seventeen-year-old I know who didn't care about getting her license and doesn't want to learn how to drive. I tell myself to go inside, to turn and leave, but instead I watch her reach into the car and hug her mom. She raises her eyes up and sees me after looking both ways for passing cars. I would rather she just outright hate me than give me the expression she levels at me, something between pity and confusion. She feels sorry for me, for the girl she thinks lied to feel better about sleeping with so many other girls' boyfriends. I open my mouth as she passes by, but she stares at the ground and leaves cold air in her wake.

"Seriously. This will be yesterday's news sooner than you know it," Faye says, wrapping her arm around my shoulder after chemistry class, which I spent staring at the back of Angela's head, willing her to turn around.

"It's not going away," I say, but I'm not thinking about the jeers and the insults and the thrown pudding cups. I'm thinking about what Charlie could have done to me. What his hands are capable of doing to Angela.

Faye and Zach talk at lunch. They're right beside me at the same round cafeteria table, but I can't hear them. My inner dialogue is too loud. *Angela hates me. She won't read the letter—she'll rip it up. Charlie brainwashed her. If she sleeps with Charlie, she'll never forgive herself. He won't give her the first time she deserves.* I push pasta salad around my plate. The yellowish color and putty texture are enough to make me gag.

"You have to eat something," Faye says, snapping her fingers. "Mercy. You have to eat something. When's the last time you had an actual meal?"

I shrug. Even that motion is exhausting.

"You need to eat. This is all going to go away, you know. Maybe sooner than you think." She bites her lower lip.

"Don't you wonder why I did it?" I say, surprised by the acidity in my own voice. "You must have at least some qualms about being my friend after what I did."

Faye props her elbows on the table and stares at the ceiling. "I did wonder why," she says. "But then I figured it out. It's like we talked about, that time you came to the store. Guys are clueless. They need guidance. That's what you wanted to give to them."

Zach casts his eyes downward. I know he wants to say something, but he stays silent.

"I guess now it's pretty obvious why I didn't want to be your girlfriend," I say with a nervous laugh. "You deserve better." *You deserve Faye.* I know she told me there was nothing going on, but I haven't forgotten what I saw when I walked into the chemistry lab.

Nobody says anything. Zach doesn't agree with me, but he doesn't disagree, either. I know he must think of Faye like that. Now that he knows what I did, he can move on. He can move on with somebody who would never hurt him like I did.

When I get to my locker, somebody is waiting there for me. Somebody I didn't expect to see here. Jillian Landry, with one foot against the door, holding her books in her arms, her back stooped slightly. Tommy used to carry her books for her, but I guess she won't let him carry them anymore.

"Hi," I say in a strangled voice.

"Why?" she says softly. "What did I do to you to deserve this? And you had the nerve to pretend to help me. I thought you actually wanted me to do well." She's not crying, but her voice is thick with unshed tears. People stop to listen around us, but Jillian doesn't pay them any attention.

I try to think of something to say to justify what I did. I remember what I told Tommy when he asked the same question, that night as he walked down my driveway *Why me? Why Jillian?* I had responded, *I just saw a chance to make myself useful.* Now those words are empty, filled with hot air and false promises.

"I did want you to do well. I do, I mean."

"That's bullshit. That's not an answer. Why?" she repeats again. I open my mouth to say something, even though I don't know what to say, but something else inside me opens instead and I start to cry, big heaving tears that almost hurt coming out of my eyes.

Jillian's eyes widen and she moves a step closer. Maybe she forgives me. Maybe she gets it, even if she doesn't understand it. But when she's right in my face, her eyes harden.

"You don't get to cry about this," she says. "You ruined my life. I was ready to give everything up for Tommy. I was even going to follow him across the country for school. Now I have no idea who I spent the last six years of my life with."

She turns on her heel and walks away, her hair flapping against her back. Jillian will have to learn how to trust people again, and that's my fault. I took that away from her. And now the one good thing I had going is gone, too. Jillian doesn't want me as a tutor. Toby doesn't, either. His girlfriend is probably freaked out, scouring the website for Toby's name in my journal. I'm not fit to teach anybody anymore.

I almost talk myself out of home economics. It would be so much easier to go home, to lock myself in my bedroom. Angela is in home economics, along with Trevor and Chase. I can't spend class staring at their backs, or having them turn around and stare at me. But Zach catches me in the hallway.

"You're not walking out," he says. "We're in this together."

Angela's seat is vacant, but Trevor and Chase both turn around when I come in. I'm met with a glare from Trevor and a wink from

Chase. Trevor is no doubt pissed off that I have ignored his Facebook messages, all six of them that have piled up in my in-box. *You said nobody would find out. What am I supposed to do now? This is all your fault.*

Mrs. Hill glances up from her desk when she sees me take a seat beside Faye, purses her lips, and focuses her gaze on the stack of papers in front of her.

"Gross," I whisper to Faye. "I think Mrs. Hill knows about the video. She just gave me the strangest look."

Faye makes a face. "She's coming over here. Don't look up."

Mrs. Hill stoops over my desk, a rather unfortunate position because it puts me in very close proximity to her sagging top.

"Mercedes, I found this on the floor. It had your name on the top. I didn't read it, but I thought you might want it back." She pushes a sheet of white paper toward me. At first I think it's an assignment, until I look at the heading.

MERCEDES AYRES'S TO-DO LIST

They're all there, every single name and nickname, every mean and cold and vulnerable thought. The same pages that Charlie posted are now floating around the school, being passed from student to student.

The color drains out of my face, and I start to feel both hot and clammy at the same time. I try to crumple the paper and hide it in my backpack, but Faye grabs it and heads to the back of the room. I can barely watch whatever it is she's going to do.

She holds it over the sink, retrieves a lighter from her jeans pocket, and lights the paper on fire. For some reason my first thought is, *Faye doesn't even smoke.* A hush falls over the class. Zach, who is at the back of the room, stands up and promptly sits down again when Faye shoots him a withering glare. She holds an edge of the sheet and watches the paper curl up while tapping her toe and smiling sweetly. Even Mrs. Hill seems lost for words. She makes little squeaking noises, which may or may not be strings of expletives, until she finally makes a move for the back of the room.

Faye drops the paper, which is by now engulfed in flames, in the sink and turns the water on.

"Detention," Mrs. Hill shouts. "Principal's office, right now."

Faye grabs her bag and winks at me. I wish I were heading to detention with her. It would be better than braving the student population on my own.

She stops at the door. "Just so you all know, there's more where that came from. She's not the only one who fucked up, so get off your goddamned high horses."

Faye will probably get detention for a week, maybe even longer. I get to hear a frazzled Mrs. Hill drone on about hormones and the female menstrual cycle. Even though Faye isn't beside me, her strength is still thrumming under my veins like a second pulse. *I will get through this. We will get through this.*

If only I could believe her. If only there were some kind of chemical formula for this, some tried-and-true solution. But there's no textbook cure, nothing that equates sleeping with people's boyfriends with forgiveness.

And there never will be.

34

"It was worth it," Faye says after school while she walks me to my car. "It's not fair that you take all the shit for this while the guys get to walk around like nothing happened. They're just as much to blame."

"I'm the one who started it," I say, kicking a beer cap across the parking lot with my shoe. "If I hadn't started it, nothing would have happened."

"Don't let them off the hook so easily," Faye snaps. "They were coming to you. It takes two to have sex. So don't defend them."

I nod, but I don't believe her. I keep telling myself that I thought I was helping, that I was doing it for them. For their girlfriends. But I know that's not true anymore.

"It's going to be okay, you know," Faye says, reaching out her hand but pulling it back and shoving it in her pocket instead. "Everything will go back to normal."

This time, I shake my head. I don't even know what normal is anymore.

A car pulls through the parking lot and up next to us. I can't see who is driving, but two girls in the passenger side pelt us with fast-food wrappers. A half-finished Coke hits me on the temple and bounces off, not hard enough to hurt, although I doubt that was the intention.

"You're never getting away with this," Laura Adams says, her skinny torso hanging out the window. Faye shoots her the middle finger and picks up the discarded can, readying herself to throw it back, even as the car speeds away.

"Don't," I say, putting my hand on her shoulder. "I deserve it."

"You don't deserve it," Faye says flatly. "None of it. And pretty soon, people are going to forget all about it."

I cock my head. "I wouldn't be so sure," I say. "What's that saying—a picture is worth a thousand words? How many words is a video worth?"

"Huh." Faye's lips curl into a little smile. "You might be right about that." She grabs my wrist and glances at my watch. "Shit. I need to get to detention now, or else I'll end up with more detention." She blows me a kiss and runs back toward the school. Her hair is being whipped around by the wind and she's holding onto the back of it with one hand and her bag with the other hand. My heart swells with something I can only describe as gratitude, gratitude for something and someone I'm not quite sure I deserve.

Instead of getting in the Jeep, I decide to walk home. I don't know how long it takes me, but I imagine Zach taking the same route, day after day, and me knowing nothing about it. How many times did I pass right by him, going too far over the speed limit to notice?

By the time I get home I'm hungry but too tired to imagine making something to eat, so I curl up in my bed. I must have fallen asleep because I wake up to a loud, obnoxious knocking on my door and a loud, obnoxious voice to go along with it.

"Mercy, sweetie, wake up. There's a boy here to see you."

I bolt upright as the door opens. This must be a joke. There's no boy who would want to see me. Unless it's Charlie, here to gloat and rub in his victory.

"No," I say, covering my face with my duvet. "I'm sick."

"Well, it would be rude to send him away. He has been waiting for you. And he brought soup."

I peek out slowly, just to make sure it's not a ruse. But there's only one guy who would bring me soup.

"Hey," Zach says, taking a seat in my swivel chair and putting a Tupperware container on my desk.

"Hey," I whisper. I almost feel like crying. Since when does soup make me so emotional?

To Kim, who is lingering in the door, I shoot what I hope is a menacing stare. "Bye."

Kim gives me the world's most obvious wink. "See you around, Zach," she says. "Maybe you'll let me win next time."

When she shuts the door behind her, I lean forward on my elbows and turn to Zach. "Win at what?" I say. "Don't—I repeat, don't—gamble with Kim. She'll take your money and run."

Zach laughs. "You were out cold, so I taught her how to play Go Fish," he says. "She had never heard of it. I told her she must be living under a rock."

This should probably be weird, Zach playing cards with Kim. I should probably be embarrassed, because she undoubtedly showed off too much of her cleavage and most likely found some way to get Zach to compliment her on how young she looks. I have kept Kim hidden from people for a reason. But with Zach, it's strangely okay somehow. If he has spent time alone with her and still isn't running for the hills, he's an even better person than I gave him credit for.

I pull back the covers and pat the mattress beside me. Zach hesitates but gets in fully clothed. We lie there like that for a minute, and I'm conscious of how much space he takes up, how long his legs and arms are. Then I lean over and do something I haven't done before. I rest my arm across his chest and close my eyes and snuggle into his neck. I'm surprised by how good it feels, how well my chin fits against him. *I fit well here.*

I'm surprised that of all the things Zach and I have done in this bed, just lying here together isn't one of them. And it feels better than anything else. He wraps the other arm around me and kisses the top of my head.

Is this what I gave up for the virgins?

But when I start tracing circles on his chest with my finger, he pulls away and his face is hard. "I didn't believe it when I first found out," he mumbles. "I didn't believe you could lie to me all that time when all I wanted to do was make you my girlfriend. I felt like a fool." He clenches his jaw. "I watched the video a hundred times and still couldn't believe it. All those guys, and I had no idea."

I reach out to touch him, but he waves away my hand.

"You didn't even write about me in that journal," he says, averting his eyes. "You wrote about everyone else. I felt like I was nothing to you."

I squeeze my eyes shut. Zach sounds like he's about to cry. Hearing his voice like that is the worst feeling in the world. "I'm sorry, Zach," I say. "I really am. You weren't nothing."

"I know," he says, his voice breaking slightly. "But part of me, this pissed-off part, wanted to be done with you. All this time I thought I had a chance with you, that you'd finally come around. Now I know it's never going to happen."

I sit up, hanging my head between my knees and gripping the sheets underneath me. My body is made up of air, and I will float away unless I anchor myself here. I will float away without Zach.

"Hey," he says, running his finger along my arm. "That was just a little part of me. I'm not done with you."

My chest shakes when I take a breath. Everything hurts. I deserve it for hurting Zach.

"I'd do anything for you," he says, squeezing my shoulder gently. "Anything. Just let me be your friend, okay? You can tell me stuff. Whatever is in your head."

"What's in my head right now is that I got what I deserved," I say quietly. "I deserved what I got."

"Never say that," he says. "Don't ever say that. You hear me?" He cups my face in his hands.

"Why do you even like me?" I say. "I'm selfish and dishonest and all I do is push people away. I wouldn't even want to be my friend."

Zach's eyes darken. "You're also real. You tell it like it is. You don't let me get away with anything. And I love that about you."

"I don't see how you can like me after all this," I say. "I wouldn't have held it against you if you decided I was a big, dirty slut and joined the angry mob in the hallway. You probably had more right than anyone."

He sets his mouth in a firm line. "Remember all the times you told me no? All the times you brushed me off when I tried to make you my girlfriend? I stuck around after that. And I'm sticking around now. You can't get rid of me that easily."

I let my lips press against his so lightly that our mouths are barely touching. When I pull away, his eyes are still closed. I stare at his face, the mouth I have kissed a thousand times. For some reason the MIT acceptance letter flits into my head again, but this time it fills me with dread. In Massachusetts, I *will* be another number. I won't be important to anybody. I won't be around people like Zach who stand by me no matter what. People I can't get rid of. People I don't want to get rid of, not ever.

Zach opens his eyes slowly and wipes a tear away from under my eye. "Penny for your thoughts," he says. "I told you mine."

"I got into MIT," I blurt out. "I haven't told anybody yet."

I wasn't planning on blurting it out. The words from the acceptance letter race through my head. *Your commitment to personal excellence and principled goals has convinced us that you will both contribute to our diverse community and thrive within our academic environment.* The words that mean less to me than all the ones Zach just said.

He squeezes my hand and gives me a lopsided half smile. "I didn't even know you had applied there," he says. "Congratulations. You deserve everything you want, and I know how hard you work at school."

I know he's proud of me, but I also know he's hurt. He's drifting away again. Friends tell friends what schools they apply to. Friends cheer friends on. I know Zach would have cheered me on if I had given him the chance.

We sit there in silence until Zach says he has to go, that he has someplace to be. I don't ask him where because it's none of my business, but for some reason I'm insatiably curious. I have no right to be insatiably curious, but I am anyway.

"You should heat up that soup," he says. "My mom says it cures everything."

I smile weakly. I wish it would cure everything that's wrong with me.

Before he leaves, he opens his backpack and takes out a binder. He rummages around in it and pulls out what looks like an essay and places it beside me on the bed.

"This is for you," he says. "I did your home economics assignment from the other day. You wrote yours on the woman's changing role in the workforce. And you did a pretty damned good job."

"Why?" I ask. "Why would you do that for me?"

He shrugs. "I figure I owe you one. You know, for all the chemistry you've done for me."

And then he's gone, with a wave and a smile I haven't seen before.

I'm left feeling like somebody I don't even know.

35

Before school on Friday, I do what I have been avoiding for the last several days.

I watch the video.

It's not hard to find. It's embedded on some website that looks like it was thrown together without a lot of effort. It doesn't look at all like something Charlie would create, and I'm sure that was exactly his intention.

The picture quality is grainy, but you can definitely tell it's me. Charlie spliced it together masterfully, cutting out all the discussions that surrounded the sexual encounters so that it's basically pure pornography. My stomach churns when I think about how many times he has seen this footage and how many times he probably jerked off to it. The entire student body of Milton High has seen every inch of my body. They have seen me on my back, on my stomach, on all fours, on my side, and even—with that idiotic mole Juan Marco Antonio—standing up.

Seeing myself doing that with so many different people makes me physically ill, like vomit could come up at any moment. I let them into my bedroom, let them into me, like it was no big deal. It's like I'm watching somebody else entirely on that screen, somebody who doesn't value herself at all. I thought I was in control, but I wasn't. It was *him* the whole time, first Luke then every other guy I let into my bed to make up for him.

I remember talking to Angela about the staying power of video and text messaging. "Once something's out there, you never get it back," she had whispered to me with wide eyes when one of the girls in our grade-ten homeroom sent a naked photo of herself to some guy she was seeing, who in turn sent it to all of his friends. Angela couldn't believe somebody would be so stupid. "Seriously. That photo will follow her everywhere. To college. To job interviews. Her future husband will probably see it." I wanted to tell her to loosen her chastity belt and stop judging people, but she was right.

And if that girl's photo made it to, say, 20 people, mine has made it to 1,601, at least if the obnoxious "visitor counter" Charlie installed at the bottom of the page can be believed. I wonder how many of them are perfect strangers, maybe some Internet perverts looking for new material to wank off to. It's a truly sickening thought.

Even worse is seeing my journal pages up there and feeling what I felt when I wrote them, all over again. It's physically painful, like being stabbed with needles from the inside. I think about the people I wrote about, if it's like that for them, too. They must be humiliated, pissed off, regretful. At least I had a choice. I could have not written anything down and spared a lot of people a lot of grief.

I read every comment people left even though I don't want to. They dig into my skin, burrow into all the parts of me I never wanted people to see.

> *Poor little bitch girl. She didn't want to sleep with him? Sure didn't seem that way.*
> *THIS GIRL IS A HEARTLESS WHORE.*
> *She thinks he'd make a good boyfriend? They deserve each other.*
> *Dear diary, I am a fucked-up slut who deserves everything I get.*

My phone starts to vibrate on the desk beside me. I jump, expecting it to be yet another nasty message, but luckily it's Faye.

"You just about ready for your fifteen minutes of notoriety to be over?" she says, sounding much too chipper for seven a.m.

"Feels more like fifteen years," I say. "But I don't think it's going away anytime soon." My throat feels like it's closing up. Faye read those comments, too. Zach read them. Angela read them.

"Don't be so sure about that," Faye says. "All you need to do is show up at today's assembly."

"No, thanks," I say. "I was planning on skipping that. Having everybody who hates me clustered into the gym just seems like a bad idea."

"Be there," Faye says. "Trust me."

I do trust her, but she doesn't give me the chance to say so. She keeps talking. "But there's something I need you to know, before this goes down. There's going to be fallout from this, and it's going to seem like I threw a lot away. But I don't care about the things a lot of people care about. I don't want to go to college like you. What I really want is to go to beauty school."

I bolt upright. "Why are you talking about all this? What exactly are you planning here? Should I be worried?"

She doesn't answer any of these questions. "Just be at the assembly today. You'll see."

I guess I don't have much of a choice anyway. Everyone goes to our assemblies. Even the kids who normally cut class—the pot-smoking slackers who take off to ride their skateboards in the park and the garden-variety slackers who take off to destinations unknown—are forced to go. Principal Goldfarb has teachers do a sweep of the school. More than once, kids have been caught when they're already in the parking lot. They get corralled back in with resigned expressions and detention slips. Although that sounds more appealing than more public ridicule, I'm not going to let Faye down.

I spot Angela and Charlie on the bleachers. My breath catches in my throat. He hasn't seen me, but just being in the same room with him makes my chest throb in terror. I almost talk myself out of the assembly, Principal Goldfarb's punishment notwithstanding, until I see the way Charlie's hand is resting in Angela's lap, with his fingers pressed into her skin. It's a simple gesture to somebody else, but not to me. He thinks he owns her. She's pulling her skirt down so the sliver of skin between her knee sock and her skirt isn't exposed. A typical Angela move, one that probably would have made me roll my eyes a few weeks ago but today makes me want to hug her and be alone with her and tell her everything. The letter I wrote is in my backpack, but I don't know if I'll ever have the chance to give it to her without her doing the same thing to it that Faye did to the piece of paper in Mrs. Hill's classroom.

Faye and Zach are notably absent, which leaves me to sit by

myself until thirty seconds before the assembly, when they both sneak in and slide into the seats beside me, which are not surprisingly vacant.

"Sorry," Faye whispers. "Technical problems." She grips my hand.

Zach stares straight ahead with his jaw clenched. I know that face well. That's the face he makes during chemistry tests, when he freezes up. It's his nervous face. But what does he have to be nervous about?

"Ahem," Principal Goldfarb says from his podium. He taps the microphone with his index finger, leaving the room with the truly horrifying sound of feedback. Most people cover their ears. I relish the screeching, because it's the first time at school since the video came out that I have heard something besides whispers about me.

"Sorry about that. Now, we have a lot of material to cover, so I'm going to get started right away. One of the topics we're going to talk about today is sexual harassment."

A wave of hushed voices crackles through the room. I can only imagine what they're saying. I resist the urge to hide my head between my knees and curl into a ball.

"I ask that you please kindly keep your thoughts to yourself. If you have questions, our guest speaker will be more than happy to answer them."

The guest speaker, a fat little man whose hands are probably much sweatier than my own, drones on about appropriate conduct, the importance of respecting each other, and how achieving personal space within an environment helps it to run smoothly for everyone. It's Common Sense 101.

"Now, we have a video that we would like you to watch. It's only a few minutes long, but I think it gets the point across." He awkwardly steps out of the way of the projector. I stifle a yawn. The only thing worse than speakers at school assemblies are speakers who insist on playing dated videos from the eighties, featuring actors with horrible hair and even worse wardrobes spouting some bullshit we already know.

For a few seconds there's no picture on the big screen. It's just white.

"Terrible fucking video!" someone yells out, taking advantage of the fact that we're in the dark.

A couple other people start talking, egged on by whoever had the nerve to shout at one of Principal Goldfarb's assemblies. Until an image comes on the screen that shuts everybody up.

Faye, blowing a kiss and waving at the camera, same as she did to me yesterday after school. But that's where the similarities end. Because when the camera pans out from her face, she's wearing nothing but lacy panties, with her hair covering her breasts.

"Are you sure nobody's going to see this? Because I don't want to ruin my reputation and all. It's a new school. I really want people to like me."

"This is the best way to get people to like you." I hear Zach's voice before I see him come up behind Faye on the screen. He puts his hands on her hips and pushes her hair to the side.

I stop breathing and dig my nails into Faye's hand.

"I'm just a nice virgin," she says. "Go easy on me." She puts her elbows on a table, probably the same table the camera is on. Her facial expression changes from a smile to shock, and the picture rattles a bit. Zach presses against her from behind, pushing her head almost against the camera.

The room erupts into yells and cheers and shouts. Shoes scuff on the gym floor. I can only imagine Principal Goldfarb and the other teachers groping in the dark, trying to find their way to the audio-video room to turn off the equipment. Somebody in the crowd screams.

"What are you doing?" I say, dropping Faye's hand. "That can't be real. You two aren't a couple. You said nothing was going on." I trusted her that nothing was going on.

Faye picks my hand up and drags it into her lap. She makes my fingers stop moving, makes my hand stay pressed against hers.

"Trust me—we're not a couple," she whispers in my ear. "But for that moment in time, we were something more."

I know my jaw is hanging open, but I don't care. I shouldn't be angry—I have no right to be angry—but I want it to stop. I don't want to see this. I don't want to see this, not after the way Zach held me in my bed last night. I know they did this for me, to take the attention away from me—to make an even bigger scandal. I think back to what I told Faye yesterday. *How many words is a video worth?* I guess she took it literally.

But watching Faye and Zach on that screen, doing a very convincing job of pretending to like each other, I wish they hadn't done this. They should have just left me for the wolves.

I take a deep breath to steady myself. I wonder if this is how Jeremy Roth's girlfriend felt when she saw me wrapped around her boyfriend. I imagine her reaction. She probably checked her e-mail that morning, expecting nothing that would ruin her life, and got the link to the website instead. Maybe she clicked on it out of curiosity. Maybe she even had plans with Jeremy that night. Plans that I ruined.

Faye on screen is wrapping her knees around Zach's chest. His hands are behind her back, pulling her against him. I want to turn away, but I keep watching, transfixed. This must be a joke. This can't be happening. I try to squeeze my eyes shut, but they stay open, like anyone's would when something truly terrible happens.

"You're blocking the money shot, man!" A guy in the crowd yells, followed by a chorus of boos.

And just like that, the screen goes blank again. Somebody flips on a light switch. And with the lights comes complete silence.

"Oh my God," I mutter under my breath, afraid if I say it too loud it might become too real. "You guys made a sex tape."

Faye clutches my hand. "I know it was drastic," she says. "But it had to be. And now your fifteen minutes are over."

36

I wait for Faye and Zach after school, but after an hour and a half of pacing back and forth down the hallway in front of Principal Goldfarb's office, it's obvious they might never come out. Questions race through my mind like ticker tape. What were they thinking? What if they get suspended, or worse, expelled? What if they ruined their lives, all because they wanted to do me a solid? And, more selfishly, what does it mean that they slept together?

Eventually I get in the Jeep and drive toward home by myself, after leaving them each about ten texts, which they may or may not ever get to read, depending on what exquisite forms of torture Principal Goldfarb has in store for them. I plan to go straight home with no detours, but I find myself driving past Angela's house instead. Maybe I'm emboldened by Faye and Zach's very public display of bravery. Maybe I just miss my best friend. Maybe both. I still can't stop thinking about her, about how Charlie plans to spend this very weekend with her. Time is running out.

I don't work up the courage to knock on her door, but I do leave the envelope in her mailbox. It's addressed simply—Angela Hirsch in blocky capitals. It doesn't look like my printing, which was the whole point. I don't want Charlie to find it and rip it up, or worse, read it himself. I never want Charlie to see the insides of that envelope. I never want anyone except Angela to see what I wrote.

After I leave the letter in the mailbox, I park down the road and wait. I don't know what I'm waiting for. Part of me just wants to see Angela, to know she's okay. Every minute that passes means the weekend is that much closer, a thought that fills me with dread.

On impulse, I pull out my phone and dial her number before I can chicken out. The phone rings and rings and eventually goes to voice mail, but I can't think of a message to leave so I say nothing and hang up.

I'm about to start the Jeep and drive away when a car pulls into the driveway. Charlie gets out of the driver's door and stretches his arms overhead, a gesture that makes me instinctively clamp my own arms around my chest. I hate how just the sight of him makes my whole body shake.

I don't want to watch, but I do. He walks around to Angela's side and opens the door for her. I can't see his face, but I know the expression on it. That smirk, the smile that says *I get everything I want, eventually.*

But Angela doesn't get out of the car and kiss him. She slams the door shut, trapping him outside. They're fighting. I lurch forward against the steering wheel, hoping for a better view. They're fighting, the day before their anniversary weekend. Maybe they won't be celebrating after all.

Charlie gestures for her to roll the window down, then he goes back around to the driver's side. I can't see what's going on in the car without pulling up for a closer look, and I'm not about to do that. If Angela saw me now, that might propel her to go through with something she doesn't want to do because she's mad at me, because she thinks I betrayed her.

And if Charlie saw me now, I don't even want to know what he might do.

My phone vibrates on the dashboard. I jump in my seat and press it to my ear. It must be Faye or Zach, finally set loose from Principal Goldfarb's office.

"What happened?" I half whisper into the phone, forgetting that Angela and Charlie are nowhere near close enough to hear me.

"What happened? You've been avoiding me all week, and now it's coming to a head. Dinner's in half an hour, and you'd better be at the house." Kim's voice floods my ear, and it's her angry voice, the one she reserves for people who seriously piss her off. She hasn't used this tone with me in a long time. Even when I try to get a reaction out of her, she still doesn't get angry. But this time, when I don't want her wrath, I don't know what I did to deserve it.

"I don't remember having dinner plans," I say coolly, keeping my eyes on Charlie's car.

"That's because you have conveniently been preoccupied this whole week," Kim says. "You could have checked the messages I left you, or the note in the kitchen."

"What's the big damned deal? Sorry if I didn't see some stupid Post-it note. It's been a busy week." My voice is laced with anger, but worst of all are the tears behind it. I want to scream at Kim. I want to blame her for letting Charlie be our gardener and for letting him dig into our lives. My life.

"You're coming home for dinner," Kim says. Now she sounds

preoccupied, like she's doing her nails and talking to me at the same time.

"Since when have we ever made dinner plans? Usually I eat alone." I think of Faye and her spaghetti and the way her eyes lit up when I ate the whole plate.

"We're having a special guest tonight." Kim sighs. "Your father."

I grip the phone, wanting to yell into it but too exhausted to bother arguing with Kim. I knew this was going to happen sooner or later. A week ago they were groping on the porch, and now my dad is coming over for dinner.

Kim takes my silence as tacit consent. "Come home, Mercedes."

I throw my phone in my purse and start up the Jeep. Angela and Charlie are still in the darkened car. Whatever they're doing in there, I can't wait around to find out.

When I walk in the door, Kim is a flurry of activity. She's wearing about eight pounds of diamonds around her neck and a black cocktail dress with matching high heels. She looks like someone ready to go on a fancy date with somebody she wants to spend a lot of money on her.

"Do I look okay?" she asks me as she stands in front of the fridge and fluffs her hair. This is definitely not normal Kim behavior. She *never* asks if she looks okay. She's nervous. I swallow the comment I was about to make about seeing her with my dad on the porch the other night.

"You better go upstairs and change," Kim says, giving me a once-over that ends with a frown.

"What's wrong with what I have on?" I say, crossing my arms. I know I'm giving her a hard time, but I shouldn't have to dress up to impress someone who hasn't been around to deserve it.

"Just put on a dress, Mercedes. Make yourself presentable."

I stomp upstairs and take off the jeans I'm wearing. I replace them with sweatpants and smirk at myself in the mirror. This will show Kim. Then I take the sweatpants off and put on a skirt and top and brush my hair. Dammit. I don't want my dad to think I'm a slob. I apply a dab of lip balm and spritz myself with perfume. Maybe Kim's antsy energy rubbed off on me, a mixture of nerves and excitement. My dad left us in his fast car so many years ago. Will I even recognize the person who walks through the door?

When the doorbell rings, I leave my room and watch from the landing as my dad comes in and gives Kim a peck on the cheek. They don't make eye contact, which must mean they're sleeping together again and don't want me to know it. Not making eye contact is the most obvious sign of all.

From my vantage point, I can see the top of my dad's head. He has a bald spot at the back that wasn't there the last time I saw him, and his hair is considerably grayer. Other than that, he's exactly as I remember, right down to the suit that's just a bit too snug around his beginning of a potbelly.

Kim clears her throat, which is either her signal to my dad that I'm in the room or her signal to me that I should come downstairs. I walk down the stairs on shaky legs and grip the banister for support. My dad is watching me, almost like he's seeing me for the first time. For some reason I start thinking I'm in a movie and this is my prom and my perfectly normal, loving parents are at the bottom of the staircase, waiting to see me off. My throat's dry and my palms are sweaty on the railing. I hope my dad doesn't want to shake my hand, because he'll know how sweaty it is. But he won't shake my hand. He'll hug me. Except he's staring at me like he doesn't know who I am, which I guess is true. So much has happened to me that he has no idea about. My dad was always good at knowing when something was bothering me. *Penny for your thoughts, kiddo*, he used to say when I was seven and stressed out about some stupid seven-year-old problem. I wonder if he can still read me. Now it would take him a lot more than a penny to know what's on my mind.

When I reach the bottom of the stairs, we stand in front of each other. I wipe my palms on my skirt, just in case he does decide to shake my hand. But he just gives me a funny smile instead and inches forward, like he's asking for permission to touch me. I like that he doesn't just expect me to want to be hugged. He's respectful of boundaries. I step forward and drape my arms loosely around his shoulders.

I don't know what I expect from the hug. I guess I'm waiting for him to pull me in and try to apologize for being missing in action for a good chunk of my life. But he just gives me a little squeeze and pats me on the back. I can feel the heat from his hand through my shirt. He's nervous, too.

When we pull away, he holds me by the arms and shakes his head. "You look so much like your mother," he says. I bite my tongue. I want to tell him that our looks are where the similarities end, but I don't want to spoil the moment when it barely started.

Kim hired a catering company to make dinner. When the three of us sit down at the dining room table, it becomes blatantly clear just how uncomfortable my dad feels in the house he used to live in. He makes little comments about the renovations Kim has had done—the ones on the house, not on her body, although I'm sure he has noticed those, too. "Great paint color," he says, along with "You finally got that hardwood floor you wanted." I keep my mouth shut until he makes a comment that sucks away my appetite completely.

"The yard looks great," he says, gesturing out the open window beside us. "You did something with that dirt garden. Those are beautiful roses."

I swallow and bite the inside of my cheeks. My hand clenches around my fork like a weapon.

"Thanks," Kim says, obviously loving his attention. "I hired a gardener. He goes to school with Mercedes."

My dad nods appreciatively. I stare at my plate. The chicken breast sitting in a pool of gravy looks gray and blubbery and totally inedible.

"And how is school, Mercedes?" My dad asks. I push the chicken around on my plate and collect peas on each tine of my fork. I have a sudden flashback of doing this very thing with peas when I was a little kid.

"School's fine," I say. "Actually, I just got into MIT, so I'll be moving away soon." I give him a tight-lipped smile. It's not like I can tell him the truth. *I lost my best friend last week because I slept with a good chunk of the senior class. My only two other friends just slept together. Now all I can do is think about what I could have done differently to change it. I can't go back, but at least I get a fresh start.*

"Wow," he says. "Very impressive." He pauses, and an awkward silence ensues. Which he breaks with an equally awkward question. "Any special men in your life?"

I shake my head. *No, the ones I used to have over aren't special at all.*

"What about the boy who brought you soup?" Kim says. "He seemed promising."

"Zach," I snap. "His name is Zach. And he's not my boyfriend, Kim."

My dad raises both eyebrows. He looks like he wants to say something but isn't sure how to phrase it, so we eat in silence. Until I ask Kim to please pass the potatoes.

"Why do you call your mother that?" he asks.

"Call her Kim? Because it's her name." I spear a potato and cut it in half much more violently than I rightfully have to. I don't even intend to eat it. I just want to slice into it.

"Okay," my dad says. "But you don't call me Roy. I mean, you could if you wanted to . . ." His voice trails off. He's trying to be the cool dad, the one who doesn't care what his daughter calls him, as long as she wants to call him something.

I shrug. "No, I'm fine with calling you Dad," I say. Maybe this is more to hurt Kim than anything. My dad is the one who left, but Kim's the real absentee parent. At least my dad up and left in body and mind. Kim pretends to be here, probably tells herself she's doing a good job as a parent. She's the biggest fraud of all.

Kim massages her fingers into her temples. My dad shoots her a sympathetic look. I roll my eyes. Kim is way too good at playing the victim. I might have inherited her cheekbones and green eyes, but I'm glad I didn't inherit that quality.

We're interrupted by the doorbell ringing. I know it must be Faye or Zach. I left my phone upstairs, and I'm sure they have both been trying to call me. I jump out of my seat and run down the hall before Kim can stop me to admonish my bad manners.

It's Faye, leaning against the door much more nonchalantly than I would be in her position. Even though I have been waiting to hear from her, I'm not sure I can handle seeing her this close right now. I want to hug her as badly as I want to push her away. I'm angry with her, angry about her and Zach and their bodies pressed together.

"What happened?" I hiss, slipping onto the porch and closing the door behind me. Whatever she says, whatever I say, I don't want Kim or my dad to overhear.

"They called Lydia, and Zach's mom, too. Lydia's working, so she won't get the message until she gets home, and I'm sure I'll have some explaining to do. Zach's mom wasn't too happy. He got two weeks of detention. I got suspended. Indefinitely." She says all of this with a smile.

I clasp my hands together. "But why'd he get detention and you got suspended?"

"Because I told Goldfarb it was my idea. Which is totally true. I told him I did the whole thing, that Zach didn't have a clue. I said Zach thought nobody else would ever see that video. God love that kid, but he's a terrible liar. I don't know if Goldfarb bought it, but Zach has such a good record, he didn't have much of a choice." She smiles. "I can be very persuasive."

"I can't believe you did this for me," I say, pressing my palms together tightly to stop them from shaking, shaking from anger or fear or both. "I don't see how you can be so okay with this. You got yourself in huge shit."

Faye leans in so close that our noses are almost touching. "What did I tell you before this went down? I said there would be fallout. And I'm okay with that."

"I'm not," I say, and my voice is high and shrill. "I'm not okay with you being suspended, and I'm not okay with you and Zach having sex." I cross my arms, wanting to push her away and pull her in but doing neither.

She moves in even closer so that she's almost speaking into my mouth. "We didn't," she says. "But it looks like we did. Everyone thinks we did."

The backs of my legs and arms start to quiver slightly. I realize they're quivering with relief. Immense relief, like even though so many terrible things have happened, everything could possibly be okay again. Faye didn't sleep with Zach. There really isn't anything going on. She smiles at me like she can read my mind, and I shift uncomfortably.

The door opens behind me. At first I don't register the sound of it, but Faye pulls back and her eyes leave my face.

"Mercedes, what's going on?" Kim says. "Oh. Hello," she says, noticing Faye.

"I'm Faye," she says, stretching out her hand, which Kim takes. "Sorry to interrupt. You guys must have been eating dinner."

"Would you like to join us?" I say before Kim can stop me. "It's a family dinner. My dad's here, too. We have lots of food."

Faye's eyes widen slightly. She knows my dad being here is a big deal. And she knows it's a big deal that I want her here for this.

"Dinner sounds great," she says. "I'm actually famished."

I don't get a chance to tell Faye thank you, but it doesn't matter. Dinner gets a hundred times less awkward when she sits down. She has my dad laughing, and even Kim breaks into a smile. You would never guess that this girl, the one helping herself to seconds of chicken and potatoes and telling my dad how to properly barbeque a steak, is the same girl who just voluntarily showed the whole school her naked body on a giant screen and got suspended as a result.

"I hope we see a lot more of you," Kim says when I get up to walk Faye to her car.

"You will," Faye says. "Thanks for dinner." She turns to my dad. "And nice meeting you, Mr. Ayres. If you're in town again, we'll have to try that steak house I told you about. Best filet mignon you ever had."

"Please, call me Roy," he says. "And it was my pleasure. Any friend of Mercy's who knows her way around a steak is a friend of mine."

I walk Faye out to the driveway, expecting to get no farther than her car. But instead of opening her door and getting in, she walks around and opens the passenger door instead.

"Take a drive with me," she says. "There's somewhere we need to go."

37

We drive in silence, which is something Faye and I haven't had much of since we met. It seems to me like she has always been talking or laughing or singing or doing something to make sure silence doesn't happen. I took her for the type who has to drive accompanied by the car stereo, but she doesn't make a move to turn it on, so I don't, either.

I have zero control.

"Where are we going?" I finally ask.

"You'll see," is all she says. Another cryptic answer.

We end up in an empty parking lot near the beach, but Faye makes no move to get out. Instead, she pushes a button and the top of her convertible folds down. She reclines in her chair and looks at me expectantly until I do the same.

"Now look up," Faye says, tipping her face up to the sky. And when I do look up, all I see is stars. I guess I never realized how much the city lights block them out.

"They look different horizontal," I say. The whole sky looks more panoramic, like it really does stretch on forever.

"Lots of things look different horizontal," Faye says. "That's why sex is so honest."

"Funny how I wasn't honest at all," I say with a bitter laugh. "Not with the people who mattered."

"Speaking of honesty," Faye says, pressing her cheek against the seat and facing me. "You have to know that what Zach and I did, it was for you and also for me. Because that's the real reason I left my old school."

"What happened?" I say slowly. "If you want to tell me."

"You're the one person I want to tell." She pushes her hair back from her forehead. "I was dating a guy at the start of this year. I really liked him. I thought he really liked me. But one night we both got drunk at a party and hooked up in one of the bedrooms. I remember not wanting to do it there, but he really wanted to, so I gave in." Her voice is airy and the words are coming out in fast-forward, almost like she swallowed helium. I can tell I'm the first person she told this story to in a long time. Maybe ever.

"Anyway, his friend was in the room with us. I was sort of out of it, but his friend videotaped us. The one thing I distinctly remember is telling his friend to leave. And my boyfriend said no. He wanted a tape, said we were the only people who would ever see it. Turns out, my boyfriend had another girlfriend, and I guess he was trying to make her jealous. By Monday, the whole school had seen that tape."

"I'm sorry," I say, wanting to reach for her hand but not moving.

"I was sorry, too," she says. "I was very angry. The guy I thought was my boyfriend dropped me like I was worth nothing. And his girlfriend made it her mission to make my life hell. Going to school was torture. Lydia saw what I was going through, and she wasn't happy in Nevada anyway."

"You must have had a hard time trusting people again," I say, finding her shoulder and squeezing it with my fingertips.

"I thought I would," she says, turning to face me. "But I trusted you right away."

I don't know what to say. I can't think of anything I could say that would equal that.

"I just wanted you to know," Faye says, propping herself up on her elbow. "I wanted to tell you where nobody else could overhear." She smiles and bites her lip. "I didn't just bring you to an empty parking lot to make out with you."

My eyes widen. "I didn't think that," I stammer, even though it's exactly what crossed my mind when we rolled in here.

"Why? Don't you want to make out with me?" she says, placing her hand on my leg and rolling over on her stomach.

I stare at her hand and then at her chest, which is moving up and down rhythmically with each breath she takes. I think about the night of the dance, when we almost kissed in the bathroom. I think back to all the little touches, the way her hair smelled when she hugged me. I think about her naked body on display on-screen.

I think about what it would be like to kiss her. It would be easy, to press my lips against hers and figure out if I was making those feelings up in my head. If I'm really attracted to Faye, or if I just like her because she's not a guy. Nobody would ever know about it. None of the people at school who want to see me make a fool of myself. Not Charlie, who thinks he ruined my life. Not Angela. Not Zach.

But that's when it hits me. I don't want to kiss Faye. I want to *be* Faye. I want to be fearless like her, bold like her. I want to figure out a way to be unapologetically myself, just like she has. Kissing Faye wouldn't make anything better. If anything, I know that it would make me feel guilty.

"You're perfect," I whisper. "But I can't make out with you."

I expect her to be disappointed, but instead her face breaks into a smile. "I thought so," she says, sitting up and doing up her seat belt.

"Are you mad?" I say, wrapping my arms across my chest.

"Of course not, silly," she says, starting the car. "I know exactly where you need to be right now, and I'm taking you there."

My heart sinks when we end up on my street. For a horrifying second I think she's taking me back to my house. Maybe she thinks I need to hash it out with Kim, find a way to forgive her and reconcile my fucked-up family life. And I don't want to disappoint her, but there's no Band-Aid big enough to put over that mess.

But we pass my house and keep driving. We keep driving until Faye pulls into Zach's driveway and stops the car.

"Why are we here?" I say, aware that my heart is pounding erratically.

Faye leans over me and raises her eyebrow. "You're a smart girl," she says, reaching over and unbuckling my seat belt. "You'll figure it out."

She makes no motion to get out of the car. When it's obvious she isn't going to, I do. I shut the car door slowly and watch her drive away. When her car disappears from view, I smooth down the front of my skirt and walk slowly to Zach's porch.

I ring the bell with shaking fingers. Nervous sweat is forming under my armpits, and I almost feel like I'm going to pass out. My mind flashes back to Evan Brown, how obvious his fright for being in a girl's bedroom was. It was so foreign to me, the concept that people could be so terrified of sex.

But here I am, just as nervous to stand at a boy's door.

Part of me doesn't want Zach to be home. When he doesn't answer the first ring, I almost turn and walk away. But then I think about Faye, about how I want to be more like her. Faye wouldn't run from this. Faye would embrace it.

Zach opens the door in flannel pajamas, the same ones he was wearing when he took care of me after the dance. They look soft and harmless, and all I want to do is wrap myself up in him.

His eyes go big and he smiles. It's his surprised smile, the one that reminds me of a hyper kid on Christmas morning, which means he had no idea I was coming over. I guess Faye has kept some secrets from him after all.

He reaches out to touch my face. "Hey."

I know what I want to say, but the words get caught in my throat and suddenly I feel more naked and exposed than I did when Charlie leaked the video to the whole school. Like I have been stripped raw and hollowed out. I can't even *think* it. If I had my notebook, I would call myself so many names. *Weakling. Idiot.* I'd rate myself a zero.

"Hey," I say, and since I can't seem to get any other words out, I wrap my arms around his neck and press my lips against his. His hands travel to the small of my back, underneath my shirt. He opens his mouth slightly, and I run my tongue along his bottom lip and curve my body firmly into his. I have the same thought I had the other night, when we were lying in my bed with our clothes on. *I fit well here.*

I've probably kissed Zach a thousand times, in countless different positions. In my bed. Pressed against the wall. In the backseat of the Jeep. In Kim's pristine kitchen. Kissing was always a gateway to sex. I always figured, if you're going to kiss a boy, you might as well have sex with him. I don't know what it's like to kiss and not have it lead to anything else. I need to know what the next thing is and go there.

This kiss feels different somehow, softer and looser and more reckless. And I don't know how to handle it.

So I grind my hips against him and move one of my hands down to his chest, to the waistband of his pants. I pull the drawstring and start to reach inside, but he grabs my hand and intertwines his fingers with mine.

We're holding hands, and I have never held hands with a boy before. All the positions I have been in in bed, as exposed as I was then, it's nothing compared to this. Now he knows my fingers are sweaty. He knows I'm terrified.

I tug at his waistband with my other hand, but he stops me again. I bite his bottom lip and stick my tongue down his throat and try to make the kiss into something familiar, something I thought Zach liked.

This time he pulls away.

"Mercy," he says. "Stop. We can't do this."

My cheeks burn with humiliation. He's rejecting me. I wiggle out of his grip and drop his hands. I wipe mine on my skirt and he watches me do it and the way his face sags makes me hate myself even more than I already do.

"But I want you," I say, even though my voice is flat and monotone and doesn't sound like me at all. It's not the voice I use in my bedroom, when I'm trying to be playful and seductive. It's nothing like that. I can't muster that right now. What is wrong with me?

"Look, nothing happened with Faye. It was all for show. I couldn't be with anybody like that. Not when . . ." His voice trails off, and he shakes his head.

Not when what? I think.

I want him to say what he said in Kim's kitchen, when I took it for granted and shrugged it off. I want him to say it again. I want to hear it now. I want to hear it now because if I have changed at all I might feel differently about hearing it.

But he says nothing and he's not smiling and his eyebrows are pulled together. That's his hurt face, and I'm becoming very familiar with it.

I follow him as he shuffles into the kitchen and opens the fridge. "Are you hungry?" he says. "My mom's at her class tonight and she made all this spaghetti. I know you liked the spaghetti that Faye made. Will you eat some?"

I come up behind him and wrap my arms around his waist. I start kissing his neck. This will make him lose interest in food. I don't think Zach and I ever actually ate lunch once during any of our lunch dates. This will make things normal again.

"Mercy," he says, spinning around to face me. "I really can't. Let's just hang out, okay? Let me heat up this food, and we'll watch TV or something."

I wring my hands in frustration. "Why not? Why can't we do what we know feels good? I'm not hungry. I don't want to eat spaghetti. I just want you."

He stares at the floor. "You don't want me," he says. "This is just your way of feeling normal again. I get it. But I can't be that guy anymore. It's too fucking difficult."

Each syllable is a knife wound, a dagger. *Too. Fucking. Difficult.*

I bite my lip. I know I'm going to cry, and I don't want to do it here. I don't want Zach to see me with puffy red eyes and wet cheeks and snot coming out of my nose. I have put him through enough without being some stupid girl crying on his shoulder.

So I turn away from him and run, down the hall and out the door, before I change my mind.

He doesn't chase me. He probably couldn't keep up anyway. I'm better at running away than he ever could be.

I don't stop running until I'm in front of my house and I'm all alone again.

"I do want you," I shout to the darkness in between heaving sobs.

I think about what I should have said to Zach, the words I can't bring myself to say out loud. *I want to feel normal just hanging out. I want to figure out how, but I have no idea. Because you're right—sex is my normal. Sex is my control. But now I'm careening off a cliff, and I have no idea where to find the brakes.*

I suck in a deep breath. It hurts my lungs, makes my insides burn.

Maybe trust is the brake I'm looking for. Faye had something bad happen to her and she still found a way to trust people again, to put her faith in them not to hurt her.

So why can't I do the same?

38

Zach has the decency to pretend the other night never happened when I get to school on Monday. He's waiting for me in the parking lot, holding a coffee, ready to walk me to class. So I pretend nothing happened, either, that I didn't break his heart and stomp all over the pieces.

"Look at us," he says, holding the door open for me as people point and stare. "The two most popular naked people in all of Milton High. That's got to be some kind of accomplishment."

I link my arm through his. "Don't give yourself so much credit," I say. "You forgot about Faye. She probably has a bigger following than the both of us."

It's weird without Faye around. I keep expecting her to come up behind us and sling an arm around each of our shoulders and laugh that seal-bark noise that I have grown to love. I realize now more than ever that Faye has been the leveling force, the glue holding everything together. Now Zach and I will have to be our own glue.

"Our trio's down to two," Zach says, humming that song from the *Lion King* as we walk down the hall to chemistry together.

"I hope I'm not the warthog," I say.

"There's that sense of humor," he says. "I miss her. Faye, not the warthog. She wasn't supposed to take the heat. We agreed to do it together."

We stop at my locker. It's not easy to miss, considering somebody took a Sharpie and drew a very anatomically incorrect penis on the front, along with **SLUT** in giant capital letters, right beside the box where Zach blacked in **WHORE** last week.

"I miss her, too," I say with a sigh.

"Look, do you think you're okay to fly solo in home economics today? I really need to camp out in the library today to study. But if you need me, I'll be there."

I shake my head. "Of course not. I'll be totally fine."

Zach's eyes widen. "Uh, Mercy—"

I whip around to see who he's staring at. For a second I think I'm going to come face-to-face with Faye, even though she's suspended. But it's somebody even less likely.

Angela. Her hands are clasped in front of her, almost like she's praying.

"Angela. Hi," I say.

"Angela. Bye," Zach says, and makes himself scarce.

She looks at her hands. I can tell by her red eyes that she has either been crying or smoking weed, and I'm willing to bet my life it's not the latter.

"Can we talk?" She looks up with a funny half smile that is more of a frown, one I haven't seen before. "Not here. After school."

"Of course," I say. "Do you want me to come over?"

"No," she says quickly. "I'll come to your house." She reaches into her backpack and pulls out something in a plastic bag, which she thrusts into my hands. She turns on her heel and scurries away before I have a chance to say anything else.

I peer into the bag. It's filled with black fabric. At first I have no idea what it is, but then I realize it's my black negligee, the one I thought Kim must have taken. But it was Angela, the one person who I didn't think was capable of stealing anything. My hands tremble slightly as I stuff the bag into my locker and slam the door. I turn to walk away but spin around and open my locker again instead. I pull out the bag and look inside again. Angela could have worn this for Charlie. Is that why she's giving it back, because it's a memory of what she did?

I ball up the bag and toss it in the nearest trash can. That's where it belongs.

We have chemistry and home economics together, but Angela doesn't so much as look at me during chemistry, and she doesn't show up for home economics. Since I'm two rows behind her in chemistry, I can tell she has horribly botched today's experiment, which is supposed to prove the heavy density of sulfur hexafluoride relative to air. Her hands are shaking, and halfway through class she drops a flask, which promptly shatters on the floor.

"What the hell did you do?" her lab partner yells.

I'm wondering the same thing. I'm wondering what Charlie did to her.

To make the day even weirder, today's home economics topic is pregnancy. I should be taking notes to fill in Faye and Angela on what they're missing, but Mrs. Hill's information is so sterile. It's nothing like what being pregnant actually is.

"This is what a baby looks like at four weeks," she says, pointing to a tiny dot on a slide with her meter stick. "It's nothing more than a speck. But that speck will grow into this." She flips to the next slide, where the speck has turned into something resembling a peanut.

"This is two months. This is what is growing inside of you at two months. And pretty soon, that turns into this." The next slide actually resembles a baby, and this is where I stop looking. Hot tears prick my eyelids. I can't sit here and watch this, so I grab my bag and dart out the door, ignoring Mrs. Hill's protestations and the stares and hushed murmurs of everyone in the classroom. I'm sure I probably left Chase Redgrave and Trevor Johnston with something much bigger than homework to think about.

I don't go right home like I plan to. I take a detour in my Jeep, one I definitely didn't plan on taking. I go back to the playground, the one Luke and I spent those summer nights at, the one I tried to go back to the other night but felt too haunted by. It looks different now, with the midafternoon sun slanting down, creating shadows underfoot. There are a few kids running around, whose moms watch from red painted benches. I stay in my Jeep and grip the steering wheel. I'm safe in here. One of the moms lifts her toddler to the top of the slide and keeps her hands on his puffy coat as he slides down. His face is contorted with tears. *I know how you feel, kid*, I want to say. *That slide did me in, too.*

I never went to this playground as a kid, probably because Kim never bothered to take me. When I finally did go, it was as an adolescent. It was where Luke and I got away from Kim, my mother and his employer. He taught me how to smoke joints here, sitting face-to-face on the seesaw. We would talk for hours about everything we thought was shitty about life. I complained about Kim. He told me about his dad, how he would smack Luke around when he had a few drinks. He said I was the only person he ever told that to, and I had no reason not to believe him.

One night, when he asked me to be his girlfriend, I felt like I was on top of the world. Then he told me what girlfriends do for their boyfriends, and he pulled his dick out of his pants. I had never seen one before, and I had no idea what to do with it. I was thirteen. But I was about to find out what to do with it, when he pushed my head down. I wanted to make Luke happy, and if I had to do this to be his girlfriend, that was okay with me.

That became our nightly ritual. We would head to the park after dark, and I would give him a blow job. And one night, when I was pressed against the slide, he told me he couldn't stop.

"You're my girlfriend," he said. "This is what girlfriends do." I still remember how his breath smelled like the beer he had chugged on the walk over. It made me want to gag, but the last thing I wanted to do was say no to Luke. The last thing I wanted was for him to think I was a baby, a stupid grade-school girl who wouldn't do the things girls in his high school would do.

"I haven't been with anyone but you," he said, kissing my neck. I wanted to push him off me, but he was so heavy, and I was trapped between the hard plastic of the slide and the hard weight of his body. He already had my skirt pushed up and my underwear pulled down.

I didn't say yes, but I didn't say no. And when I felt the burning pain between my legs, like I was being ripped in two, I bit my lip hard enough to draw blood, but I still didn't tell him to stop.

Afterward he did up his pants and barely talked to me on the way home. He stopped calling after that, and he stopped showing up at our house for work. A week later, I heard through a mutual friend that he had been dating a girl from his class for the past year.

I never told anyone about Luke, especially not Kim. Kim was the one who hired Luke to be our gardener that summer, and she thought he did great work with roses, which never grew in our garden before Luke. I was afraid of what Kim would say, afraid she would blame me for leading him on. Terrified she would roll her eyes and tell me to just grow up and get over it. Besides, I was more embarrassed than anything. I thought I did something wrong. Maybe I was bad at sex, and that was why he stopped wanting to see me. I made a promise to myself to get better.

I pushed it out of my mind, something I got good at doing after Luke. I figured I could write it off as a life experience, something that might give me an edge when I started high school. I had one up on most thirteen-year-olds, who spent their summers at the mall blowing their allowances on designer skinny jeans and bright makeup. They wanted to make themselves look older, but I *was* older. I convinced myself that what happened with Luke was the best thing that could have happened to me.

Until I missed my period. I spent days in denial, unsure if I should talk to Kim but uncertain of what I would say. I got the sex talk early from Kim. The one hard-and-fast rule she stressed was, "Use a condom." And I even got that wrong. I figured maybe my period was just late. I had only started it the year before. I read that it was normal for girls my age to be irregular. I couldn't possibly be pregnant after my first time.

I let myself believe that for almost a week, until the other signs were too hard to ignore. I looked them up online. Morning sickness. Fatigue. Back pain. I had them all. I bought a pregnancy test in the mall, the one nearby that I could get to on foot. I was only thirteen, so I couldn't drive, and I wasn't going to ask Kim to drive me.

I couldn't think straight when I saw the two lines on the stick. I figured I did it wrong, so I was glad I bought two tests. The second one had two lines as well. I remember not being able to breathe. My life was over. I couldn't be a mom. But how could I get an abortion without Kim finding out?

It took me two more days to get up the nerve to call Luke. I dialed his number from the pink phone in my bedroom, my hands trembling and my heart pounding. I could barely hear my own voice over the blood rushing to my head.

"I have something to tell you," I started.

"Who's this?" he said. Just two words. *Who's this?* If he would have punched me in the gut, it would have hurt a lot less.

I should have stopped talking there and realized he wanted nothing to do with me. But I wanted to do the right thing. And I needed him. I needed to tell somebody what was happening to me, that I was a hostage in my own body.

"It's Mercedes," I said. "Can you come over?"

"I'm busy," he said. "Sorry."

"It's important," I said, to which he said nothing. Finally I just blurted it out.

"I'm pregnant."

A long pause. Then he said something I'll never forget. "How do you know it's mine?"

His words hung there in the air, suspended like the humidity outside. There were so many things I could have said. *It's yours because you're the only person I have slept with. You made me. I didn't even want to.* But I said nothing. I didn't cry, either. I didn't make a sound.

"It's not mine," he said. "Look, Mercy. We had fun. But now you're trying to keep me around and it's not working. I moved on. You should, too."

He hung up without saying good-bye. He never said good-bye to me.

I looked up abortion clinics online. I made an appointment at one for the next week. I still didn't know what I would tell Kim. I could keep a lot of things from her, but not something that big. Every day leading up to that appointment, I prayed to a God I didn't believe in. I prayed for the baby to go away. I begged, with my hands pointed to the ceiling and tears streaming down my face, for God to give me a second chance. I promised I wouldn't screw up my life again. I told God I would never ask for anything ever again, as long as He gave me my life back.

And it turns out, somebody up there heard me, because I woke up in the middle of the night with the worst cramps of my life and knew I was losing the baby the size of a speck inside me. I sat on the toilet and bit the insides of my cheek and waited for it to disappear. When it was over with, I flushed the toilet without even looking. It was just a speck anyway, not a real person. My prayers came true. It was everything I asked for.

I should have been happy, but I was mad. I felt like God must have taken something else inside me away, too, because I just felt empty.

I thought a baby was the worst thing that could happen to me. I thought being pregnant would ruin everything.

But it turns out I ruined everything on my own.

39

I told Angela all about Luke in the letter, and I told her about the baby. I told her that I don't blame Luke for what I have been doing, that what he did to me doesn't make it right for me to sleep with other girls' boyfriends. I told her that I don't even know if I really enjoy sex or if I just like the control I feel during it. I told her that I really did want to make them better at it so that their girlfriends would have better first times than I did. That was a big part of it for me, no matter how wrong it sounds out loud or how bad it looks on paper. But I'm still expecting an onslaught of questions from her, if she even gives me the chance to answer them.

I wait on the porch for her for almost an hour, staring at every blond head that saunters down the sidewalk. When she doesn't show up, I open the front door to let myself in. She's not coming. She thought twice about it and doesn't want anything to do with me.

But Angela is on the other side of the door and looks just as surprised as I feel.

"Your mom let me in," she says. "She seemed happy to see me. Even though she forgot my name. I guess you probably haven't told her about . . . you know."

Considering this is the most Angela has said in over a week, I'm much more optimistic than I was alone on the porch.

"God, no. Kim knows nothing about my life."

Angela frowns.

"Sorry. I won't say God anymore. Bad habit."

We head upstairs. Usually we would sit on my bed, but that seems wrong somehow. I sit cross-legged on the floor, and Angela does the same.

I open my mouth to speak, but she starts talking first and cuts me off.

"I'm sorry I stole your nightgown," she says. "I don't know what made me do it. I never stole anything in my life, not even a chocolate bar. Stealing is a sin. And I was only looking for a cardigan, I swear. But then I found the nightgown and thought it was pretty and Charlie kept hinting around about sex and all of my pajamas are old and ratty and one pair even has feet attached and I couldn't wear them in front of him so—"

"Seriously, don't worry about it. I would have just given it to you," I say, stopping her before she forms the world's longest run-on sentence. Her face is turning red, and her voice is high pitched.

"I don't want it. I never wore it. That's why I gave it back."

"Fine." I say. "But that's not important."

I stop talking when her words hit me. *I never wore it.* With those words, I feel about ten pounds lighter, like an elephant has stepped off my chest and I can breathe normally again.

She inhales deeply. "My mom found your letter in the mailbox and gave it to me. At first it made me sick. I was mad. Then it just made me sad." She looks down at her fingers, where she is methodically peeling the skin off her cuticles. She must have picked up that habit from me. Thankfully it's the only habit she picked up from me.

"I know. It was a lot of information. That's stuff I never told anybody before, and I probably never will."

"No, Mercy. I'm glad I read the letter, because Charlie is kind of like Luke. What he said, to get you to do things." Her voice gets hushed and she looks at the door, like somebody might be eavesdropping outside.

"No, Ange," I say. "Please tell me he didn't make you do anything."

"He didn't," she whispers. "But he tried. He told me we were as good as married, that being engaged is the same thing. I kept telling him I wanted to wait. I still want to wait."

I want to hug her, but her body language indicates that she might not want to be hugged. So I listen to the story unfold.

"He got us this hotel room on the weekend, while my parents were gone, and tried to get me to drink wine with him. But I was nervous and didn't need anything that would make my head cloudier than it already was. So I said no, and he started acting kind of funny. Kind of mean, actually. I told him we could sleep in the same bed, and we could kiss and stuff, but that I wasn't ready for, *you know*."

"Sex."

"Exactly. And he knew that." She looks at me and sighs. "That was when he started to say stuff like, if you're not ready now, when are you ever going to be ready? We're already dealing with a long engagement. When are we ever going to do stuff normal couples do?"

"I can't believe he said that," I say through gritted teeth, even though I'm not surprised at all.

"Anyway. This is so embarrassing, but when I got in bed, I faced away from him and just wanted to go to sleep. But he didn't let me. He was naked and kept wanting me to touch, you know, *it*. Then he grabbed my wrist and made me. That was when I ran to the bathroom and locked myself in and pretended to be sick."

"I'm so sorry, Ange. I didn't want anything to happen to you." I want to add that I would love to cut the offending *it* right off his body, but I restrain myself.

"Well, nothing did. I stayed in the bathroom all night, even though he hammered and pounded on the door. He started saying things like, I'm so lucky that he has stayed with me and how he could find somebody else. Eventually he fell asleep, and I slipped out before he woke up. He has been calling me nonstop ever since, saying he's sorry, blaming it on the wine."

She starts to cry. This time I do hug her. She cries into my hair, taking shuddering breaths. I wish I could find Charlie and punch him in the face. Or worse.

"The thing is, I was mad at you," she says, her voice muffled by my hair. "I was mad at you because he kept saying that you were ready and willing to give it up for him. I was mad at you because I didn't know who else to be mad at. But now I just never want to see him again." She wipes her nose on her sleeve. I grab a box of tissues off my nightstand, but she waves them away.

"You had a right to be confused," I say. "I don't blame you. Especially after everything I have done. Or, everyone," I say, cracking a little smile. Angela laughs weakly, but I haven't heard her laugh in so long that it's a beautiful sound.

"The thing is, I had been starting to feel pressured by Charlie before I even found out about you. He kept talking about it. We used to talk about other things, but then he only ever wanted to talk about sex. When I changed the subject, he would get all sullen and moody. He asked me not to wear skirts to school, because other guys were looking at my legs. He got really controlling. And I let him be."

"Trust me, I know what it's like," I say, and I realize exactly who I sound like. Faye. *Trust me*—her life motto. And if I can be half the friend to Angela that Faye has been to me, I might just be deserving of that trust.

"But your story, about how he threatened you, I really didn't know who to believe. He kept saying you seduced him. And he had that book of names to back it up. And you said he came onto you, but I guess I needed proof."

Now it's my turn to pick at my cuticles.

"There's something else I don't understand," she continues. "I mean, you don't have to tell me. But I don't get why you never told the police about what happened with Luke. Why didn't you report him? You were thirteen! And pregnant!"

I knew Angela was going to ask me this if she ever decided to speak to me again. And I don't blame her. It's something I have asked myself about a million times—something I probably won't ever stop asking myself. I read the news, about guys like Luke who get a second chance to do it all over again because some timid victim didn't come forward. And now I have to tell my best friend why.

"Here's the thing, Ange. It was my word against his. None of Luke's friends knew I existed. Nobody knew about our secret little relationship. He told me not to tell anybody, that it was more special because only the two of us knew."

Angela pulls a tissue out of the box and shreds it into little pieces of confetti, which she promptly pushes around the carpet with her fingers. For a long time she says nothing, and I don't, either. I give her time to absorb it. Considering not a day has gone by where I haven't thought about Luke and wondered if I should have done things differently, I can't expect Angela to process the information on the spot.

When she does say something, it's not what I expect.

"I hope you can forgive me," she says quietly. "I believe you, and it makes me sick that Charlie almost turned me against you."

I hug Angela fiercely, relief flooding through me. I have my best friend back. And that's something I'll never take for granted again.

"I have one more question for you," she says when we pull away.

"Ask away," I say. "I'm not hiding anything from you ever again."

"Why did you do it? Why did you sleep with all those guys?" She looks at the carpet.

"I think a lot of it was about control." I exhale shakily. "When I was the one who had it, even for a few minutes, I felt powerful. And the more guys I slept with, the more I craved it." With every word, I realize how terrible it sounds out loud. That I got greedy for that feeling. That it became an obsession. It wasn't about helping the virgins.

It was about helping myself.

Angela reaches for my hand. She will never understand it, but she loves me.

"You asked me before if I was in love with Luke," I say. "The answer is no. Luke was using me, and I was too young and naïve to figure it out. I might have a lot of experience, but I don't think I've ever been in love."

"Well, it's not like I'm any authority on relationships," Angela says. "I thought I loved Charlie. I mean, I thought I wanted to marry him. But maybe I was just under his spell. I don't think I really know what love means at all."

I smile. "Some lucky guy will be very happy to be your boyfriend," I say. "And he will respect you and never pressure you, because that's what love is. He'll want to be around you all the time. And nothing you do will make him leave, no matter how many times you push him away. And you'll never have to be afraid of him."

Angela narrows her eyes, and I'm not sure if she's about to laugh at me or chastise me.

"What?" I ask. "Sorry, that was cheesy. But it's true."

She takes my hand in both of hers, her delicate little hands with fingernails that will never have blood under them.

"There is no fear in love, but perfect love casts out fear."

I cock my head. "What?"

Angela rolls her eyes. "First John 4:18. If you had been paying attention during prayer group, you would know."

"I'm sorry I lied about prayer group, Ange. I promise I won't lie to you ever again."

"That's great, but how about lying to yourself?"

I shrug. "What do you mean?"

"I mean," she says slowly, drawing out each syllable, "it sounds like you might have more experience with love than you're giving yourself credit for."

I roll her words around in my head. *Perfect love casts out fear.*

Then, my own words. *Nothing you do will make him leave, no matter how many times you push him away.*

I stand up so fast that the blood rushes to my head.

"Angela," I say, "there's somewhere I really need to be."

40

The Jeep can't get there fast enough. Every second is wasted time, grains of sand slipping through my hand. By the time I screech into my usual parking spot and run for the door, I realize I have no idea what I'm even going to say.

But I don't let that stop me.

He's not in the library, where he said he was going to be. I dart down every aisle and check every cubicle, hoping to see the top of his head. A few people look up as I dash by, but no Zach.

I sprint down the hallway, passing my locker. The blacked-out **WHORE** and **SLUT** have been joined by **BITCH**, but I don't let any of those words slow me down.

I almost run right past the chemistry lab. It's mostly dark and the door is closed. But something stops me. Instinct, or some greater force. When I look in the window, I see him at our old desk, with his head in his hands.

I don't hesitate. I don't give myself the chance to chicken out or change my mind and run away. I open the door and stride up to the whiteboard. I clear my throat and pick up a whiteboard marker, just like I did that day when I didn't know Jillian was watching.

"Today, we're going to be talking about ionic and covalent bonds," I say, surprised at how steady my voice sounds, how sure of myself I seem.

Zach leans forward in his chair. "Mercy, what are you doing here?"

I keep talking. "You're probably wondering what the difference is. Well, in an ionic bond, the oppositely charged ions are strongly attracted to each other." I use the whiteboard to draw two little stick people, the extent of my artistic ability.

"Ionic compounds have high melting and boiling points." I add arrows to one of the stick people. Highs and lows, ups and downs. "Lots of energy is required to melt ionic compounds or cause them to boil."

Zach taps his pen against his notebook and squints at the board.

"Ionic compounds are hard and brittle." I draw a box around the stick person, trapping it inside. "Hard because the positive and negative ions are strongly attracted to each other and difficult to separate." I erase the first stick person and redraw it closer to the one in the box.

"But the electrostatic repulsion can be enough to split the crystal, which is why ionic solids are also brittle." I rub out the box with my finger and whip around to face him. "Is any of this ringing a bell?"

Zach scrapes his chair back and raises his hand, something

he never does during class because he never knows the answer. "Opposites attract," he says. "Two things come together and make something stronger. Like table salt. Sodium and chloride."

The corners of my mouth start to twitch into a smile. "You're learning," I say.

Zach grins. "Told you I wasn't a lost cause," he says, standing up and walking toward me. He stops when he's right in front of Mr. Sellers's desk. "I never thought I'd see the day when you'd actually tutor me."

"I figure I have some lost time to make up for," I say.

Zach leans over and I know he's going to kiss me, but I step back. "Wait," I say, holding out my hand. "I need to tell you something."

I swallow hard and start speaking before I can talk myself out of it.

"I didn't not write about you in my journal because you were nothing, Zach. That wasn't the reason why."

He cocks his head quizzically. "Why, then?"

I ball up my hands so hard that my nails dig into my palms.

"Because you were everything. You weren't one night, one experience I had to record for proof that it happened. You were so much more than that. I didn't write about you because I took it for granted that I would always have you." I bite the inside of my cheek and try to stop myself from crying, but it doesn't work, and I know my mascara is running, but this time I don't care.

Zach reaches across and wipes my cheek with his thumb. "What are you saying?"

I smile through quivering lips. "I'm saying I want to eat spaghetti with you."

Zach takes my hand and laces our fingers together, and I don't stop him. I'm holding hands with a boy, and it feels so much better than I could have imagined.

"You know what this means," he says slowly. "We can't just be Wednesday friends anymore. This will probably involve more days of the week."

I shake my head. "I don't want to be just Wednesday friends."

"Good," he says, stepping around the desk and wrapping his arms around me. "Because I'm busy that day. I mean, I switched into this home economics class just to be closer to this girl I'm totally crazy for, and I have all this extra homework now because she's such a slacker."

I press my face into his chest. There's so much I want to say, so much to tell him about myself that he doesn't know. But there will be time for that. There's no need to rush.

"I don't know how to be a girlfriend," I say. "I've never done it before."

Zach kisses the top of my head. "It's okay," he says. "That's something we can figure out together." He pulls away and puts his hands on my shoulders. "Now, former Wednesday friend, can you help me with this covalent bonds thing now? Because they still make no sense. Maybe one of your diagrams would help?"

I smile, bigger than I'm sure I ever have before, and his lips are on mine, and if this isn't the best kind of chemistry, I don't know what is.

41

It's funny how giving up control can actually end up putting things back in place. But that's what I'm learning, that too much of something ends up yielding the opposite reaction. It's a logic that has taken me the longest time to figure out but the shortest time to mend. And in two weeks, my life goes from complete shambles to something resembling almost normal.

The best part—besides Angela and I being best friends again—is that Faye is allowed to come back to school. I don't know exactly how it happened, and Angela won't tell me the specifics, but she went into Principal Goldfarb's office early one morning and didn't come out for almost two hours. She must have had some serious ammunition.

"What did you say to Goldfarb?" I ask when she finally emerges, with a serene smile on her face. "If there's one thing I know about Goldfarb, it's that he never changes his mind."

Angela just shrugs. "Maybe I'll tell you, maybe I won't. But come on. We're late for prayer group."

I'm still not sure I buy into prayer group, but I'm definitely starting to see the importance of having faith in something, or somebody. Even if that somebody is your best friend. Today's prayer-group topic hits especially close to home. It's forgiveness.

"Everybody open your Bibles to Ephesians 4:31," Angela says with a broad smile. She clears her throat and reads with confidence.

"Get rid of all bitterness, rage and anger, brawling and slander, along with every form of malice. Be kind and compassionate to one another, forgiving each other, just as in Christ God forgave you."

"Everybody" no longer includes Charlie, who hasn't shown his face at prayer group since Angela gave back her engagement ring. Prayer group is a place I can count on never seeing Charlie again. I wish I could say that about everywhere, but I can't. There's no magic chemistry formula that will make Charlie disappear, but there is a little thing called the truth. And now that the former virgins know that Charlie was the one responsible for that video, I don't think I'm the most hated person at Milton High anymore.

Plenty of people do still hate me, and there's not much I can do to change that. But now I have Angela back. She doesn't physically hold my hand when somebody hisses *slut* or *whore* at me in the hall, but she doesn't have to. She is my strength just the same. Charlie didn't get to be her first. That becomes my mantra.

Angela still wears her promise ring. When I asked her about it, she had a good reason.

"I'm keeping this," she said, twirling it around her finger. "I

picked it out. But it's not a promise to Charlie anymore, it's a promise to myself, that I'm always going to trust my gut."

The best part is, she got me one to match and told me to make
my own promise on it. Which I did, but I didn't tell her what it was.

I owe Faye more than I could ever tell her. She somehow got
the website Charlie made taken down from the Internet. I could
have let it ruin my life, but I let it die a quick death at Faye's hands
instead. She's another best friend now, somebody I trust with my
life. But I don't want to be her anymore. I'm still getting the hang
of being myself.

Faye was right and wrong. I'm not quite old news yet. People
still whisper when I approach them, and there are several girls who
wouldn't mind seeing me get hit by a car. I still have to deal with
death stares in the hallway, and I probably always will, at least until senior year is over. I left a lot of pissed-off ex-girlfriends in my
wake, and I'll never be able to explain to them why I did what I
did. I considered trying to, but maybe they're trying to move on as
much as I am. And no reason will ever justify what I did to them.

I guess the only thing I can do is leave the past in the past. Most
of the couples are done for good. Laura Adams dumped Trevor
Johnston in a profanity-laced text message. Isabella reportedly
threw her shoe at Juan Marco Antonio's face during soccer practice and told him she couldn't wait for him to go back to his home
country. Rafe Lawrence found himself at the receiving end of
Caroline's wrath, just like he wanted, although rumor has it he
wants her back now and she's not having any of it. Good for her.

Jillian Landry decided to give Tommy Hudson another chance.
I still pass them in the hall, and they still hold hands. I don't tutor
her anymore, but sometimes I swear Jillian gives me the faintest
hint of a smile, like she knows more than I have told her. Like
she forgives me for what happened. I hope Tommy and Jillian
make it.

I wasn't expecting it when Toby Easton found me at my locker, waving his midterm report card in my face. He got an A in polymers. If he noticed the covered-over words on the locker door, the blacked-out **WHORE** and **SLUT** and **BITCH**, he didn't show it. He lunged forward like he wanted to hug me but stopped short. He had probably seen the website, read the notebook pages. He was probably saying thanks, but no thanks. I didn't blame him.

I waited for him to say good-bye, but he didn't. He said something else.

"Same time, same place today?"

I nodded. Something swelled in my chest. I got to keep tutoring Toby. That meant everything to me.

"You really did save my life," he said as he walked away.

Nobody else tells me that anymore. And if Toby is the last person I ever hear it from, I'm okay with that.

Some people think I'm a bitch, some people think I deserve to die, and some people think I'm a glorified prostitute. I hear all kinds of rumors about myself, most of which have absolutely no root in reality. They don't just go away, but I knew they wouldn't. They linger, but they're no longer insults hurled across the cafeteria. They're more like whispers, echoing off the walls.

"I heard she quit sleeping with high school guys and moved onto college ones," I heard somebody say when I was sitting on the toilet taking a pee.

"I heard she got herpes," another girl said.

"No, she didn't get herpes. She got pregnant," a third voice chimed in.

"No, you guys are wrong. She has an actual boyfriend now. I saw them holding hands yesterday," a fourth girl said to a chorus of disbelieving laughter.

Thankfully, only the last of those rumors is true.

And tonight is a particularly special night. Tonight, Zach and I are having our first real date. My first real date ever.

"It's about time," Faye says with a wink. She and Angela are over at my place, helping me get ready. Angela is thumbing through Kim's old copies of *Us Weekly* magazines, and Faye is trying to make me sit still while she does my makeup.

"I'll say," Angela says. "Mercy's first date. This is a big deal."

I roll my eyes. "Don't make me more nervous than I already am," I say. "You're supposed to be helping me feel like I'm ready."

"Please," Faye says, swiping mascara across my upper lashes with a flourish of her hand. "You were born ready." She squints at me and frowns. "Now close your eyes. I need to do your eyeliner."

I do what she says. I never thought I would be able to sit like this, to give somebody control over even something as simple as my makeup. But I'm learning to take baby steps.

"So what's the plan?" Angela says. "Knowing you, there's a big elaborate plan. I'm dying to know, and you haven't said anything."

I smile, despite Faye's instructions not to move my face.

"Nope," I say. "There's no plan. We're playing it by ear."

"There must at least be an outfit," Angela says. "You have so many nice dresses to pick from."

She's right—I have a closet full of nice dresses that I never wear, dresses that Kim bought me for random charity events and dinner parties and other occasions I found a way to weasel out of. I have a closet full of dresses and drawers full of lingerie, some of which I have worn for Zach on multiple occasions. Lingerie that was supposed to say something. *I'm playful. I'm fun. I'm sexy. I'm a bombshell.*

So maybe it's telling that I'm wearing a cotton bra and underwear set that I haven't worn in years. My days of letting my lingerie speak for me are long gone.

"No dress," I say. "I'm wearing exactly what I have on."

That statement is met with silence. I crack my eyes open and see the disappointment on their faces.

"What? You don't like my jeans?"

"It's just, you wore them all day," Angela says. "I thought you were going to wear something more girly."

"Nope," I say, blotting my lips against a piece of tissue paper that Faye presses against them. "I've spent enough time pretending to be somebody else's fantasy. Tonight, I'm just going to be myself. I think Zach will approve."

Faye narrows her eyes. I can see a smile tugging at the corner of her mouth.

"It's not about what you've got on top. It's about what you have on underneath. Let me guess. Leather and lace."

Angela pretends to cover her eyes and hide her head, but I can tell she's laughing. I tug at the corner of my shirt, exposing an unembellished nude bra strap, and see Faye's face fall again.

"That's, like, the world's most boring bra," she says. "If this is a real date, he probably wants to see your boobs."

I bend over to rummage under my bed for my Cons. "Really, Faye," I say. "It's a first date. I'm not that easy."

Angela claps. "I think this is great," she says. "You found someone you really like."

Faye plops down on my bed. "Well, I want details later," she says. "I'll be expecting a late-night phone call with all the specifics."

The doorbell rings. Seven o'clock—right on time.

I grab my purse off the back of my chair and head for the door. "I don't think so," I say with a grin. "I think the whole school has heard enough about my love life. From now on, the rest of it will take place behind closed and locked doors."

42

I'm nervous to see Zach. Nervous because I have never actually been on a real date, and nervous because I hope I'm okay at it. I'm just about the furthest thing from a virgin, but I guess there are some things that are still virgin territory for me.

But Zach makes it easy. Kim has already answered the door by the time I get downstairs, and Zach is standing in the foyer wearing a button-down shirt and carrying a bouquet of flowers. Daisies, not roses. They're the most beautiful flowers I have ever seen.

"For you," he says, handing me the bouquet.

This time I don't chuck them at the bottom of the stairs. I let Kim put them in a vase. Later, I'll bring them to my bedroom and leave them on my nightstand. Flowers from my boyfriend.

"Ready?" Zach says, placing his hand on my lower back and guiding me to the door.

"Ready," I say.

"I'll have her home by curfew, Mrs. Ayres," he says as he opens the door for me.

Kim idles in the foyer, and I wait for her to make an embarrassing comment, but for once she doesn't. "You kids have fun," she says instead. I glance back at her and for the first time in forever, I don't scowl or roll my eyes or blow her off. I meet her eyes and smile. Because Kim might suck at being a mom, but she's the only one I've got. Maybe she's trying, in her own misguided way. And I guess I can understand something about that.

I look up the stairs one more time, and there are Faye and Angela, standing on the landing, waving at me. And in this moment I have never felt more normal, more like a regular girl going on a date with a boy she likes.

I have never felt luckier, either.

Zach leads me down the driveway to where a white sedan is hidden behind my Jeep and Kim's convertible. "I borrowed my mom's car," he says. "It's a hunk of junk and it only goes one speed, but it should get us there in one piece."

I smile. "It's perfect," I say.

He holds my car door open and shuts it gently once I get in. He lets me pick the music on the radio and reaches for my hand as he pulls away from the house.

"Where to?" he says. "What big adventure did you decide on?"

Zach let me design our whole date, not because he's indecisive but because he knows I like to have a plan. But I think I'm about to surprise him.

"Actually," I say, "I do have an idea. Keep driving. Straight for the beach."

Zach raises an eyebrow. "Are you trying to get me out of my

clothes?" he says. "Because if you wanted to see me naked, there was already this video that went around."

I punch him in the arm. "No, silly. You'll see."

When I finally tell him to stop the car, he gives me a quizzical look. "This doesn't look like a fancy restaurant," he says. "Or a movie theater, or bowling. So where exactly are we going?"

"Well," I start, "I was kind of in the mood for milkshakes."

And this is our date. It's not fancy or over-the-top or adventurous or even what most people would describe as romantic. But to me, it's perfect. My life has been dramatic enough. We order milkshakes and French fries, and I eat in front of Zach without feeling self-conscious at all. He makes me laugh and finds little ways to touch me, in places I never thought I'd like being touched. On my wrist, on my knee, on the tip of my nose.

We even sit on the same side of the table.

"You know, I've been thinking," he says as we walk on the beach afterward. "California will be awfully lonely without you next year."

"There's always phone sex," I say, bumping up against his shoulder. I take a deep breath before what I'm about to say next. "Or you could just come with me. Go to school somewhere it snows in the winter."

Zach hasn't let go of my hand, but now he squeezes it gently. "Mercedes Ayres, is it possible we're driving the same speed for once?"

A smile twitches at my lips. "Well, you know. I'm trying this thing where I go a bit slower. Like a minivan, instead of a Mercedes."

Zach stops and pulls me toward him and traces the shape of my face with his finger. A month ago, I wouldn't have let him. It would have been too intimate, too meaningful. But today, I don't pull away.

"You can't be a minivan," he says. "I love that you're a Mercedes. But I'll do my best to keep up with you."

"You already are," I say, brushing my lips against his and letting him lift me off the sand.

Here's the thing. I can't make up the speed limit any more than I can take back time. I can't fix what has already happened to me, and I certainly can't fix what happened because of me. But what I can do is drive beside the somebody who is beside me now. I could drive away in a few months like I planned and start fresh. Or I could stay here and love the people I'm with and the life I have with them. Maybe Zach and I will be together forever, and someday we'll tell our kids that we were high school sweethearts, a much tamer version of what really happened. Maybe we're soul mates. Maybe we really have come together to make each other stronger, like sodium and chloride. Or maybe a year from now, we'll be on opposite sides of the coast and decide we're better off as friends. But all those maybes aren't important, because I can't control them.

I can control what happens in the chemistry lab. There's a formula and an equation, and I know exactly what the reaction will be when I mix one thing with another. Life, not so much. Love, not at all. No matter what elements you combine, you really have no idea what happens next.

It's scary not knowing what comes next.

But not knowing might also be the best part.